ROGUE PLANET

ROGUE PLANET

GREG BEAR

 THE BALLANTINE PUBLISHING GROUP
NEW YORK

A Del Rey® Book
Published by The Ballantine Publishing Group

Copyright © 2000 by Lucasfilm Ltd. & ™.
All Rights Reserved. Used Under Authorization.

All rights reserved under International and Pan-American
Copyright Conventions. Published in the United States by The
Ballantine Publishing Group, a division of Random House, Inc.,
New York, and simultaneously in Canada by Random House of
Canada Limited, Toronto.

Del Rey is a registered trademark and the Del Rey colophon is a
trademark of Random House, Inc.

www.starwars.com
www.randomhouse.com/delrey/

Library of Congress Card Number: 00-190283

ISBN 0-345-43538-9

Text design by Michaelis/Carpelis Design Assoc. Inc.

Manufactured in the United States of America

First Edition: May 2000

10   9   8   7   6   5   4   3   2   1

For Jack, and Ed, and
Doc Smith,
for Isaac,
and for George—
Masters of adventure

ROGUE PLANET

A LONG TIME AGO IN A GALAXY FAR, FAR AWAY....

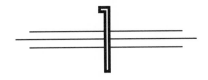

Anakin Skywalker stood in a long, single-file line in an abandoned maintenance tunnel leading to the Wicko district garbage pit. With an impatient sigh, he hoisted his flimsy and tightly folded race wings by their leather harness and propped the broad rudder on the strap of his flight sandal. Then he leaned the wings against the wall of the tunnel and, tongue between his lips, applied the small glowing blade of a pocket welder, like a tiny lightsaber, to a crack in the left lateral brace. Repairs finished, he waggled the rotator experimentally. Smooth, though old.

Just the week before, he had bought the wings from a former champion with a broken back. Anakin had worked his wonders in record time, so he could fly now in the very competition where the champion had ended his career.

Anakin enjoyed the wrenching twist and bone-popping jerk of the race wings in flight. He savored the speed and the extreme difficulty as some savor the beauty of the night sky, difficult enough to see on Coruscant, with its eternal planet-spanning city-glow. He craved the competition and even felt a thrill at the nervous stink of the contestants, scum and riffraff all.

But above all, he loved *winning*.

The garbage pit race was illegal, of course. The authorities on Coruscant tried to maintain the image of a staid and respectable metropolitan planet, capital of the Republic, center of law and civilization for tens of thousands of stellar systems. The truth was far otherwise, if one knew where to look, and Anakin instinctively knew where to look.

He had, after all, been born and raised on Tatooine.

Though he loved the Jedi training, stuffing himself into such tight philosophical garments was not easy. Anakin had suspected from the very beginning that on a world where a thousand species and races met to palaver, there would be places of great fun.

The tunnel master in charge of the race was a Naplousean, little more than a tangle of stringlike tissues with three legs and a knotted nubbin of glittering wet eyes. "First flight is away," it hissed as it walked in quick, graceful twirls down the narrow, smooth-walled tunnel. The Naplousean spoke Basic, except when it was angry, and then it simply smelled bad. "Wings! Up!" it ordered.

Anakin hefted his wings over one shoulder with a professionally timed series of grunts, one-two-three, slipped his arms through the straps, and cinched the harness he had cut down to fit the frame of a twelve-year-old human boy.

The Naplousean examined each of the contestants with many critical eyes. When it came to Anakin, it slipped a thin, dry ribbon of tissue between his ribs and the straps and tugged with a strength that nearly pulled the boy over.

"Who you?" the tunnel master coughed.

"Anakin Skywalker," the boy said. He never lied, and he never worried about being punished.

"You way bold," the tunnel master observed. "What mother and father say, we bring back dead boy?"

"They'll raise another," Anakin answered, hoping to sound tough and capable, but not really caring what opinion the tunnel master held so long as it let him race.

"I know racers," the Naplousean said, its knot of eyes fighting each other for a better view. "You no racer!"

Anakin kept a respectful silence and focused on the circle of murky blue light ahead, growing larger as the line shortened.

"Ha!" the Naplousean barked, though it was impossible for its kind to actually laugh. It twirled back down the line, poking, tugging, and issuing more pronouncements of doom, all the while followed by an adoring little swarm of cam droids.

A small, tight voice spoke behind Anakin. "You've raced here before."

Anakin had been aware of the Blood Carver in line behind him for some time. There were only a few hundred on all of Coruscant, and they had joined the Republic less than a century before. They were an impressive-looking people: slender, graceful, with long three-jointed limbs, small heads mounted on a high, thick neck, and iridescent gold skin.

"Twice," Anakin said. "And you?"

"Twice," the Blood Carver said amiably, then blinked and looked up. Across the Blood Carver's narrow face, his nose spread into two fleshy flaps like a split shield, half hiding his wide, lipless mouth. The ornately tattooed nose flaps functioned both as a sensor of smell and a very sensitive ear, supplemented by two small pits behind his small, onyx-black eyes. "The tunnel master is correct. You are too young." He spoke perfect Basic, as if he had been brought up in the best schools on Coruscant.

Anakin smiled and tried to shrug. The weight of the race wings made this gesture moot.

"You will probably die down there," the Blood Carver added, eyes aloof.

"Thanks for the support," Anakin said, his face coloring. He did not mind a professional opinion, such as that registered by the tunnel master, but he hated being ragged, and he especially hated an opponent trying to psych him out.

Fear, hatred, anger . . . The old trio Anakin fought every day of his life, though he revealed his deepest emotions to only one man: Obi-Wan Kenobi, his master in the Jedi Temple.

The Blood Carver stooped slightly on his three-jointed legs. "You smell like a *slave*," he said softly, for Anakin's ears alone.

It was all Anakin could do to keep from throwing off his wings and going for the Blood Carver's long throat. He swallowed his emotions down into a private cold place and stored them with the other dark things left over from Tatooine. The Blood Carver was on target with his insult, which stiffened Anakin's anger and made it harder to control himself. Both he and his mother, Shmi, had been slaves to the supercilious junk dealer, Watto. When the Jedi Master Qui-Gon Jinn had won him from Watto, they had had to leave Shmi behind . . . something Anakin thought about every day of his life.

"You four next!" the tunnel master hissed, breezing by with its midsection whirled out like ribbons on a child's spinner.

Mace Windu strode down a narrow side hall in the main dormitory of the Jedi Temple, lost in thought, his arms tucked into his long sleeves, and was nearly bowled over by a trim young Jedi who dashed from a doorway. Mace stepped aside deftly, just in time, but stuck out an elbow and deliberately clipped the younger Jedi, who spun about.

"Pardon me, Master," Obi-Wan Kenobi apologized, bowing quickly. "Clumsy of me."

"No harm," Mace Windu said. "Though you should have known I was here."

"Yes. The elbow. A correction. I'm appreciative." Obi-Wan was, in fact, embarrassed, but there was no time to explain things.

"In a hurry?"

"A great hurry," Obi-Wan said.

"The chosen one is not in his quarters?" Mace's tone carried both respect and irony, a combination at which he was particularly adept.

"I know where he's gone, Master Windu. I found his tools, his workbench."

"Not just building droids we don't need?"

"No, Master," Obi-Wan said.

"About the boy—" Mace Windu began.

"Master, when there is time."

"Of course," Mace said. "Find him. Then we shall speak . . . and I want him there to listen."

"Of course, Master!" Obi-Wan did not disguise his haste. Few could hide concern or intent from Mace Windu.

Mace smiled. "He will bring you wisdom!" he called out as Obi-Wan ran down the hall toward the turbolift and the Temple's sky transport exit.

Obi-Wan was not in the least irritated by the jibe. He quite agreed. Wisdom, or insanity. It *was* ridiculous for a Jedi to always be chasing after a troublesome Padawan. But Anakin was no ordinary Padawan. He had been bequeathed to Obi-Wan by Obi-Wan's own beloved Master, Qui-Gon Jinn.

Yoda had put the situation to Obi-Wan with some style a few months back, as they squatted over a glowing charcoal fire and cooked shoo bread and wurr in his small, low-ceilinged quarters. Yoda had been about to leave Coruscant on business that did not concern Obi-Wan. He had ended a long, contemplative silence by saying, "A very interesting problem you face, and so we all face, Obi-Wan Kenobi."

Obi-Wan, ever the polite one, had tilted his head as if he were not acquainted with any particular problem.

"The chosen one Qui-Gon gave to us all, not proven, full of fear, and *yours to save. And if you do not save him . . .*"

Yoda had said nothing more to Obi-Wan about Anakin thereafter. His words echoed in Obi-Wan's thoughts as he took an express taxi to the outskirts of the Senate District. Travel time—mere minutes, with wrenching twists and turns through hundreds of slower, cheaper lanes and levels of traffic.

Obi-Wan was concerned it would not be nearly fast enough.

The pit spread before Anakin as he stepped out on the apron below the tunnel. The three other contestants in this flight jostled for a view. The Blood Carver was particularly rough with Anakin, who had hoped to save all his energy for the flight.

What's eating him? the boy wondered.

The pit was two kilometers wide and three deep from the top of the last accelerator shield to the dark bottom. This old maintenance tunnel overlooked the second accelerator shield. Squinting up, Anakin saw the bottom of the first shield, a huge concave roof cut through with an orderly pattern of hundreds of holes, like an overturned colander in Shmi's kitchen on Tatooine. Each hole in this colander, however, was ten meters wide. Hundreds of shafts of sunlight dropped from the ports to pierce the gloom, acting like sundials to tell the time in the open world, high above the tunnel. It was well past meridian.

There were over five thousand such garbage pits on Coruscant. The city-planet produced a trillion tons of garbage every hour. Waste that was too dangerous to recycle—fusion shields, worn-out hyperdrive cores, and a thousand other by-products of a rich and highly advanced world—was delivered to the district pit. Here, the waste was sealed into canisters, and the canisters were conveyed along magnetic rails to a huge circular gun carriage below the lowest shield. Every five seconds, a volley of canisters was propelled from the gun by chemical charges. The shields then guided the trajectory of the canisters through their holes, gave them an extra tractor-field boost, and sent them into tightly controlled orbits around Coruscant.

Hour after hour, garbage ships in orbit collected the canisters and transported them to outlying moons for storage. Some of the most dangerous loads were actually shot off into the large, dim yellow sun, where they would vanish like dust motes cast into a volcano.

It was a precise and necessary operation, carried out like clockwork day after day, year after year.

Perhaps a century before, someone had thought of turning the pits into an illegal sport center, where aspiring young toughs from Coruscant's rougher neighborhoods, deep below the glittering upper city, could prove their mettle. The sport had become surprisingly popular in the pirate entertainment channels that fed into elite apartments, high in the star-scrubbing towers that rose everywhere on the capital world. Enough money was generated that some pit officials could be persuaded to turn a blind eye, so long as the contestants were the only ones at risk.

A garbage canister, hurled through the accelerator shields, could easily swat a dozen racers aside without damage to itself. The last shield would supply it with the corrective boost necessary to compensate for a few small lives.

Anakin watched the flickering jump light on the tunnel ceiling with focused concentration, lips tight, eyes wide, a little dew of sweat on his cheeks. The tunnel was hot. He could hear the roar of canisters, see their silver specks shoot through the shield ports to the next higher level, leaving behind blue streaks of ionized air.

The pit atmosphere smelled like a bad shop generator, thick with ozone and the burnt-rubber odor of gun discharge.

The tunnel master twirled up to the exit to encourage the next team.

"Glory and destiny!" the Naplousean enthused, and slapped Anakin across the brace between his wings. Anakin stayed focused, trying to sense where the currents would be at this level, where the little vortices of lift and plunge would accumulate as they formed and rotated between the shields. Ozone would always be in highest concentration in the areas where the winds would be strongest and most dangerous. And for every volley of canisters, following a prearranged formation through the shields, another volley would soon follow, taking a precisely determined series of alternate routes.

Easy. Like flying between a storm of steel raindrops.

Anakin's fellow racers took their places in the tunnel's exit, jockeying for the best position on the apron. The Blood Carver gave Anakin a jab with his jet-tipped right wing. Anakin pushed it aside and kept his focus.

The Naplousean tunnel master lifted its ribbon-limb, the tip curling and uncurling in anticipation.

The Blood Carver stood to Anakin's left and closed his eyes to slits. His nostril flaps pulsed and flared, filled with tiny sensory cavities, sweeping the air for clues.

The Naplousean made a thick whickering noise—its way of cursing—and ordered the contestants to hold. A flying maintenance droid was making a sweep of this level. From where they waited, the droid appeared as a flyspeck, a tiny dot buzzing its way around the wide gray circumference of the pit, issuing little musical tones between the roar and swoosh of canisters.

Managers could be bribed, but droids could not. They would have to wait until this one dropped to the level below.

Another volley of canisters shot through the shields with an ear-stunning bellow. Blue ion trails curled like phantom serpents between the concave lower shield and the convex upper shield.

"Longer for you to live," the Blood Carver whispered to Anakin. "Little human boy who smells like a slave."

Obi-Wan, against all his personal inclinations, had made it his duty to know the ins and outs of anything having to do with illegal racing, anywhere within a hundred kilometers of the Jedi Temple. Anakin Skywalker, his charge, his responsibility, was one of the best Padawans in the Temple—easily fulfilling the promise sensed by Qui-Gon Jinn—but as if to compensate for this promise, to bring a kind of balance to the boy's lopsided brace of abilities, Anakin had an equal brace of faults.

His quest for speed and victory was easily the most aggravating and dangerous. Qui-Gon Jinn had perhaps encouraged this in the boy by allowing him to race for his own freedom, three years before, on Tatooine.

But Qui-Gon could not justify his actions now.

How Obi-Wan missed the unpredictable liveliness of his Master! Qui-Gon had spurred him to great effort by what appeared at first to be whimsical japes and always turned out to be profound readings of their situation.

Under Qui-Gon Jinn, Obi-Wan had become one of the most capable and steady-tempered Jedi Knights in the Temple. Obi-Wan, for all his talents, had been not just a little like Anakin as a boy: rough-edged and prone to anger. Obi-Wan had soon come to find the quiet center of his place in the Force. He now preferred an orderly existence. He hated conflict within his personal relations. In time, he had become the stable center and Qui-Gon had become the unpredictable goad. How often it had struck him that this topsy-turvy relationship with Qui-Gon had once more been neatly reversed—with Anakin!

There were always two, Master and Padawan. And it was sometimes said in the Temple that the best pairs were those who complemented each other.

He had once vowed, after a particularly trying moment, that he would reward himself with a year of isolation on a desert planet, far from Coruscant and any Padawans he might be assigned, once he was free of Anakin. But this did not stop him from carrying out his duties to the boy with an exacting passion.

There were two garbage pits inside Anakin's radius of potential mischief, and one was infamous for its competition pit dives. Obi-Wan searched for guidance from the Force. It was never too difficult to sense Anakin's presence. He chose the nearest pit and climbed a set of maintenance stairs to the upper citizen-observation walkway at the top.

Obi-Wan ran along the balustrade, empty at this hour of the

day—the middle of the afternoon bureaucrat work period. He paid little attention to the roaring whine of the canisters as they soared through the air into space. Sonic booms rang out every few seconds, quite loud on the balustrade, but damped by sloping barriers before they reached the outlying buildings. He was looking for the right turbolift to take him to the lower levels, to the abandoned feed chambers and maintenance tunnels where the races would be staged.

Air traffic was forbidden over the pit. The lanes of craft that constantly hummed over Coruscant like many layers of fishnet were diverted around the launch corridor, leaving an obvious pathway to the upper atmosphere, and to space above that. But within this vacant cylinder of air, occupied only by swiftly rising canisters of toxic garbage, Obi-Wan's keen eyes spotted a hovering observation droid.

Not a city droid, but a 'caster model, not more than ten or twenty centimeters in diameter, of the kind used by entertainment crews. The droid was flying in high circles around the perimeter, vigilant for enforcement droids or officers. Obi-Wan looked for, and found, six more small droids, standing watch over the upper shield.

Three flew in formation above a cupola less than a hundred meters from where Obi-Wan stood.

These droids were guarding a likely exit point for the crews should metropolitan officials decide, for whatever reason, to ignore their bribes and shut down the races.

And no doubt they were marking the turbolift Obi-Wan would have to take to find Anakin.

The next dive had been postponed until the observers were certain that the pit watch droid had passed to the next lower level. The tunnel master was very upset by the delay. The air was thick with its nauseating odor.

Anakin drew on his Padawan discipline and tried to ignore the stench and keep his focus on the space between the shields. They could dive at any moment, and he had to know the air currents and sense the pattern of the canisters, still flying through the accelerator ports in endless procession, up and out into space.

The Blood Carver was not helping. His irritation at the delay was apparently being channeled into ragging the human boy at his side, and Anakin was soon going to have to put up some sort of defense to show he was not just a stage prop.

"I hate the smell of a slave," the Blood Carver said.

"I wish you'd stop saying that," Anakin said. The closest thing he had to a weapon was his small welder, pitiful under the circumstances. The Blood Carver outmassed him by many tens of kilos.

"I refuse to compete with a lower order of being, a *slave*. It brings disgrace upon my people, and upon *me*."

"What makes you think I'm a slave?" Anakin asked as mildly as he could manage and not appear even more vulnerable.

The Blood Carver's nose flaps drew together to make an impressive fleshy blade in front of his face. "You bought your wings from an injured Lemmer. I recognize them. Or someone bought them for you . . . a tout, I would guess, slipping you into the race to make someone else look good."

"You, maybe?" Anakin said, and then regretted the flippancy.

The Blood Carver swung a folded wing around, and Anakin ducked just in time. The breeze lifted his hair. Even with the wings on his own back, he quickly assumed a defensive posture, as Obi-Wan had taught him, prepared for another move.

The bad smell abruptly grew more intense. Anakin sensed the Naplousean right behind him. "A duel before a race? Maybe a holocam is needed here, to amuse our loyal fans?"

The Blood Carver suddenly appeared entirely innocent, his nostril wings folded back, his expression one of faint surprise.

The long curved corridor circumnavigating the pit was filled with old machinery, rusting and filthy hulks stored centuries ago by long-dead pit maintenance crews: old launch sleds, empty canisters big enough to stand up in, and the tarnished plasteel tracks that had once guided them down to the loading tunnels.

It was in this jumble that Obi-Wan found a thriving trade in race paraphernalia.

"Flight starting soon!" cried a little lump of a boy even younger than Anakin. The boy had obviously come from off-world, born on a high-gravity planet, strong, stout, fearless, and almost unbelievably grimy. "Wagers here for the Greeter? Fifty-to-one max, go home rich!"

"I'm looking for a young human racer," Obi-Wan said, bending down before the boy. "Sandy brown hair cut short, slender, older than you."

"You bet on him?" the stout boy asked, face wrinkled in speculation. This child's life was guided by money and nothing more.

So much distortion, Obi-Wan thought. *Not even Qui-Gon could save all the children.*

"I'll wager, but first I want to have a look at him," Obi-Wan said. He waved his hand slightly, like a magician. "To observe his racing points."

The stout boy watched the hand, but no scarf appeared. He smirked. "Come to the Greeter," the boy said. "He'll tell you what you want to know. Hurry! The race starts in seconds!"

Obi-Wan was sure he could sense Anakin somewhere near, on this level. And he could also sense that the boy was preparing for something strenuous, but whether for a fight or the competition he could not tell.

"And where will I buy a set of race wings?" Obi-Wan asked, aware there was no time for niceties.

"You, a racer?" The stout boy broke into howls of laughter. "The Greeter! He sells wings, too!"

Something was wrong. Anakin should have been aware of any anomalies earlier, but he had been focused on preparing for the race, and what confronted him now was another matter entirely.

The Naplousean tunnel master had been alerted by an accomplice that the maintenance droid had dropped to the next level, and that had distracted it from Anakin. In that instant, the Blood Carver withdrew one arm from a wing and reached into his tunic.

That made no sense. Anakin suddenly realized the Blood Carver's primary mission was not to race.

He knows I was a slave. He knows who I am, and that means he knows where I am from.

The Blood Carver swung out a twister knife. His arm seemed to telescope, all the joints going straight at once, then doubling back into a neat U.

"Padawan!" he hissed, and the spinning tips of the three blades glittered like a pretty gem.

Anakin, hampered by the bulk of the wings, could not move fast enough to completely avoid the thrust. He bent sideways, and the knife missed his face, but one blade gouged his wrist and the other two blades jammed against the left main strut. Pain shot up Anakin's arm. Quick as a snake, the Blood Carver drew his arm back and aimed another thrust.

Anakin had no choice.

He kicked away from the tunnel, skidded down the sloping apron, and spread the race wings to their full width.

Without hesitating, the Blood Carver followed.

"Race not yet!" the tunnel master husked, and a dense plume of stink shot from the tunnel, leaving the other contestants gagging.

Obi-Wan had only seconds to grasp the main points of this new piece of equipment he had purchased. He hefted the wings onto one shoulder and ran down the long tunnel, the loose and rattling struts scraping the ceiling. He hoped this was the tunnel from which the racers were flying, but found himself at the end, standing alone on the apron, staring across the vast lens-shaped space of the pit between two acceleration shields.

His newly purchased wings did not fit. Fortunately they were larger, not smaller, and the Greeter had not cheated him too badly, selling him wings intended for a biped with two arms. He cinched the thorax straps as tight as the buckles would allow, then ratcheted the arm clamps until the struts threatened to bend. Whether the wings were charged and fueled, he did not know until he swung up a little transparent optical cup and attached it over his eye.

The red and blue lines in his field of vision showed one-quarter charge in the small fuel tank. Hardly enough for a controlled fall.

Dying in a stupid garbage pit race, tangled in antique race wings, was not what Obi-Wan had hoped for as a Jedi.

He looked to his left, saw a blank space of wall, then turned right, grabbing a broken metal bar to lean out. The wings nearly pulled him out of balance, and he hung precariously for a moment. Recovering his footing, his race wings rattling ominously, Obi-Wan saw Anakin standing on the apron of the tunnel to his immediate right, about fifty meters away. He was just in time to witness the confused tangle of limbs and the flash of a weapon.

Obi-Wan leapt just as Anakin fell or jumped, and barely had time to observe a Blood Carver, Anakin's assailant, leap after.

His wings spread wide with almost no effort, and the tiny motors at their tips coughed and whined to life. Sensors on the struts searched for the intense tractor fields that permeated the space between the huge, curved shields. By themselves, the wings could not have supported a boy, much less a man, but by using the stray fields from the accelerator ports, a flyer could perform all sorts of aerobatics.

The first maneuver that Obi-Wan mastered, however, was to fall straight down.

Almost three hundred meters.

Anakin's confusion and pain quickly re-formed into a clarity he had not experienced in many years—three years, to be precise, since his final Podrace on Tatooine, when he had last been so close to death.

It took him almost three seconds to roll to a proper position, feet angled slightly down, wings folded by his side, head tilted back against the brace. Like diving into an immense pool. Then, slowly, the wings seemed to spread without his conscious volition. The motors coughed and sputtered to a sharp, well-tuned whine, like the skirling of two large insects. He felt the sensors twirling just beyond his fingertips, perceived the faint vibrating signal in the palms of both hands that a gradient field was available.

He had fallen less than a hundred meters. The wings, spread
to their full width of five arm spans, quivered and shuddered like
living things as they caught the air and the fields, and as the motors responded to subtle jerks of his arms, he gained complete
control—and *soared!*

The optical cup that gave him fuel and other readings
flopped uselessly below his chin, but he could get along without it.

Not bad, he thought, for someone so close to dying! The
clarity became a rush of energy throughout his small frame. For
an instant he forgot the race, the pain in his arm, the fear, and felt
a thrill of complete victory over matter, over the awkward bundle
of metal and fiber on his back, over the space between the huge
curving shields.

And, of course, over the Blood Carver who had wanted to
kill him.

Out of the corner of his eye, he saw what he thought might
be the Blood Carver, twirling like a falling leaf below and to his
left. He saw the figure scrape the wall of the pit and tumble,
catch a gust and go right again.

But this hapless flier was not the Blood Carver. With another
spin of sharp emotion, he realized his assailant had leapt from the
apron after him and was now soaring on a parallel, about twenty
meters to his right.

No doubt their status as contestants had been canceled by
the tunnel master. *Very well,* Anakin thought. He never cared
much for the formalities of victory. If this was a contest solely between him and the murderous Blood Carver, so be it.

The prize would be survival.

No worse than Podracing against a Dug.

* * *

Obi-Wan did not fear dying, but he resented what this kind of death implied: a failure of technique, a lack of elegance, a certain foolhardy recklessness that he had always tried to eliminate from his character.

The first step to avoiding this unhappy result was relaxation. After the first glancing contact with the wall, he went completely limp and tuned all his senses to how the air, the tractor fields, and the wings interacted. As Qui-Gon had once advised him when training with a lightsaber, he let the equipment teach him.

But such a process could take hours, and he had only a few seconds before he smacked himself flat on the lower shield. Best to make do with what he had learned so far.

And follow the apprentice's example.

Obi-Wan looked right and saw Anakin assume his flight position. Obi-Wan spread the wings and let his feet drop below the level of his head. He knew enough about lift-wing racing to catch the vibrations in his palms, to understand what they implied, to grab the strongest gradient field available to him, and to soar out across the shield like a leveret pulling out of a stoop.

The sensation was exhilarating, but Obi-Wan ignored that and focused instead on the tiniest indications from the wings, from the excruciating bind of the straps around his chest where he hung in their loose embrace. He had gained just a little more time.

The buzz in his palms ceased. The sensors rotated noisily, and again he started to drop. The increased thrust of the wingtip engines at this point in the race was more for control than for lift, but with the wings spread to maximum—nearly pulling his arms from their sockets—the toes of his boots came within scant centimeters of grazing the shield.

Then the buzz in his palms became frantic. He saw a ten-meter-wide hole, passed over it, felt the tractor field strengthen near the next port, and swerved to one side just in time to avoid the ear-stunning bellow of a garbage canister.

The updraft and roil of air in the canister's wake pulled him up like a fly caught in a dust devil. Deafened by the noise, wings shuddering uncontrollably, his palms hot with the frantic buzz of the sensors, he wrapped the wings tightly to his sides to break loose from the strongest part of the field, fell for some distance, caught the field gradient at a usable intensity, and spread the wings once again. The result: at least an illusion of control.

Across the pit, another canister roared through a port in the lower shield and was shunted by the tractor fields to its next port. And another. A volley was under way.

Obi-Wan had no idea where Anakin was, or whether he was still alive. And until he gained more than just rudimentary control of the wings, with less reliance on luck, his Padawan's circumstance mattered little.

The goal of the garbage pit race was to fly across the convex surface of the lower shield, drop through a port not currently fully charged with an acceleration field or filled with a rising canister, and then do it all again for the next two shields below that, until one arrived at the bottom of the pit.

Once at the bottom, all a contestant had to do was grab a scale from a garbage worm, while still airborne, stuff the prize into a pouch, and then ascend through the shields and fly into another tunnel to present the scale to the judge—that is, to the Greeter, who controlled nearly all the action in these affairs.

Garbage not packaged for export into space was gathered from the pit's municipal territory, mixed into a slurry of silicone oils, spewed from the lowest ring of outfall tunnels, and processed by the worms. The worms took this less-toxic garbage and chewed it down to tiny pellets, removing any last bits of organics, plastic, or recoverable metal.

Garbage worms were huge, unfriendly, and essential to the efficient operation of the pit. The garbage worms had natural ancestors on other worlds, but Coruscant technicians, masters of the vital arts, had long since bred these monsters away from the limits of their origins. Arrayed in the silicone slurry like jumbled nests of thick cable, the slowly writhing worms reduced millions of tons of preprocessed pellets to carbon dioxide, methane, and other organics that floated in thick islands of pale yellow froth on the roiled surface of the silicone lake. Discarded metals and minerals and glasses sank and were scraped from the bottom of the basin by ponderous submerged droids.

It was said a garbage worm could actually eat a defunct hyperdrive core and survive . . . for a few seconds. But that was seldom expected of them.

There were a great many worms in the lake of silicone at the bottom of the pit. Their scales were large and loose, glittered like diamonds, and were prized by the Greeter, who sold them to a small but select market of collectors as sports memorabilia.

Anakin performed a roll and looked up. The Blood Carver was on his left now. The other contestants had leapt after them, so the race was on after all. The tunnel master must have decided that the disruption only added to the sport.

Anakin could think of no better plan than to win the race by staying far from the reach of the Blood Carver, present a worm scale to the Greeter, and return to the Temple before anyone noticed he was missing. He could be back in training with Obi-Wan inside of an hour, and he would sleep well tonight, with no bad dreams, exhausted and justified on a deep level not yet penetrated by Jedi discipline.

He would have to disguise his wrist wound, of course. It did not appear too bad, on cursory inspection, all he could manage in flight.

Time to pick his port, tuck, and drop like a stone once again—a stone in complete control.

Which is where Anakin always wanted to be.

Obi-Wan picked himself up from the broad curved surface of the shield and quickly, with Jedi expertise, assessed his physical condition. He was bruised, frustrated—he quickly damped that, for frustration could easily lead to self-defeating anger—but he had avoided breaking any bones. He was also winded, but he recovered even as he looked for the other racers.

Anakin circled in a slowly ascending spiral over the center of the shield and about a hundred meters above it. A second golden figure performed a quick, leaflike downward spiral about a hundred meters above Anakin. A third and fourth were ascribing broad arcs around the perimeter.

Obi-Wan focused on Anakin. He prepared his wings for another liftoff, just as he saw his Padawan tuck like a diver and drop out of sight through the shield's central hole.

Obi-Wan ran to the lip of the nearest port, about twenty meters distant. He made sure his wings were properly folded and could be easily swept out and expanded. His feet broke through gluey tractor fields on the shield's curved surface. The air sizzled around him. His insides felt as if he were marching through the worst thunderstorm on the most violent gas-giant planet.

Drifts of frozen moisture flurried around him in the wake of a canister as it screamed through a port less than fifty meters to his right. The cyclonic updraft nearly lifted him from his feet, and he did not know if he could muster the strength to stand upright once more against the local field lines.

Obi-Wan Kenobi, like Qui-Gon Jinn, was no supporter of training by punishment. Recognition of mistakes by the apprentice was almost always sufficient. Still, with shame, he saw in a dark part of his thoughts that he was planning harsh words, extreme trials, and many, many extra chores for Anakin Skywalker, and not just to improve his Padawan's perspective on life.

Anakin felt a pure kind of joy as he spread his wings and caught a field on the next lower level. The beauty of the ion trails, the lightning that played continuously between plumes of discharge smoke and brightened the distant walls of the pit, the drumbeat roar every five seconds of ascending canisters was beautiful, but more important, they all, with one almost-living voice, called out a challenge greater than anything he had experienced on Tatooine, including the Boonta Eve Podrace.

This was a place most would find terrifying, where most beings would certainly die, yet he was only a boy, a *mere child,* a former slave, relying not on Jedi training so much as raw native courage. He was alone, happy to be alone! He would gladly live out the rest of his life in this kind of immediate peril if he could simply forget the past failures that haunted him at night, whenever he tried to sleep. The failures—and the terrifying sense of carrying something beyond his power to control.

The dark empty boots that trod the worst of his nightmares.

Again, he picked out his port, near the shield center, where few canisters were launched. He could feel the pulse of the huge gun carriage beneath this lowest shield. His senses were tuned to the rhythm of that rotating launcher, bigger than the entire Jedi Temple. Anakin listened for the hesitation, the brief silence followed by a bass grind and *chuff* before a ring of canisters was chambered and fired. Best, of course, to drop through a port during a lull between discharges, and away from a port where a canister had recently passed, with its flux of gases, updrafts, lightning, and blue ion trails.

Before he made his decision, Anakin marveled at a phenomenon he had only heard about from other racers in tones of awe: rising circles of plasma spheres, drifting as if imbued with purpose in the void above the first shield. They glowed orange and greenish blue, and he could even hear their fierce sizzle. To touch them was to be instantly fried. He watched a circle of these spheres explode with tinny pops, and through the space where they had been, a particularly fierce bolt of lightning flew like a javelin through a hoop.

This raised his neck hair in a way no static discharge could explain. It was as if he faced the primitive gods of the garbage pit, the real masters of this place, yet to think this even for a moment went against all of his training. *The Force is everywhere and demands nothing, neither obeisance nor awe.*

But this, of course, was what he needed to experience in order to forget. He needed to strip down to pure savagery, to that place below his name, his memory, his self, where ominous shadows dwelled, and where one could turn in an instant from the light side of the Force to the dark and hardly know they were different.

Anakin, pure instinct, a mote of dust in the game, tucked his wings once more and dropped through the central port in the shield.

He did not notice, fifty meters above him, that the Blood Carver did the same.

The gun carriage sat on its elevated mount two hundred

meters below the shield, going through its automated motions. From tracks on all sides it received loaded and charged canisters, each falling into a firing chamber with only a bulbous tip protruding. Each canister bore a specific designation in the carriage program, a specified route through the four shields, with four chances to be accelerated into a specific orbit. The charge beneath the canister would carry it only the first three hundred meters, to the first shield. Thereafter the tractor fields and magnetic-pulse engines took over. It was a sophisticated yet centuries-old design, rugged, durable, duplicated all over Coruscant.

The air above the rotating carriage was almost unbreathable. Fumes from the exploding charges—simple chemical explosives—could not be vented and processed fast enough to prevent a toxic pall forming below the first shield. Added to this perpetual burnt-rubber haze were the miasmic vapors from the silicone-filled basin below the gun carriage.

It was here that the most primitive—not to mention the largest—creatures on Coruscant lived and performed their functions in a perpetual twilight, illuminated only by the fitful glows of work lights hung from the undersides of the gun carriage supports. The largest worms were hundreds of meters long and three or four meters wide.

Anakin glided to one side of the lowest level and alighted on a carriage support. He could feel through his feet the rotation and launching of the chambered canisters. The immense mass of the ferrocarbon structure shuddered under his flight slippers.

He had conserved most of his fuel for this moment. The tractor fields below the carriage were weak, sufficient only to discourage the worms from rising to suck at the supports. Once he had plucked loose a glassy worm scale, he would have to jet upward to the first shield and catch a canister updraft, then be pulled through a port to the void above the first shield.

This would be insanely difficult.

All the better. Anakin, eyes wide open, surveyed the dim, chaotic brew of worms below. He locked one wing briefly, pulled loose an arm, and wrapped a breather mask over his mouth and nose. He then took this opportunity to attach his optical cup and pulled down bubble goggles to protect his eyes from the silicone spray. Then he tensed to leap.

But he had made a Jedi apprentice's first mistake—to direct all one's attention to a single goal or object. Focus was one thing, narrow perception another, and Anakin had ignored everything above him.

He felt a prickle in his senses and looked to one side just in time to catch, with the top of his head, a blow aimed at his temple. The Blood Carver glided past and landed on the next stanchion, watching with satisfaction as the young Jedi tumbled headlong toward the churning worm-mass.

Then the Blood Carver followed, long neck stretched forward, nostril flaps clapped together in a wedge, gliding down to finish his day's work.

Anakin's fall was cushioned by an island of the thick, smelly froth that floated across the lake of worms. He sank slowly into the froth, releasing more noxious gases, until a burst of ammonia jerked him to stunned consciousness. His eyes stung. The blow to his head had knocked his goggles and breather mask awry.

First things first. He spread his wings and unbuckled his harness, then rolled over to distribute his weight evenly along the wings. They acted like snowshoes on the froth, and his rate of sinking slowed. The wings were bent and useless now anyway, even if he could tug them from the foaming mass.

The Blood Carver had just murdered him. That death would take its own sweet time to arrive was no relief from its certainty. The broad island of pale yellow undulated with the rise and fall of worm bodies. A constant crackling noise came from all around: bubbles bursting in the froth. And he heard a more sinister sound, if that was possible: the slow, low hiss of the worms sliding over and under and around each other.

Anakin could barely see. *I'm a goner.* Reaching out to put himself in tune with the Force might be soothing, but he had not yet reached the point in his training of being able to levitate, at least not more than a few centimeters.

In truth, Anakin Skywalker felt so mortified by his lack of attention, so ashamed by his actions in being here, in the pit, in the first place, that his death seemed secondary to much larger failures.

He was not made to be a Jedi, whatever Qui-Gon Jinn had thought of him. Yoda and Mace Windu had been correct all along.

But acid awareness of his stupidity did not require that he take further insults in stride. He felt the noiseless flight of the Blood Carver a few meters overhead and almost casually ducked in time to miss a second blow.

A Jedi does not contemplate revenge. But Anakin's brain was in full gear now, his thinking clarified by the ache in his skull and the dull throb in his arm. The Blood Carver knew who he was, where he was from—too much of a coincidence to be called a slave, this far from the lawless fringe systems where slavery was common. Someone was either stalking Anakin personally or Jedi in general.

Anakin doubted he had attracted much attention during his short life, or was worthy of an assassin's interest by himself. Far more likely that the Temple was being watched and that some group or other was hoping to take down the Jedi one by one, picking the weakest and most exposed first.

That would be me.

The Blood Carver was a threat to the people who had freed Anakin from slavery, who had taken him in and given him a new life away from Tatooine. If he was never to be a Jedi, or even live to maturity, he could remove at least one threat against that brave and necessary order.

He pulled up his breather mask, took a lungful of filtered air, and examined his foundering platform. A wing brace could be broken free and swung about as a weapon. He stooped carefully, balancing his weight, and grasped the slender brace. Strong in flight, the brace yielded to his off-center pressure, and he bent it back and forth until it snapped. At the opposite end, where the wings socketed in the rotator, he made another bend, stamping quickly with his booted foot, then jerked the end free and snatched away the flimsy lubricating sheath. The rotator ball made a fair club.

But the entire set of wings weighed less than five kilograms. The club, about a hundred grams. He would have to swing with all his might to give the impact meaning.

The Blood Carver swooped low again, his legs drawn back, triple-jointed arms hanging like the pedipalps on a clawswift on Naboo.

He was focused completely on the Padawan.

Making the same mistake as Anakin had.

With a heart-leap of hope and joy, Anakin saw Obi-Wan winging over the Blood Carver. The boy's master extended the beam on his lightsaber as he dropped with both feet on the assailant's wings and snapped them like straws.

Two swipes of the humming blade and the outer tips of the Blood Carver's wings fell away.

The Blood Carver gave a muffled cry and flipped on his back. The fuel in his wingtip tanks caught fire and spun him in a brilliant pinwheel, elevating him almost twenty meters before sputtering out.

He fell without a sound and slipped into the lake a dozen meters away, raising a small, gleaming plume of oily silicone. Ghosts of burning methane swirled briefly above him.

Obi-Wan recovered and raised his wings just in time to end up buried to his waist in the froth. The look on his face as he collapsed the lightsaber was pure Obi-Wan: patience and faint exasperation, as if Anakin had just failed a spelling test.

Anakin reached out to help his Master stay upright. "Keep your wings up, keep them high!" he shouted.

"Why?" Obi-Wan said. "I cannot *vault* the two of us out of this mess."

"I still have fuel!"

"And I have almost none. These are terrible devices, very difficult to control."

"We can combine our fuel!" Anakin said, his upper face and eyes bright in the murk.

The froth rippled alarmingly. At the edge of their insubstantial island of foam, a gleaming silver-gray tube as wide as four arm spans arched above the silicone slurry. Its skin was crusted with stuck-on bits of garbage, and its side was studded with a lateral line of small black eyes trimmed in brilliant blue.

The eyes poked out on small stalks and examined them curiously. The worm seemed to ponder whether they were worth eating.

Even now, Anakin observed the prize scales glittering along the worm's length. *The best I've ever seen—as big as my hand!*

Obi-Wan was sinking rapidly. He blinked at the haze of silicone mist and noxious gases wafting over them.

Anakin reached down with all the delicacy and balance he could muster and unhooked the fuel cylinders from his wings, taking care to disconnect the feed tubes to the outboard jets and pinch off their nozzles.

Obi-Wan concentrated on keeping himself from sinking any deeper into the sticky foam.

Another arch of worm segment, high and wide as a pedestrian walkway, thrust itself with a liquid squeal from the opposite side of the diminishing patch. More eyes looked them over. The arch quivered as if with anticipation.

"I'll never be this stupid again," Anakin said breathlessly as he attached the tanks to Obi-Wan's wings.

"Tell it to the Council," Obi-Wan said. "I have no doubt that's where we'll both be, if we manage to accomplish six impossible things in the next two minutes."

The two worm segments vibrated in unison and hissed through the silicone like tugged ropes, proving themselves to be one long creature as they rose high overhead. More coils surrounded them: other, bigger worms. Obviously, the Jedi—Master and apprentice—looked tasty, and now a competition was under way. The segments whipped back and forth, striking the edges of the island. The froth flew up in hissing puffs, until there was hardly more remaining than an unwieldy plug.

Anakin gripped Obi-Wan's shoulder with one hand. "Obi-Wan, you are the greatest of all the Jedi," he told him earnestly.

Obi-Wan glared at his Padawan.

"Could you give us just a little boost . . . ," Anakin pleaded. "You know, up and out?"

Obi-Wan did, and Anakin lit off their jets at the very same instant.

The jolt did not distract him from reaching out with outstretched fingers, grazing a curve of worm skin, and grabbing a scale. Somehow they lifted to the first shield and slipped into the updraft of a discharged canister. Spinning, knocked almost senseless, they were drawn up through a port.

Obi-Wan felt Anakin's small arms around his waist.

"If that's how it's done . . . ," the boy said, and then something—was it is his Padawan's newfound skill at levitation?—lifted them through the next shield as if they lay in the palm of a giant hand.

Obi-Wan Kenobi had never felt so close to such a powerful connection with the Force, not in Qui-Gon, nor Mace Windu. Not even in Yoda.

"I think we're going to make it!" Anakin said.

The opportunities are endless," Raith Sienar said as he walked along the factory parapet. Beside him strolled Commander Tarkin of the Republic Outland Regions Security Force. They might have been brothers. Both were in their early thirties. Both were thin and wiry, with high-arching bony brows, piercing blue eyes, aristocratic faces, and attitudes to match. And both wore robes of senatorial favor, showing extraordinary service to the senate over the past decade.

"You're speaking of the Republic?" Tarkin asked with more than a hint of disdain. His training—he came from an old and well-established military family—gave his voice a particular edge, both world-weary and amused.

"Not at all," Sienar said, smiling at his old friend. Beyond and below the parapet, four Advanced Project ships approached completion, black, sleek, smaller than previous models, and very fast indeed. "I haven't received an interesting contract from the Republic for seven years."

"What about these?" Tarkin asked.

"Private contracts with the Trade Federation, several mining firms, others. Very lucrative, so long as I don't sell my very best weapons to the wrong buyers. Every ship I make, I equip with weapons, as you doubtless know. Much more profitable that way, but tricky at times. So I keep the best in reserve . . . for my most generous customers."

Tarkin smiled at this answer. "Then I may have useful news for you," he said. "I've just come from a secret meeting. Chancellor Palpatine has finally forced a stand-down over the Naboo incident. The Trade Federation security forces will soon be disbanded. In the next few months, they are to be assimilated into Republic forces and placed at the disposal of the senate. All will comply—even Outland Mining—or face a centralized and much more powerful military response." Tarkin used a small hand scope to look over the details on the new ships. Each was twenty meters wide, with broad, flat cooling vanes terminating their wings. The compartments were compact, spherical, hardly luxurious. "If they are your main source of income, your position now is, shall we say, compromised?"

Sienar tipped his head to one side. He had already caught wind of Chancellor Palpatine's decree. "The Trade Federation had large reserves of money, and granted, they gave me many more interesting contracts than the Republic did, but I've kept my friends in the senate. I will miss Trade Federation patronage, but I don't see a complete collapse of Trade Federation influence for some time. As far as the Republic is concerned . . . their specifications are neither inspired nor inspiring. And when I do take a Republic contract, I'm forced to work with aging engineers the senators trust. I hope that changes."

"I've heard they do not look favorably upon you. You criticize them too freely, Raith. When your present customers pass into history, have you considered subcontracting?" Tarkin asked with a slightly taunting air.

Sienar gestured with his spidery fingers. "I hope you recognize I am versatile. After all, we've known each other for ten years."

Tarkin gave him an *oh, please!* glance. "I'm still a young man, Raith. Don't make me feel old." They advanced to the end of the parapet and along a suspended walkway leading to an octagonal, transparisteel-walled room suspended thirty meters above the center of the factory floor. "These, pardon me, look like advanced *fighters* to me. Very pretty they are, too."

Sienar nodded. "Experimental models for protecting freight haulers on the fringe. The Republic no longer polices some of the most lucrative routes. I presume with the Trade Federation forces integrated, they will once more. At any rate, these ships have already been paid for."

"They are storable?"

"Of course. Multistack in spare holds. All to spec. A true surprise for raiders. Now. Enough about my business worries. About *our* relationship—"

Tarkin rested his hands on the rail. "I've made new contacts," he said. "Very useful contacts. I can tell you very little more."

"You know I'm an ambitious man," Sienar said with a look he hoped seemed both hungry and dignified. Tarkin would not be easy to fool. "I have plans, Tarkin, extraordinary plans, which will impress anyone with imagination."

"I know plenty of people with *imagination,*" Tarkin said. "Perhaps too much imagination at times . . ." They continued walking. Assembly droids bustled beneath them, and a suspended crane hauled three fuselages in a nested carrier just meters away. "In truth, I've come to pick your brains, tell you a remarkable fairy tale, and enlist you in my cause, old friend. But not out here, not out in the open."

Inside the transparisteel-walled design room, closed to all but Sienar and his special guests, Tarkin sat in a comfortable chair of inflatable plastic, one of Sienar's design. Next to him a large dark gray holographic table hummed faintly.

Sienar dropped black security curtains all around the lighted center. The men were absorbed by an eerie silence.

Tarkin tried to speak, but no sound could be heard. Sienar handed him a small, nut-sized silver vocoder connected by a flexible wire to a beautifully machined plasteel mouthpiece. He showed Tarkin how to insert the button into his ear and allow the mouthpiece to float just in front of his lips.

Now they could hear each other.

"I do small favors for certain people," Tarkin said. "I once balanced these favors between opposing sides. Lately, my efforts have become a bit more lopsided. Balance is no longer necessary."

Sienar stood before his old friend and listened intently. His tall, cleanly muscled body seemed to reject repose.

"Some of these people have an appreciation for fingers—not tentacles, my friend, not palps, but human fingers—reaching into a great many stellar soup bowls, testing the temperature to see if they are ready for the eating."

"Why the concern that they be human?"

"Humans are the future, Raith."

"Some of my best designers are not even remotely human."

"Yes, and we employ nonhumans wherever they are useful, for now. But mark my words, Raith. *Humans are the future.*"

Raith noted the tension in Tarkin's voice. "So marked."

"Now listen closely. I'm going to tell you a tale of intrigue, wonderfully ornate, yet at its heart very simple. It involves a kind of spacecraft rare and little-seen, very expensive, of unknown manufacture, supposedly a toy for the wealthy. It may ultimately lead to a lost planet covered by a peculiar kind of forest, very mysterious. And it may soon involve the Jedi."

Sienar smiled in delight. "I adore stories about the Jedi. I'm quite the fan, you know."

"I myself am intrigued by them," Tarkin said with a smile. "One of my assignments—I will not tell you who does the assigning and how much they pay—is to keep track of all the Jedi on Coruscant. Keep track of them—and discourage any increase in their power."

Sienar lifted an eyebrow. "The Jedi support the senate, Tarkin."

Tarkin dismissed this with a wave. "There is a youngster among the Jedi with a curiosity for droids and all sorts of machinery, a junk collector, though with some talent, I understand. I have placed a small, very expensive, very broken droid in the way of this youngster, and he has taken it into the Jedi Temple and made it mobile again, as I suspected he would. And it has been listening to some curious private conferences."

Sienar listened with growing interest, but also growing puzzlement. The Jedi had not once, in his lifetime of designing and constructing fine ships and machines, ever shown an interest in contracting for spacecraft. They had always seemed content to hitch rides. As far as Sienar was concerned, for all their gallantry and discipline, the Jedi were technological ignoramuses—but for their lightsabers, of course. Yes, those were of interest . . .

"Please pay attention, Raith." Tarkin jerked him out of his reverie. "I'm getting to the good part."

Half an hour later, Sienar replaced the security vocoders in their box and lifted the curtains. He was pale, and his hands shook slightly. He tried to hide his anger.

Tarkin's moving in on what could have been mine!

But he quelled his chagrin. The secret was out. The rules had changed.

Absently, and to create a distraction from his reaction to Tarkin's story, he switched on the hologram display, and millions of tiny curves and lines assembled in the air over the dark gray table. They formed a slowly rotating sphere with a wide slice removed from the side. Two smaller spheres appeared above and below the poles, linked by thick necks bristling with spiky details.

With a contentedly prim expression, Tarkin turned to the hologram. His thin, cruel lips pressed tightly together, revealing thousands of years of aristocratic breeding. He bent over to examine the scale bars, and his eyebrow lifted.

Sienar was pleased by his reaction.

"Impossibly huge," Tarkin commented dryly. "A schoolboy fancy?"

"Not at all," Sienar said. "Quite doable, though expensive."

"You've piqued my curiosity," Tarkin said. "What is it?"

"One of my show projects, to impress those few contractors with a taste for the grandiose," Sienar said. "Tarkin, why have these . . . people . . . chosen me?"

"You haven't forgotten you're human?"

"That couldn't be their main criteria."

"You'd be surprised, Raith. But no, likely at this stage it is not crucial. It's your position and your intelligence. It's your engineering expertise, far greater than my own, though, dear friend, I do exceed you in military skills. And, of course, I do have *some* influence. Stick with me, and you'll go places. Fascinating places."

Tarkin could not take his eyes off the slowly rotating sphere, with its massive core-powered turbolaser now revealed. "Ah." He smiled. "Always a weapon. Have you shown this to anybody?"

Sienar shook his head sadly. He could see the enticement was working. "The Trade Federation knows precisely what it needs and shows no interest in anything else. A deplorable lack of imagination."

"Explain it to me."

"It's a dream, but an achievable dream, given certain advances in hypermatter technology. An implosion core with a plasma about a kilometer in diameter could power an artificial construct the size of a small moon. A couple of large ice asteroids for fuel . . . common enough still in the outer fringe systems . . ."

"A small crew could police an entire system with one vessel," Tarkin mused.

"Well, not so small a crew, but one vessel, certainly." Sienar walked around the display and made large, vaguely designing sweeps of his hands. "I'm considering removing the extraneous spheres, sticking with one large ball, ninety or a hundred kilometers in diameter. A more wieldy design for transport."

Tarkin smiled proudly. "I *knew* I picked the right man for this job, Raith." He admired the design with brows tightly knit. "What a sense of scale! What unutterable *power!*"

"I'm not sure I have any free time," Sienar said with a frown. "Despite my lack of connections, I still manage to keep very busy."

Tarkin waved his hand dismissively. "Forget these shadows of a past life and focus on the future. What a future it will be, Raith, if you satisfy the right people!"

The Jedi Temple was a massive structure, centuries old, well and beautifully made, but like much on Coruscant, the exterior had of late suffered from neglect. Below the five spotless and gleaming minarets, at the level of the dormitories and the staff entrances, paint flaked and bronze gutters dripped long green streaks down broad curved roofs. Molded metal sheets had lost their buffers of insulation and were beginning to electrically corrode, creating fantastic rainbow patterns on their surfaces where they touched.

Within the Temple, the domain of the Jedi Knights and their Padawans, the chambers were cool, with lighting at a minimum, except in the private quarters, which were spare enough, but provided with glow lamps for reading the texts taken from the huge library. Each cubicle was also equipped with a computer and holoprojector for accessing the later works of science and history and philosophy.

The overall effect, to an outsider, might have been one of studious gloom, but to a Jedi, the Temple was a center of learning, chivalry, and tradition unparalleled in the known universe.

It was meant to be a place of peace and reflection, commingled with periods of rigorous training. Increasingly, however, the Jedi Council devoted its time to troublesome matters of politics and the large-scale repercussions of a decades-long economic collapse.

The Republic could not afford too much reflection, however, nor too much study. This was soon to be an age of action and counteraction, with many forces arrayed against freedom and the principles that had guided the Jedi in their zealous guardianship of the senate and the Republic.

That explained why so many of the Masters were away from the Temple, scattered around the crumbling fringes of the Republic.

It did not explain why Mace Windu maintained a bemused smile even as he presided over the distressing case of Anakin Skywalker.

In truth, Obi-Wan Kenobi had never quite gotten the range of Mace Windu. Many declared that Yoda was the most enigmatic of the Jedi Knights, habitually teaching by trick rather than example, conundrum rather than pointed fact. Mace Windu, in Obi-Wan's experience, seemed to lead by rigorous example, using concrete guidelines and steady discipline rather than startled revelation. Yet of all the Jedi, he was quickest to appreciate a joke, and often to spring a devious philosophical trap during debates.

In physical training, he was among the toughest to best, because his moves could be so unexpected. Whatever he seemed to propose, or to oppose, might in fact be a ploy to encourage quite a different result.

There was a creative whimsy to the man that defied intellectual analysis. And that was one reason why Mace Windu was ranked a Jedi Master.

Decadent cynics in the Senate District who knew little about the Jedi regarded them as somber, stuffy preservers of a fusty old religion, like shreds of an aging fabric soon to give way to a gleaming new garment, an age of surgical precision and cold, hard facts. Mace Windu reminded all who came in contact with him that the Jedi Knights were a vibrant, living order, rich in contradictions, possessing a vitality very difficult—some said impossible—to extinguish.

Obi-Wan and Anakin, as soon as they had scrubbed and showered away the silicone and stench, climbed the steps and took an ancient but beautifully maintained turbolift to the heights of the gleaming Council Tower. Late-afternoon sun poured through the broad windows in the Council chamber. The circular room was suffused by an antique golden glow, but this glow did not fall upon Anakin, whose slight form was obscured by the shadow of a tall and vacant chair.

The Padawan looked more than a little bewildered.

Obi-Wan stood beside him, as a Master must when his apprentice is in peril of dismissal.

Four Masters were present. The other chairs were empty. Mace Windu presided. Obi-Wan remembered several disciplinary hearings for his own Master, Qui-Gon Jinn, yet none had been held in such a charged atmosphere as this, no matter Mace Windu's amused expression.

"Anakin Skywalker has been with us three years now, and has shown himself a capable student," Mace began. "More than capable. Brilliant, with abilities and strengths we have all hoped to see developed and controlled."

Mace rose and walked around the pair, his robes swishing

faintly with the movement of his long legs. "Strength of character is a challenge to be overcome by a Padawan, for it may be a mask for careless will lacking center and purpose. What seems bright in youth tarnishes in maturity, and crumbles in age. A Jedi is allowed no such weakness." He stopped in front of the boy. "Anakin Skywalker, what is your error?"

Obi-Wan stepped forward to speak, but Mace's hand shot up, and his eyes sparked with warning. Though a Master must defend his Padawan, it was clear the Council was beyond that here.

Obi-Wan suspected the worst: that a judgment had already been rendered, and that Anakin was to be released from the Temple.

Anakin watched Mace with large eyes, uncharacteristically subdued.

Mace was unrelenting. "I ask again, what was your error?"

"I brought shame upon the order and the Temple," Anakin responded quickly now, his voice high and soft.

"That is hardly precise. Again, your error?"

"To break the laws of the municipality, and . . . and . . ."

"No!" Mace declared, and his smile vanished, replaced by a stern expression, like the dark underside of a cloud heretofore painted by sun.

Anakin flinched.

"Obi-Wan, explain to your Padawan his error. It does, after all, arise from the same roots as your own." Mace regarded Obi-Wan with a lifted brow.

Obi-Wan considered this intently for a long moment before answering. Nobody tried to rush him. Inner truth was a perilous journey, even for a Jedi.

"I see it," he said. "We both want certainty."

Anakin stared at his master with a puzzled frown.

"Explain to us all how you have failed your Padawan," Mace said, gently enough, considering the turnabout in the proceedings.

"He and I are far too young for the luxury of certainty," Obi-Wan began. "Our experience is insufficient to earn us even momentary peace. As well, I have been more concerned with his growth than my own, distracted by his obvious flaws, rather than using his mirror to guide me, so that I may in turn guide him."

"A good beginning," Mace allowed. "Now, young Skywalker, explain to the Council how you can find peace by seeking cheap thrills among the most deluded occupants of this planet."

Anakin's frown deepened.

"You are defensive," Mace warned.

"What I did, I did to fill a lack in my training," Anakin shot back testily.

Mace's expression turned stolid, and his eyes became heavy lidded, languid, as he placed his arms behind his back. "And who is responsible for this lack?"

"I am, Master."

Mace nodded, his rugged face like ancient hewn stone. No trickster here, no humor now. Behind that face, if one knew how to sense it, burned an unbearably brilliant flame of concentration, easily worthy of the legendary Masters of past millennia.

"I seek to escape pain," Anakin said. "My mother—"

Mace lifted his hand, and Anakin instantly fell silent. "Pain can be our greatest teacher," Mace said, barely above a whisper. "Why turn away from pain?"

"It . . . it is my strength. This I see."

"That is not correct," Obi-Wan said, placing his hand on Anakin's shoulder. The boy looked between them, confused.

"How is it wrong, teacher?" Mace asked Obi-Wan.

"Lean upon pain like a crutch and you create anger and a dark fear of truth," Obi-Wan said. "Pain guides, but it does not support."

Anakin cocked his head to one side. He seemed slight and even insubstantial among these Jedi Knights, all this overwhelming experience. His face collapsed in misery. "My most useful talents are not those of a Jedi."

"Indeed, you throw your spirit and your anguish into machines and useless competitions, rather than directly confronting your feelings," Mace said. "You have cluttered our Temple halls with droids. I stumble over them. But we are away from the crux of our present matter. Try again to explain your error."

Anakin shook his head, caught between stubbornness and tears. "I don't know what you want me to say."

Mace took a shallow breath and closed his eyes. "Look inward, Anakin."

"I don't want to," Anakin said breathlessly, his voice jerking. "I don't like what I see."

"Is it possible you see nothing more than the tensions of approaching adulthood?" Mace asked.

"No!" Anakin cried. "I see . . . too much, too much."

"Too much what?"

"I burn like a sun inside!" The boy's voice rang out in the chamber like a bell.

A moment of silence.

"Remarkable," Mace Windu admitted. Curiously, a smile flickered on his lips. "And?"

"And I don't know what to do with it. I want to run. It makes me reckless, so I seek sensation. I don't blame any of you for—" He could not finish that sentence.

Obi-Wan felt the boy's anguish like a small knife in his own gut.

"My own mother didn't know what to do with me," Anakin murmured.

The door in the far wall swung open slowly. Mace and Obi-Wan looked up to see who was there.

A small female figure clad in Temple robes stepped into the circle, and a clear voice sang through the chamber. "Just as I thought. A little inquisition going on here, eh?"

Mace got to his feet, smiling broadly at the sarcasm. "Welcome, Thracia."

Obi-Wan bowed his head in respect.

"Anakin, may I stand beside you?" Thracia Cho Leem walked slowly toward the center of the chamber where Obi-Wan and Anakin stood. Her gray hair was cut to a close cap on her long skull, and her aquiline nose sniffed at the cool air as if she judged all by their scent. Her eyes, large and bright, irises like ultramarine beads, swept the empty seats. She gathered her long dark robes and pulled up her sleeves to reveal strong, thin arms. Then she thrust out her chin. "I should have warned you I'd return, Mace," she said.

"It is always an honor, Thracia," Mace said.

"You seem to be ganging up on this boy."

"It could be worse," Mace said. "Most of the Council are away today. Yoda would be much harsher—"

"That big-eared tree stump knows nothing about human children. And for that matter, neither do you. You've never married, Mace! I have. I have many sons and daughters, on many worlds. Sometimes I think you should all take a break, as I did, and sniff the real air, see how the Force manifests in everyday life, rather than mope around learning how to swing lightsabers."

Mace's smile became one of delight. "It is wonderful to have you with us, Thracia, after so many years." There was not a hint of irony in his tone. He was, in fact, pleased to have her in the room, and seemed even more pleased that she had surprised them. "What do you suggest for young Skywalker?"

"There's something wrong with me," Anakin interrupted, and then clamped his mouth shut, glancing around the chamber.

"Nonsense!" Thracia cried, her face wrinkled in irritation. She was about Anakin's height, and looked him straight in the eyes. "None of us can see into another's heart. Mercifully, the Force does not do that for us. I ask you, boy, what do you want to prove?"

"You know what happened?" Obi-Wan inquired of her.

"You came back this afternoon covered with slime and smelling of garbage. It's the talk of the staff in the Temple," Thracia said. "Anakin amuses them. He's brought more energy and spark to this gloomy old pile than anyone in recent memory, including Qui-Gon Jinn. Now, boy, what do you want to prove?"

"I don't want to prove anything. I need to know who I am, as Obi-Wan tells me over and over."

Thracia sniffed once more and regarded Obi-Wan with a mix of affection and sharp judgment. "Obi-Wan has forgotten ever being a child."

Obi-Wan gave her a small grin. "Qui-Gon would have disagreed."

"Qui-Gon! Now *there* was a child, all his life a child, and wiser than most! But enough banter. I sense there is real danger here."

"There was an assassination attempt," Obi-Wan said. "A Blood Carver."

"We suspect involvement from dissident forces within the Republic," Mace said.

"He knew all about me," Anakin added.

"All?" Thracia inquired, arching a brow at Mace.

"I let him—" The boy's eyes widened in realization. He stared at Obi-Wan. "Master, I realize my error!"

Thracia pressed her lips together and turned to Obi-Wan.

Obi-Wan folded his arms. He and Anakin might have been brothers, separated by only a double handful of years, yet Obi-Wan was the closest thing the boy could ever have to a father. "Yes?"

"I sought out personal peace and satisfaction in the pit race, rather than thinking of the greater goals of the Jedi."

"And?" Obi-Wan encouraged.

"I mean, I know it was wrong to sneak out of the Temple, to mislead my master, to engage in illegal activity that could have brought disrepute on the order—"

"A long list," Mace Windu said.

"But . . . I pursued personal goals even after it should have been obvious to me that the Temple was being threatened."

"Very serious, indeed," Thracia murmured. She took Anakin by the shoulders, then glanced at Obi-Wan to see if she could intervene. He assented, though with some misgivings. Thracia was renowned for training female Jedi, not for preparing young males.

"Anakin, your powers, someday, could surpass those of anyone in this room. But what happens when you push something harder?"

"It moves faster," Anakin said.

She nodded. "You are propelled by an inheritance few can understand." Thracia dropped her hands from his shoulders. "Obi-Wan?"

"Moving faster gives you little time to think," Obi-Wan continued where she had left off. "You must temper your passions, but be less concerned, for now, with being free from your pain. Youth is a time of uncertainty and unrest."

"Couldn't have put it better myself," Thracia said. "Anakin, *be a child*. Revel in it. Test your limits. Irritate and provoke. It is your way. Time enough for wisdom when you've worn more holes in your shoes. Run your master ragged! It'll be good for him. It'll remind him of when he was a boy. And . . . tell us what you need, *now*, to go where you must finally go in your training."

Mace Windu seemed about to violently disagree with this, but Thracia gave him a radiant smile, brows high on her wrinkled forehead, and his shoulders drooped. Thracia was one of the few who could outjape Mace Windu, and he knew it.

Anakin looked around the room, realizing that whatever the mood at the beginning of the meeting, there was little chance now of his being expelled from the Temple. Thracia had made her point, as only she could, by lightly stinging them all.

"I need a job, a mission," he said, his voice cracking with emotion. "I need something to do. Something real."

"How can we give you our trust?" Mace asked, leaning forward and staring at the boy. Anakin did not avert his eyes. The power of his spirit, of his personality, was almost frighteningly apparent.

"Indeed, Padawan, how *can* we trust you, after all these errors?" Thracia asked, her voice level. "It is one thing to be what you are, quite another to drag others into danger." Anakin stared at her for long seconds, searching her face as he might look over a map, trying to find his way home.

"I never make the same mistake twice," he finally said, blinking slowly. He faced the other Council members. "I'm not stupid."

"I agree," Thracia said. "Mace, give these two something useful to do, rather than stewing in the Temple pot."

"I was approaching that conclusion," Mace said.

"Taking all day and terrifying the boy!" Thracia exclaimed.

"Anakin is not easily frightened, not by us," Mace said wryly. "Thracia, there must be another reason you honor us today."

"How observant!" she said. "The danger grows daily, and our enemies, whoever they are, within the senate or without, may again try to target our students before they are ready to defend themselves." Thracia flapped out her sleeves and sat in an empty Council seat beside Mace. "You sent my former apprentice, Vergere, on a mission, and we have heard nothing from her in a year. Vergere is self-reliant, as Jedi are trained to be. It is possible she has extended her mission, or found another. In any case, I request that Obi-Wan Kenobi be sent as backup."

"With me?" Anakin asked, his face eager. He remembered Vergere, an intense, trim, and diminutive female who had treated him with polite reserve—as if he were an adult. He had liked her. He had especially liked the patterns of feathers and short whiskers around her face and her large, quizzical eyes.

"Would this be a long mission?" Obi-Wan asked.

"To the far side of the galaxy, far beyond the rule of the Republic," Mace said thoughtfully. "If we agree."

"A chance for adventure and growth, away from the seethe and intrigue of the capital world," Thracia said. "Obi-Wan, you are not enthusiastic?"

Obi-Wan stepped forward. "If the Temple is in danger, I would rather stay and defend it."

"I see the path we all tread," Mace said. "Thracia is concerned about her apprentice, even now that Vergere has become a Jedi Knight. This mission involves mystery, long journeys, and an exotic world—all things that could focus the attention of a young Padawan."

"We must not encourage adventurism for its own sake," Obi-Wan protested. Anakin looked up at him, dismayed.

Mace's somber face showed he shared some of Obi-Wan's concerns, but not all. He raised his hand. "Matters are not yet at crisis on Coruscant. That may be decades away. While you are gone, Obi-Wan, we can *probably* fend for ourselves." Mace's lips cracked the faintest of smiles. "A Padawan must attend his Master. Anakin, do you agree?"

"Absolutely!" Anakin squirmed with the hope of being out from under so many critical eyes. "Is the meeting over?"

"In due time," Mace said, eyes languid once more. "Now, explain to me again how you got involved in this race."

Anakin lay on his cot in the small room, twirling a droid verbobrain in his hands. His face was utterly intent in the pool of light from his small glow lamp. His brows cast deep shadows over his eyes. He ran his hands over his short hair and peered deep into the unit's connectors.

He did not like the fact that he had won. It seemed wrong that he had stepped so far out of line, and yet had been retained as a Padawan. He did not like the unease this victory, if victory it was, produced in him. Above all weaknesses, arrogance was the most costly.

They keep me here because I have potential they've never seen before. They keep me in training because they're curious to see what I can do. I feel like a rich man who never knows whether his friends are true—or whether they just want his money.

This was a particularly galling thought, and certainly neither true nor fair. *Why do they put up with me, then? Why do I keep testing them? They tell me to use my pain—but sometimes I don't even know where the pain comes from! I worried my mother—and I tested her, again and again, to make sure she loved me. She sent me away so I could be brought up by stronger people. So I could control myself. And I still haven't learned.*

He sat up in a squat and plugged a test wire into the verbobrain. Small criticality lights flickered to dull red on the perimeter of the knobby sphere.

A compact protocol droid filled a corner of the room. Anakin stood and lifted the droid's access panel, inserted the verbobrain, and arranged the leads again at different test points. Criticality lights showed that this unit could direct its own actions once more. With a flick of his finger, Anakin started the verbobrain spinning. It rolled back and forth on high-speed gimbals faster than even his quick eyes could track, seeking inputs from the many sensor brushes arranged within the droid's head.

Another droid repaired. The Jedi had no use for them, but they were yet one more eccentricity they somehow tolerated. *Usually.*

One of Anakin's smaller droids, a fancy home-maintenance model he had picked up half-crushed on the street, had been found in the Council chamber, working on light fixtures that did not need repair. That one had been returned to him neatly cut in half, the edges fused in an easily recognizable way.

A comparatively gentle warning.

Anakin took some comfort in this. Too much tolerance for deviation showed weakness, and the Blood Carver's attempt on his life indicated there was real danger on Coruscant.

He sucked in a deep breath and resolved that these were probably the only people in the galaxy who *could* teach and train and direct him. And, of course, the weight of that job lay on Obi-Wan, whom Anakin loved and respected, and for that reason, needed to test all the more.

Tomorrow they would leave Coruscant, the destination not yet specified. He needed to get some sleep.

Anakin dreaded sleep.

It seemed, in his dreams, that something inside was testing *him,* something very strong, and it did not care whether it was loved or feared.

Vergere was my most able apprentice. I was with her from the time she was an infant fresh from her egg. She herself chose this mission." Thracia Cho Leem accompanied Obi-Wan and Anakin onto the passenger ramp of the orbital transport. Alone, the transport occupied a special bay reserved for Jedi travel in the Capital Terminal. She handed Obi-Wan a small data card. Anakin stood with hands clasped behind him, watching the older Jedi with an eager expression.

"The details are too sensitive to talk about here," Thracia said. "When you are with Charza Kwinn, he will give you another card, necessary to unlock the contents. Charza may seem a little difficult, a little strange, but he has served the Jedi well for over a century. I entrusted Vergere to him, and now, I entrust you. May the Force be with you!"

The transport carried them effortlessly into space. Anakin sat in the forward compartment as Obi-Wan closed his eyes and meditated in the seat across from him. The Republic transport was in good mechanical repair, as befitted a *Senate*-class vessel, but Anakin felt the decorative details were less than first-rate. Not that he appreciated luxury. He was just very much in tune with the way people maintained their machines.

"Master, this isn't the mission you wanted, is it?"

Obi-Wan opened his eyes. His meditation had not gone very far, just to the point of isolating his thoughts from all language and social connections, to the edge of a simple unity with the Force, and he returned easily enough. Anakin seldom meditated, though he certainly knew how. "I have learned to accept what the Council assigns us," Obi-Wan said, clearing his throat.

A service droid rolled forward and presented them with a variety of juices in squeeze bulbs. They were the only passengers this trip. Obi-Wan finished a bulb. Anakin took two and juggled them for a moment before sucking them dry.

"Where would you rather be?" Anakin asked. "If you didn't have to be my teacher."

"We are where we are, and our job is important."

"Where do you go when you meditate?" Anakin asked.

Obi-Wan smiled at the boy's chatter. "To a state of mind and body where I reacquaint myself with simplicity."

Anakin wrinkled his nose. "I don't meditate very often."

"I've noticed."

"I get to a certain point and I just overload. It's like I'm plugging into a supernova. Something goes blooey in me. I don't like it."

Anakin had not told him this before. Getting away from the Temple was already showing benefits. Thracia had been right. "We should work on that during our journey. As for now, direct your energy," Obi-Wan suggested. "There are many Jedi texts yet to be learned. Mace insisted you keep up your studies."

"I'll work on them once I know where we are and where we're going," Anakin said.

Obi-Wan knew better than to question this. Anakin was no slouch at his studies. Indeed, he was much quicker than Obi-Wan had been at his age.

Once in orbit, the transport quickly sidled up to a transfer dock. Anakin recognized the class of ship on the opposite side of the dock: a small cargo transport, probably a modified YT-1150. It resembled a long oval loaf of bread sliced lengthwise into three pieces, the center fuselage the largest. Judging from the changes Anakin could see in the nacelle that held the outboard stabilizers and the hyperdrive integrator, the modifications easily made it a Class 0.8, faster than anything in the Republic or the Trade Federation listings.

Anakin eagerly watched as the connection tunnels linked. The smell of the air inside changed drastically.

Charza Kwinn's ship smelled like an ocean, Obi-Wan thought. A not-very-fresh tide pool.

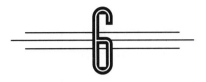

Charza Kwinn was a male Priapulin. In a galaxy of a great variety of life-forms, which any cosmopolitan traveler would find unremarkable, Priapulins still looked like an angler's bad dream. Obi-Wan had heard of this legendary auxiliary to the Jedi many times, of course, but was still not quite prepared for his actual presence.

Most worms were without backbone. Charza had five knobby notochords arranged around his tubular length. Flattened lengthwise, he stretched at least four meters from tip to tail when fully straightened, which was rare.

As he greeted his two travelers, he was curled in an upright radical **S**, the top of that **S** nearly touching the bend in its first curve, like a squashed hook. His eyes rose in three pairs along the upper curve of this hook. His underside was covered with a brush of thick bristles that constantly rubbed against each other as if in speculation. His lower tail, or foot, rode on a similar stiff brush, scrubbing with a hiss through the thin film of water that covered the floor. Along his outside edges, long flexible spines stuck out like the fringe of a starched carpet.

Anakin was most fascinated by the shapes of these spines. Some were like tiny hooks, others were spatulate, and still others formed tiny thorny balls. Charza Kwinn used them as hundreds of exquisitely capable fingers.

"Welcome to the *Star Sea Flower*," he greeted them. "Good once more to have Jedi accompany me between the stars."

For all his dreadful majesty, Charza spoke in a smooth sibilant whisper, making these tones by rubbing bristles together near his spiracles, his breathing vents. That he spoke at all was remarkable. That his speech was clear, and his words disarmingly friendly, was startling.

The darkened and damp interior of Charza's ship was enlivened by small wriggling things. Larger animals hid in corners and peered out as Charza escorted Obi-Wan and Anakin through his ship. Pumps and filters whined faintly and kept the water as refreshed as could be expected. The scant illumination came from a scattered glow of instruments and thin laser beams stretched at intervals across the corridors. Tiny spotlights tracked the larger creatures, including Anakin and Obi-Wan.

Obi-Wan took all this in stride, though he hoped there were special quarters for passengers less aquatic than Charza.

"It's an honor to work with you, Charza Kwinn," Obi-Wan said, and introduced Anakin. Anakin was both wary and fascinated.

Charza issued something like a chuckle. "Jedi young have big eyes when they come aboard the *Star Sea Flower*. Do not mind the fragrances. All will be freshened once we are away, cruising in hyperspace. Until then, energy is conserved, comfort reduced."

Charza took them down a narrow tunnel toward the center

of the fuselage, well away from the drives, and brushed against a large chrome button at the end of the tunnel. The hatch swung outward with a sigh, and warm dry air wafted over them like a draft out of the deep deserts of Tatooine.

Obi-Wan entered their travel quarters and rubbed his hands with satisfaction. "Most excellent, Charza," he said. Anakin stepped through and wiped his feet on the absorbent mat just below the hatch.

Charza hung back, clearly uncomfortable with the dry air. The small but well-equipped room was bright and warm, furnished with two acceleration couches that doubled as beds. Looking up, Anakin saw they had a direct view of space through a broad circular port, radially ribbed for additional strength.

"We depart in a tenth of a tide . . . one standard hour," Charza announced. "There are waterproof shoes, boots, that will adjust to fit, should you decide to keep me company forward, in the pilothouse. That would bring me no end of delight." Charza backed away, and the hatch closed.

Anakin settled in and dropped his small bag in a closet. "Vergere must have stayed here," he observed.

"Unless she preferred swimming," Obi-Wan said.

"What do you think happened to her?"

"I wouldn't dare hazard a guess. Her skills are exceptional. She is as resourceful as Thracia, and almost as adventurous as you."

Anakin smiled at this. "But more sensible?"

Obi-Wan inclined his head. "You can be sensible," he allowed.

"But it's a sometime thing," Anakin said. "Now, can you tell me where we're going?"

Obi-Wan stowed his own travel kit and sat on the end of one couch. He folded his hands and looked steadily at Anakin. "I won't know all the details until we match our data card with Charza's. I do know this: The Jedi received knowledge of a world in the Gardaji Rift, within the Tingel Arm, far beyond the bounds of Republic rule. There had been intelligence from free-lance traders about an outlying community that built exceptional starships, small personal craft, sleek and beautifully made, and rated easily at zero-point-four."

Anakin's eyes goggled. He sat across from Obi-Wan, eager to hear more.

"The rumors were associated with a mysterious planet, called Sekot by some, Zonama Sekot by others."

"Sea-coat?"

"Zonama Sekot, sources told us, was the actual name of the planet, which circles a small dwarf star at the far spinward and galactic north side of the rift. But charts from expeditions in that region of two centuries past show only rocky rubble, protoplanets, nothing of interest but to future hardscrabble miners. Nothing alive, certainly. Still, other sources confirmed that a kind of diffuse trade route had been established, and that rich connoisseurs of star travel were coming by secret appointment to have ships made. While the ships have been observed in certain systems, no one in Republic security has ever examined one in detail."

"Sounds like a legend," Anakin said. "Maybe a hoax."

"Perhaps. However, an intrusion was reported three years ago in the Gardaji region, from an unknown spacefaring species. It was that which Vergere was sent to investigate, and inciden-tally, to see if she could locate Zonama Sekot. She found the planet . . . and sent to our farthest outlying station a brief mes-sage. But nothing has been heard of her since. The transmission was garbled. We have only interesting fragments."

"And what did she find?"

"A world covered with dense jungle, of a kind never observed before. Huge treelike life-forms and hidden factories. Her report did little more than confirm that the legend is true."

Anakin shook his head in wonder. "Rugged," he said admiringly. "Absolutely rugged!"

"We'll look over the full reports once we're under way," Obi-Wan said. "Now, we should join Charza."

"He's rugged, too," Anakin said. "I'd like to see him go up against a Hutt."

"Charza comes from a species devoted to peace," Obi-Wan said. "He regards overt conflict as the grossest breach, and would rather die than fight. Still, he is intensely intelligent and extremely ambitious."

"So he makes a great spy?"

"A great spymaster. And an extraordinarily resourceful pilot," Obi-Wan said.

Raith Sienar was a very wealthy man. His scrupulous attention to markets, his extraordinary skill in managing his workers—human and otherwise—and his strategy of always keeping operations relatively small and localized had brought him profits beyond his wildest dreams of youth.

This new prospect—of joining with Tarkin in an enterprise both nebulous and risky—made him nervous, but something deep inside pushed him forward nonetheless.

Instinct had moved him this far, and instinct said this was the pulse of the future. In truth, he might know a few more things about that future than Tarkin.

Still, it was wise to be cautious, knowledgeable, prepared, in all times of change.

Another contributor to his success had been his habit of hiding excesses. And he did indeed have excesses—that was the word he used, much better than foibles or eccentricities.

Not even Tarkin knew about Sienar's collection of failed experiments.

Sienar walked slowly down the long hall that lay over a kilometer beneath the central factory floor of Sienar Systems' main Coruscant plant. Holograms appeared just ahead of him, holoprojectors turning on as he passed, showing product rollouts for the Republic Defense Procurement plan ten years before, commendations from senators and provincial governors, prototype deliveries for the early contracts with the many branches of the Trade Federation, which had become more and more cloaked in secrecy as it tightened its central authority.

He smiled at the most beautiful—and so far, the largest—of his products, a thousand-passenger ceremonial cruiser rated at Class Two, designed for triumphal receptions on worlds signing exclusive contracts with the Trade Federation.

And then there was his fastest and most advanced design, most heavily armed, as well, made for a very secretive customer—someone of whom Sienar suspected Tarkin was completely ignorant. *He should not underestimate my own contacts, my own political pull!* he thought.

But in fact, Sienar had never learned with certainty just who that customer was, only that he—or she, or it—favored Sienar designs. But he suspected the buyer was a person of great importance. And he suspected much more, as well. *A buyer whose name it is death to even whisper.*

So the Republic was changing, perhaps dying, perhaps being murdered around them day by day. Tarkin intimated as much, and Sienar could not disagree. But Sienar would survive.

His ships had likely ferried between star systems the very personages that Tarkin could only hint at. That made him proud, but at the same time . . .

Raith Sienar knew that extraordinary opportunity also meant extraordinary danger.

Tarkin was sufficiently intelligent and very ambitious, and also as venal as they came. This amused Sienar, who fancied himself above most of the comforts of the flesh. The comforts of the intellect, however, he was perfectly willing to wallow in.

Luxurious intellectual toys were his weakness, and the best of those toys were the failures of his competitors, which he bought cheap whenever he could, saving them from the scrap heaps of technological disgrace. Sometimes he had had to rescue these unhappy products from a kind of execution. Some were too dangerous to be kept operational, or even intact.

He keyed in his entry code to the underground museum and sniffed at the cool air, then stood for a moment in the darkness of the small antechamber, savoring the peace. Sienar came here most often to think, to get away from all distractions, to make key decisions.

Recognizing him, the chamber turned on its lights, and he keyed another code into the door to the museum's long underground nave. With an anticipatory sigh, Sienar entered this temple of failures, smiled, and lifted his arms in greeting to the ranks of exhibits.

Standing among these glorious examples of overreaching and bad planning helped clear his mind wonderfully. So much failure, so many technical and political missteps—bracing, tart, like a cold, astringent shower!

A group of his favorites occupied a transparent cube near the museum entrance: a squad of four hulking universal combat droids equipped with so many weapons they could hardly lift themselves from the ground. They had been manufactured in the factory system of Kol Huro, seven planets totally devoted to turning out defense systems and starships for a petty and vicious tyrant vanquished by the Republic fifteen years ago. Each was over four meters tall and almost as broad, with very tiny intelligence units, slow, awkward, as stupid in conception as the tyrant who had ordered their design. Sienar had smuggled them past Republic customs ten years ago, and they had not been disarmed, nor were their weapons nonfunctional. Their core intelligence had been removed, however. Not that it had made that much difference. They were kept on minimum power, and their sensors tracked him slowly as he walked past, their tiny eyes glowing, their weapons pods jerking in disappointment.

He smiled, not at *them*, pitiful monstrosities, but at their makers.

Next in his rank of prizes came a more insidious machine, one that actually revealed both ingenuity and some care in execution: a landing pod designed to invade the metal-bearing asteroids of an unexploited star system and set up shop, making small invasion droids out of the raw ore. The mining equipment had been very well made. The unit had failed, however, in the finesse of its droid factories. Less than one out of a hundred of the droids had proven functional.

Sienar had thought often about this approach, creating a machine to make more machines, all of them programmed to carry out offensive strategies. But the Republic had too many scruples to show much interest in such weapons, and the Neimoidian leaders in the Trade Federation had rejected them out of hand as impractical. Not much imagination there, at least as of a few years ago . . .

Perhaps that was why their leadership had capitulated to Chancellor Palpatine.

The lights came on for the major rank of cubicles, stretching off five hundred meters to the end of the nave. Two thousand and twelve exhibits of failed weapons and ship design. So many minatory admonishments—*you are fallible, Raith Sienar. Always think three times before acting, and then, always prepare three alternatives.*

A small cubicle between two larger exhibits held a rather ugly assassin droid, with a long cylindrical head and rudimentary thorax. These assassins had failed on two accounts: they were depressingly obvious in appearance, and they were likely to go completely out of control and kill their makers. This one had had its verbobrain crisped by high-security droids. Sienar kept it here because a former classmate from Rigovian Technical University had been involved in the design, and this very unit had killed her. It was a cautionary reminder not to overstep one's competence.

Anticipating a change in political psychology, Sienar had recently begun to contemplate his own weaknesses, his own narrow focus. He had always preferred elegance, finesse, and pinpoint expression of power. And he had always dealt with leaders who more or less agreed—a widespread ruling class used to centuries of relative calm, used to dealing with isolated system wars through embargo and police action. Who would replace such a ruling class?

Those who espoused elegance and finesse?

He did not think so. Entering his museum of failures, he had begun to see himself mounted in the center of his own prize exhibits, rigid, inflexible, outdated, outmoded . . . and so young!

Those who replace effete elites rule by brutality. This was a law in the history of the galaxy. A kind of political balance, frightening but true.

Months ago, coming at his craft from another angle—brutal and centralized strength—Sienar had begun work on the Expeditionary Battle Planetoid, whose design had so entranced Tarkin. Tarkin's reaction suggested that Sienar's guess—stab in the dark might be more accurate—had hit its mark. These new leaders might be far more impressed by high melodrama than style.

Tarkin himself had always been easily impressed by size and brute force. That was why Sienar had kept up their friendship. Tarkin was astute politically and militarily, but in Sienar's own expertise—the machines of transportation and war—he was decidedly inferior. Tarkin had admitted as much in their interview.

Yet . . . Admitting a weakness, the need for a partner, was unlike Tarkin in so many ways.

Who was playing with whom?

"Most interesting," a voice behind him said. Sienar nearly jumped out of his skin. Spinning about, he looked between two cubicles and saw the tall, thin form of Tarkin, half in shadow, his blue eyes gleaming like small beads. Standing tall behind him, a being with multijointed limbs, an incredibly broad nose, and iridescent gold skin watched Sienar closely.

"Suddenly I find there's very little time, and we need something from you," Tarkin said. "You are either with us on this venture, or we move without you. But I must have a certain piece of information. If you decide against joining us, and give us that information, then out of respect for our friendship, and knowing you can keep a few secrets if there's profit in it, my young acquaintance here will not kill you."

Sienar knew he could not afford the time to be surprised. Times were changing. Friendships could be expected to change as well. To ask how Tarkin and his associate happened to gain access to his private sanctuary would be fruitless and, in the discourse of the moment, possibly even rude.

"You want something from me," Sienar rephrased, with a wry smile. "Something you don't think I'll give willingly. But all you had to do was ask, Tarkin."

Tarkin ignored this. There was now no humor in him at all and no tolerance. His face looked surprisingly old and malevolent. Evil.

Sienar sensed desperation.

"You were once a major subcontractor in a retrofit of the YT light trade class of vessels."

"That's a matter of record. Most of them have long since been put out of service by their original owners. Later models are so much more efficient."

Tarkin waved that away. "You placed a tracking unit in the integument of every vessel you retrofitted. One you could activate with a private code. And you did not reveal this fact to the owners, or for that matter, to any authorities."

Sienar's expression did not change. *He needs the codes necessary to switch on one of the trackers.*

"Hurry," the Blood Carver said, its voice thin but self-possessed. Sienar noticed the tall gold being was recovering from a number of wounds, some superficial, but at least two more serious.

"Give me the ship's serial number, and I'll give you the code," Sienar said. "As a friend. *Really,* Tarkin."

Tarkin gestured quickly to the Blood Carver. He held out a small datapad on which the number was displayed, blinking rapidly in red. Beneath the number, an orbital registry account was also blinking, indicating the docking slot would soon be open for another Senate-sponsored vessel.

It took him no time at all to reconstruct the code string for that particular vessel. He had created the code based on an equation that utilized the serial number. He told them the code, and the Blood Carver entered it into his comlink and transmitted it.

Sienar shifted in his clothes, hoping to find the small spy droid that had obviously been set upon him during Tarkin's last visit. "The tracker will be useless in hyperspace," he told Tarkin. "It's low-power and unreliable at extreme distances. I've since learned how to build better."

"We'll have a newer tracker partner with yours before the ship leaves orbit. We need the code for them to communicate. Together, they'll serve our purposes."

"A senatorial vessel?" Sienar asked.

Tarkin shook his head. "Owned by an auxiliary of the Jedi. Stop fiddling with your pants, Raith. It's unseemly." Tarkin showed a small control unit fitted into his palm. He waved it casually, and something rustled in Sienar's pants. He squirmed as it dropped down his leg and crawled away from his booted foot. It was a tidy little droid of a kind Sienar had not seen before, flat, flexible, able to change its texture to match that of clothing. Even an expert might have missed it.

Sienar wondered how much this knowledge was going to cost him. "I was about to agree to your proposal, Tarkin," he said with petulance.

"I say again, we are very pressed for time."

"No time even for simple manners . . . between old friends?"

"None at all," Tarkin said grimly. "The old ways are dying. We have to adapt. I have adapted."

"I see. What more can I offer?"

Tarkin finally saw fit to smile, but it did not make him seem any friendlier. Tarkin had always shown a little too much of the skull beneath the skin, even as a youth. "A great deal, Raith. It's been some time since you used your military training, but I have faith you haven't forgotten. Now that I'm sure you're with us—"

"Wouldn't dream otherwise," Sienar said softly.

"How would you like to command an expedition?"

"To this exotic planet you spoke of earlier?"

"Yes."

"Why tell me of this world before now? If you couldn't trust me enough to give you such a thing as a tracker code."

"Because I have recently been informed that to you, this world was no secret."

Raith Sienar drew his head back like a serpent about to strike and sucked in his breath. "I *am* impressed, Tarkin. How many of my most trusted employees will I have to . . . dismiss?"

"You know the planet is real. You hold one of its ships."

Sienar did not like being caught out in a ruse, however innocent. "A dead hulk," he said defensively, "acquired from a corrupt Trade Federation lieutenant who had killed its owner. The ships are useless unless their owners are alive."

"Good to know. How many of these ships have been manufactured, do you think?"

"Perhaps a hundred."

"Out of twenty million spacecraft, registered and unregistered, in the known galaxy. And how much do they cost their owners?"

"I'm not sure. Millions, or billions," Sienar said.

"You have always thought yourself smarter than me, one step

ahead of me," Tarkin said tightly. "Always on top of things. But this time, I can save your career, and perhaps your life. We can pool our sources, and our resources—and both come out far ahead."

"Of course, Tarkin," Sienar said evenly. "Is now the time, and is this the place, for a good, firm handshake?"

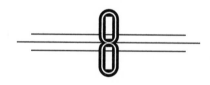

Obi-Wan and Anakin donned their boots and joined Charza in the pilothouse in the starboard nacelle. Through the broad ports surrounding the pilot's position, they could see Coruscant's night side below them, the endless metropolis twinkling like a Gungan deep-sea menagerie. Anakin stood beside a line of small, hard-shelled, many-clawed creatures that fidgeted in the pool of water behind the pilot's backless couch. Obi-Wan stooped to sit in a smaller, empty seat on the opposite side of the couch.

Charza Kwinn did not need to turn his body to look them over with a pair of silver-rimmed, deep purple eyes. "I'm told you possess a scale from a garbage worm," Charza said to Anakin. "Won during a pit competition."

"Not a formal competition," Obi-Wan said.

"You wouldn't let me hand it over to the Greeter and claim my rank," Anakin said resentfully.

"I enjoy watching the pit races," Charza Kwinn said. "My

kind engages in so little competitive behavior. It is amusing to watch more aggressive species rush to their fates." With this, he suddenly arched over backward, swept his spike fringe along the line of clawed creatures, and grabbed two. They were guided into a seam that opened between the thick bristles on his underside and quickly consumed.

The remaining members of the line kept their formation, but clacked tiny claws as if applauding.

"You are most welcome," Charza said to the survivors.

Anakin shuddered. Obi-Wan shifted in his seat and said, "Charza, perhaps you should explain your relations to my Padawan."

"These are friends, confidants, shipmates," Charza told the boy. "They aspire to be consumed by the Big One."

Anakin screwed up his face, then quickly blanked it as he realized Charza could still see him. He glanced at Obi-Wan, feeling at a loss.

"Never assume the obvious," Obi-Wan cautioned in an undertone.

"We are all partners," Charza said. "We help each other on this ship. The little ones provide food, and once they are consumed I carry their offspring inside me. I give birth to and take care of their babies. Their babies become shipmates and partners . . . and food."

"Do you eat all of your partners?" Anakin asked.

"Stars, no!" Charza said with a scrubbing, shuffling imitation of human laughter. "Some would taste terrible, and besides, it's simply not done. We have many different relationships on this ship. Some food, some not. All cooperate. You'll see."

Using controls mounted on struts that curved along his

sides, Charza pulled the ship away from the orbital dock and engaged the sublight engines.

For its age, the YT-1150 accelerated with remarkable smoothness, and in minutes they were out of Coruscant orbit, moving for the point where they would make their jump into hyperspace.

"Good ship," Charza said, and his bristles and spikes stroked the closest bulkhead. "Good friend."

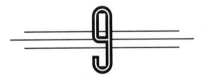

Raith, you've been angling for this kind of opportunity for years," Tarkin said as he poured a glass of chimbak wine from Alderaan. Tarkin's private apartment was small but choice, high on the residential level of Prime Senate Spire, two kilometers higher than most of the city. "Whether you knew it or not, you've always wanted to be there for the dawn of a new way of doing business."

Sienar was not a drinking man, but for the time being, he was acting friendly and cooperative. He did not enjoy the presence of the Blood Carver. He took the glass and pretended to savor it. The merest comforting twinkle in his ring's bright green stone told him the thick red fluid was neither drugged nor poisoned. Indeed, as wine went, it was mellow and delicious.

"But you must find it interesting that you have no friends you can trust," Tarkin continued. "Friendship is a thing of the past. All now is alliance and advantage. Reliance on trust is a great weakness."

It was possible Tarkin had lost this innocence long before Sienar. "You still haven't introduced me," Sienar said.

Tarkin turned to the Blood Carver. "This is Ke Daiv, from a famous political family on Batorine. Ke Daiv was formerly part of a select assassination corps loosely affiliated with the Trade Federation. Some last, inept attempt to exact a measure of revenge, against the Jedi, I believe."

Sienar turned his lips down at this audacity. "Really?" he said with a small and false shiver of wonder. He knew more about this matter than Tarkin suspected, and knew that somehow Tarkin had been involved—but his sources could provide few details.

"An ill-considered attempt, at best," Tarkin said, glancing at Sienar.

"Blood Carvers are not known to be involved in outside politics," Sienar observed.

"I am an individual," Ke Daiv observed. "Opportunity expands with freedom from the past."

"Well-spoken," Tarkin said. "I asked for him, actually. His skills are quite substantial, and he failed against a Jedi Knight. I'll forgive him that, wouldn't you?"

"I will try again, and succeed, given the opportunity," Ke Daiv said.

"Blood Carvers are an artistic people," Sienar said. "Refresh my memory, but the most famous product from Batorine is sculpture . . . carved from the bright red wood of the indigenous blood tree?"

"It has a double meaning," Ke Daiv said. "Assassination, too, is a kind of sculpting, chipping away what is not needed."

Sienar finished his glass and complimented Tarkin's taste. Tarkin nodded to Ke Daiv, and the Blood Carver left them.

"Impressive," Sienar observed after the narrow door had

closed. Space was at a premium all over Coruscant, and even now, in the economic downturn, Tarkin's quarters, while high over the city, were much less spacious and certainly less well-appointed than Sienar's own.

"It could take decades to make humans the supreme race in this galaxy," Tarkin said with a sniff. "The tolerance and weakness of our predecessors have made it necessary to be magnanimous, for the time being." He listened to a tiny beep on his comlink, held tightly in one hand. "Our quarry has departed from Coruscant orbit. The tracker is in place and is communicating with your unit."

"What will the Neimoidians do—and all the other founding members of the Trade Federation—when they discover they are expendable? This new deal with the senate could easily cause trouble all by itself."

"Let us just say that we have powerful forces behind us. Forces even I shudder to consider." Tarkin lowered the comlink and rubbed his forearm with the other hand. "Let's discuss more immediate matters, however. This is a high-stakes game we're involved in. As you've noticed, I have some distance to cover in this new hierarchy. Eventually, I hope to be awarded a provincial governorship, and to control many star systems. You . . . will be selling equipment to whatever political force emerges from this turmoil. Together, we can find this mysterious planet and exploit it to our mutual advantage."

"It is intriguing," Sienar said. "Ships rated zero-point-four could be a remarkable discovery." *Indeed,* he thought. Given such a technological advance, and ten years of steady development, Sienar himself might have been wealthy enough to personally choose the leadership of any new galactic government.

What might have been, however, was of little concern now.

"I won't be able to go with you, unfortunately," Tarkin said. "I have to keep my juggling act here on Coruscant for the time being. But you will be well equipped." His comlink beeped again.

"Now comes a few tense days," Tarkin said. "Our ship of interest has entered hyperspace. We have positioned subspace transponders at several points within a few hundred light-years of where this planet is likely to be."

"So . . . I'll be dealing with an entire planet, as a commander of former Trade Federation forces?"

"Of droids, with a small contingent of ship's crew and troops," Tarkin said. "Your crew and adjutants will all be Trade Federation–trained, of course. The Republic has not yet taken charge of certain ships held in reserve. Ke Daiv will go with you. He has experience working with Trade Federation weaponry, and he will answer directly to me."

"Fine," Sienar said, but thought differently. He had never fancied droid armies. Droids, in his opinion, were poor replacements for living troops. They were limited in intelligence and flexibility.

Tarkin seemed to sense his distaste. "You'll be using a new variety of battle droid," he said. "These have enhanced intelligence and are no longer centrally controlled. The Trade Federation has learned from recent debacles."

"Good," Sienar said, still less than enthused.

"You'll get your affairs in order, of course," Tarkin said.

"That might take a couple of months."

"I hope you'll be ready in a couple of days."

"Of course," Sienar said. He tapped his chin in speculation. "Ke Daiv failed on a mission. Yet this looks like a promotion, to be moved from failed assassin to assistant commander of . . . what? A fleet?"

"A squadron, actually," Tarkin said. He made a face. "Ke Daiv will have no position in your command structure. Agreed, however. In some respects this is awkward."

"Let me guess. Dark forces are playing with us all, and Ke Daiv has connections? *Nonhuman* connections that are still useful?"

Tarkin made a sour face but did not answer this. "Just prepare, Raith," he said. "And for all our sakes, don't ask too many questions."

Obi-Wan listened to the steady rhythm of the boy's breath. Anakin had been exhausted by the day's events and was sound asleep. His face, gently outlined by the soft luminance of the cabin's blue emergency lights, was young and perfect and quite beautiful.

Obi-Wan lay back on his couch, both hearing and feeling the tingle and thrum of the hyperdrive. They were well away—yet Obi-Wan felt a distinct unease. There was something about this mission—a simple adventure, really, a journey to the far reaches of the galaxy to make contact with a planet that apparently was unknown to the Republic and to the enemies of the Republic. He had been to regions outside the reach of the law often enough. The mission was not, of course, without its dangers, but they would be far from the immediate dangers of Coruscant.

Perhaps what bothered Obi-Wan was that he would be entirely in charge of Anakin. In the Temple Anakin had been surrounded by many Jedi and Jedi auxiliaries, including the staff, who had taken some of the burden off Obi-Wan. They had played the role of family, and Anakin had eaten up their attention.

The truth was, Obi-Wan was not sure he was up to the task. Obi-Wan tended to arrange his thoughts and his life in orderly rows. Anakin Skywalker kicked those orderly rows asunder whenever he could.

There were the tricks. Anakin had once taken a battered protocol droid he had found abandoned somewhere, repaired its motivator, and dressed it up in Jedi robes. The droid's intellectual capacity had long since been depleted in some accident or another, and Anakin had supplied it with the simple verbobrain from a kitchen droid, then set it loose in the hallway outside Obi-Wan's quarters. Unable to see its droid face behind the hood, Obi-Wan had spoken with it for two minutes before realizing the form was not a Jedi, not even a living thing. His perceptions and his guard had been down, inside the Temple. Anakin had actually ragged him about that—the apprentice ragging the master!

Obi-Wan smiled. It was something Qui-Gon might have done. With Anakin, the boundaries between Master and apprentice were often erased. It was all too common for him to realize he could learn from the boy. In his weaker moments he felt that was not the proper way of things.

But there it was.

The danger—and it was a real danger—was that Anakin could not and did not exercise a proper control over his talents, his brilliance, his power. He was, most of the time, just a boy on the edge of manhood, and liable to all the mistakes one would normally expect.

It had not happened yet, but Obi-Wan was certain that someday soon the danger would come not from boyish energy and adventurous hijinks, but from a misapplication of the Force.

Perhaps that was what caused him unease.

Perhaps not.

He drew himself into an alert meditative state. For the last couple of years, Obi-Wan had tried to cut down on his need to sleep. While all of the Jedi he knew slept, he had heard that some did not. He was certain that meditative alertness performed all the functions of sleep, and would give him time to examine his own thoughts at their deepest levels, to maintain vigilance.

You do not trust yourself yet, Jedi. You do not trust your unconscious connection to the Force.

Obi-Wan turned his head and looked around the darkened cabin. That had sounded like Qui-Gon Jinn speaking, yet he had *heard* nothing. Nor had the boy made a sound.

Strange that this did not disturb Obi-Wan more.

"No, Master, I do not," Obi-Wan said to the empty air. "That is my strength."

Qui-Gon would have debated that point fiercely. But there was no reply.

Sienar tried to focus on his mount and ignore the seethe of concerns that had occupied him since his last encounter with Tarkin.

The animal, a gray-blue trith prancer, trotted on six graceful legs around Sienar's private arena, responding to his faintest ankle tap or tug on upward-jutting shoulder bones. A trith prancer's back formed a natural saddle—if the genetic manipulation of a thousand generations could be considered natural. Sienar's animals—he owned three prancers—were the finest money could buy, another luxury he was reluctant to put at risk. *Too soft, too attached, too inflexible!*

Nevertheless, Sienar rode and tried to enjoy himself.

He pulled back gently, and the trith rose up on its two rear pairs of legs, pawing the air elegantly. It emitted musical fluting noises that thrilled Sienar to his core. Once, he could have ridden a trith across open prairie for days and been perfectly happy—happy, that is, until another spacecraft design occurred to him.

Now it was likely he would be neither riding nor designing

for some months. Tarkin seemed to think he could alter Sienar's life, intrude into his business affairs, threaten him, and dine opulently from his table of secrets.

The difficulty was, Tarkin was probably correct: buried in this morass of obligation and coercion was a real opportunity. Still, Tarkin himself was likely to benefit the most from Sienar's participation.

He spun his animal around and pushed with his ankles to get it to gallop on two rear sets of legs. This was a difficult behavior, and Sienar was proud of how well his animals performed. They had won many prizes at competitions on several planets.

A commotion broke out near the wide double door to the arena. Security droids backed into the arena, gesturing frantically. Sienar quickly dismounted and hid behind the trith, staring over the smooth fur of its back.

Tarkin walked between the droids, ignoring their warnings. Astonishingly, he carried a Senate-grade ionic disruptor, which rendered security droids harmless.

Sienar smiled grimly and walked around the trith, which blew out its breath in some alarm at the stranger. Fortunately, Tarkin had come this time without his Blood Carver.

"Good morning, Raith," Tarkin called out cheerfully. "I need to view this Sekotan ship of yours. Now."

"By all means," Sienar said pleasantly. "Next time, you should give me some warning. Not all of my security droids are vulnerable to disruptors, you know. It's good I anticipated your rudeness . . . and programmed them to recognize you. Otherwise they would have shot you as soon as you passed through that door."

Tarkin looked over his shoulder and paled slightly. "I see," he said, putting away the disruptor. "No harm done."

"Not this time," Sienar muttered.

Sienar had kept two of his old factory sites in the ancient depths of the capital city, long after he had moved all operations to fancier locations. The rent was cheap, and any curious intruders could be disposed of with little legal difficulty. In fact, this was where he posted most of his offworld and noncompliant security droids, the finest money could smuggle. They took orders only from Sienar.

As guards, droids were fine. Their wits could not be dulled by boredom.

Tarkin followed, for the first time visibly nervous. His own security droids seemed small and inconsequential beside the large, heavily armored silver machines that guarded the remains of the Sekotan ship in its dark, dry, cavernous hangar.

"Just this hulk cost me a hundred million credits," Sienar said, switching on a few key lights around the echoing hangar. "As you can see, it's not in very good shape."

Tarkin walked around the scabrous hulk in its shimmering refrigeration field. The once-graceful curves had subsided into a wrinkled, deflated mass, despite deep-freezing and less obvious efforts at preservation.

"It's biological," Tarkin observed, nose wrinkling.

"I thought you would have known that already."

"I didn't think it was . . . *this* organic," he said. "I had been told the ships were in some sense alive, but . . . Not much use when dead, are they?"

"A curiosity, like some preserved deep-sea monstrosity, rarely seen," Sienar said. "As for understanding its capabilities, well, there's not much left to analyze."

"I have some images," Tarkin said. "Ships in outlying ports, taking on fuel."

"And nutrients, no doubt," Sienar said. He probably had seen the same images.

"Is it plant, or animal?"

"Neither. It cannot reproduce by itself. No cellular structure, dense and varied tissues that can incorporate both metals and a variety of high-strength, heat-resistant polymers . . . A marvel. But without its owner, it quickly dies, and quickly decays."

"Reminiscent of Gungan technology on Naboo, perhaps?" Tarkin suggested.

"Perhaps," Sienar said. "Perhaps not. The Gungans manufacture their ships from organic matter, but the ships are not themselves alive. This . . . seems to be very different. Before your generous offer, I was looking for an owner willing to allow me access to a fully functioning Sekotan ship. So far, however, there are no takers. It seems secrecy is part of the contract, and betrayal could end an owner's relationship with his vessel. This was the best I could do."

"I see," Tarkin said. "I chose the right man for this mission, Raith. I had a feeling you'd be up on all this."

"Now that you've seen my expensive but disappointing prize," Raith said, "can I offer you some breakfast? It's late, and I haven't had time to dine."

"No, thank you," Tarkin said. "I have many more visits to make today. Keep your schedule open, my friend. Something could happen at any minute."

"Of course," Raith said. *My time is yours, Tarkin. I am patient.*

Obi-Wan paused on the way to the bridge and leaned into the small cubicle where the food-kin, the small crablike creatures, made their homes when they were not working. Anakin sat on a small stool in a circle of food-kin. His brow was knit in concentration.

He looked up at Obi-Wan. "I can't decide whether I like this or not," he said.

"Like what?"

"This arrangement they have with Charza. They seem to revere him, but he *eats* them."

"I would trust their feelings rather than your own, in this case," Obi-Wan said.

Anakin was not convinced. "I don't feel comfortable around Charza."

"He's an honorable being," Obi-Wan said.

Anakin stood, his waterproof boots splashing. The food-kin backed away, clattering their claws. "I understand a lot of what they're saying. They're smart, for being so small. They tell me they're proud that Charza only eats *them*."

"Eating food or being food—simply matters of timing and luck," Obi-Wan said, perhaps a little too lightly. He admired the discipline and self-sacrifice he saw in the crew of the *Star Sea Flower*. "We're due for a briefing from Charza in a few minutes. And we'll be making our first emergence from hyperspace in an hour."

Anakin snapped his fingernails in farewell to the little food-kin and sloshed out of the cubicle to join Obi-Wan in the central corridor. "You just like the arrangement because they obey orders without question," he said.

Obi-Wan drew himself up, indignant. "It's deeper than that," he said. "Surely you sense the underlying structure here."

"Of course," Anakin said, walking ahead of him. They passed a fall of freshened seawater. It slid down a wall from a duct near the ceiling, filled with tiny shelled creatures no bigger than a fingertip. Three food-kin lined up beside the base of the fall, where it dropped into a pool and was carried away behind the bulkhead. They fished busily with their claws and ate ravenously.

Just beyond the fall, the Padawan and his master entered the pilothouse. Charza Kwinn was surrounded by a host of helpers and kin. Obi-Wan had not seen them all together before. The sight was impressive. There did not seem a square centimeter of the bridge's equipment that was not attended by several creatures, ranging in size from the food-kin, about as broad as his hand, to meter-long replicas of Charza himself.

Charza sat on his backless couch waving tools clutched in his spikes. The bristles of his "head" scrubbed against the upper curve of the foot, making a loud, rhythmic sound like ocean breakers striking a shore.

Charza stopped when he noticed his passengers had arrived. The food-kin clacked in disappointment. Apparently, Charza had been singing to them. He shifted his bristles slightly around his spiracles to imitate human speech.

"Welcome. The quarters are comfortable?"

"Quite," Obi-Wan said.

"I'll tell you more now about this place you go to. First, size. Zonama Sekot is nine thousand salt pans broad, that is, in Republic measure . . ." He conferred with one of his smaller duplicates. "Eleven thousand kilometers. Its star system is a triple, in a hidden region of the Gardaji Rift, surrounded by great dust clouds. Two stars, a red giant and a white dwarf, orbit close to each other. Zonama Sekot circles the third star, a bright yellow sun, which orbits much farther out, several light-months distant. It is almost impossible to find if you don't know the way."

Charza paused as two food-kin enthusiastically offered themselves for his breakfast. He waved his head gently back and forth, and they retreated in apparent disappointment. "Their biological clocks chime," Charza explained. "Must eat them before the day is over, or their children spoil. But I am so full now!"

Obi-Wan observed Anakin's reaction. Charza was perhaps not the most appropriate father figure for the boy to puzzle over at this time in his life.

"Now," Charza said, leaning to one side and pulling two heavy, parallel levers, "we come out of hyperspace."

The forward ports opened again. The strange display outside collapsed to a dazzling point. With a sharp lurch, the stars returned—the stars, and the distinctive flaming red and purple pinwheel that dominated the skies of Zonama Sekot.

"Wow," Anakin said, eyes wide. The display was stunning, perhaps the most beautiful he had ever seen. "Where's our planet?" the boy asked eagerly.

"Zonama Sekot's sun is behind us," Charza said. "These two spectacular dancers, the red giant and the white dwarf, with their long spiral tail, are its companions."

The pinwheel began as a ribbon of starstuff pulled from the red giant. It then curled around the white dwarf, which flung it outward in interwoven braids of ionized gas.

"You can see Zonama Sekot itself . . . it is that tiny green point just ahead." Charza grabbed a long rod with his bristles and tapped it on the port. "There. See?"

"I see it," Anakin said.

The little food-kin scrambled for a better view and chittered in admiration. Two perched on Anakin's shoulders. A smaller fringed wormlike creature curled around one of the boy's legs and made contented gurgling sounds.

"They do not bother you?" Charza asked Anakin.

"They're fine," Anakin said.

"They feel you are safe," Charza said approvingly. "You have a rare attraction for them!" He swung his couch around and played some of his spikes over another instrument panel. The green planet was already as wide as a thumb tip held at arm's length. "When I came to Zonama Sekot last, I released Vergere on a mountain plateau high in the northern hemisphere, near the pole. I fervently hope she is still alive."

"It is believed she is alive," Obi-Wan said.

"Perhaps," Charza said with a chuffing of his bristles. "There are no pirates here, no commerce centers—indeed, the only inhabited planet for many light-years is Zonama Sekot. But Zonama Sekot is very close to the edge of the galaxy. Beyond this point, there is much that is not known. Anything could happen."

"The edge of the galaxy!" Anakin said, still entranced by the picture. "We could be the first beings to go beyond the edge!" He looked at Obi-Wan. "If we wanted to."

"There are still frontiers," Obi-Wan agreed, "and that is a comforting thought."

"Why comforting?" Charza asked. "Empty places without friends are not good!"

Obi-Wan smiled and shook his head. "The unknown is a place where we can discover who we truly are."

Anakin regarded his master with some surprise.

"So Qui-Gon taught me," Obi-Wan concluded, drawing the long sleeves of his robe in over his booted knees.

"Zonama Sekot itself is not empty," Charza said. "There are beings there, not native to the planet. They arrived many years ago, not known how long. But they invite guests only recently, mostly rich buyers from worlds that do not owe strong allegiance to the Republic or trade with the Trade Federation. I will show you a picture now that Vergere sent to my ship before I left the system."

Charza chuffed orders to a cluster of food-kin perched on one console. They danced on buttons and tugged levers, and a viewer swung into place.

"Best for humans," Charza murmured, and the food-kin adjusted the colorful but blurry image. It floated in the middle of the bridge, suddenly sharpened and took on motion.

Obi-Wan and Anakin leaned forward and stared.

An intensely green landscape, viewed at sunset, spread before them. The scale of treelike growths that filled most of the image was not immediately apparent until Anakin spotted a structure in the lower left, a kind of balcony with what looked like humans standing on it. Then it became apparent that the trees were easily five or six hundred meters tall, and that the great green domes of foliage in the upper right were easily hundreds of meters across. Green was the dominant color, but the foliage was also rich with gold, blue, purple, and red.

"They do not look like trees," Obi-Wan commented.

"Not trees," Charza said. "Not trees at all. Vergere called them boras."

The planet's yellow sun, setting in a golden haze between the ranks of huge growths, was not the only light in the sky. The vast pinwheel of red and purple gas covered all they could see of the northern sky beyond the boras.

"That is all I know," Charza continued. "I dropped off Vergere, then waited until I was dismissed, and returned to orbit. There was no message to retrieve her, so I departed, as she had ordered. At that time, I detected six ships of known types in the region. All were private craft, I think belonging to customers of the shipbuilders on Zonama Sekot."

"You did well, Charza," Obi-Wan said, getting to his feet. "Perhaps nothing is amiss."

"She may be alive," Charza said, "but I do not think all is well."

"Your instinct?"

Charza burred and lifted his head to the ceiling, then twisted around to regard them with all of his eyes. "Simple observation. Where one Jedi travels alone, perhaps no cause for alarm. Where a Jedi falls silent, and other Jedi follow . . . mishap and adventure!"

Tarkin marched ahead of Raith Sienar down the tunnel toward the waiting shuttle. "There is no time to lose," Tarkin shouted over his shoulder. "They've emerged from hyperspace, and we've received the tracker signal. We have less than an hour before you must join your squadron and leave Coruscant."

Sienar clutched his travel bag and passed last-minute instructions to his protocol droid, which followed at a quick if lurching pace a few steps behind.

"Come on, man!" Tarkin shouted.

Sienar handed the droid the last thing he had packed earlier that morning: a small disk containing special instructions should he not return.

The droid halted at the embarkation slip and gestured a formal good-bye as Sienar joined Tarkin inside the well-appointed shuttle lounge. The hatch slid shut with an ear-popping hiss, and the shuttle immediately pulled from its tower berth and punched through a clear space in the traffic lanes.

It rose rapidly into orbit.

"I hope you understand what could be at stake here," Tarkin said, his thin face grim. His blue eyes grew large and deadly serious as he looked at Sienar. With such wide eyes, his face once more took on the aspect of an animated skull. "At the moment we are merely useful lackeys. We are below the level of awareness of those who will command the galaxy. If this planet and its ships are as useful as they appear to be, we will be richly rewarded. We will be *noticed*. Some already share my belief that this could be very big. All will share in our success, so our mission has been given level-two priority, Raith. *Level two!*"

"Not level one?" Sienar asked innocently.

Tarkin frowned. "Your cynicism may not serve you well, my friend."

"I keep an independent mind," Sienar said.

"In the long run, that could be extremely unwise," Tarkin told him, and his eyes narrowed to slits.

Charza Kwinn brought the *Star Sea Flower* into a high orbit above Zonama Sekot. As Obi-Wan and Anakin prepared their belongings in the dry cabin, Obi-Wan brought out a pouch he had concealed in his robes, drew open a cord, and laid it out on top of his travel kit.

Anakin looked at it hopefully. "Another lightsaber?" he asked.

Obi-Wan smiled and shook his head. "Not yet, Padawan. Something more appropriate for a planet run by merchants. Old-style aurodium credits. Three billion's worth, in several large ingots."

"I've never *seen* that much money!" Anakin said, stepping closer. Obi-Wan shook his finger in warning, then opened the packet and showed its contents to Anakin.

The ten pure aurodium ingots sparkled like tiny flames. Each held a depth of mysterious light that refused to fix on one color.

"What they say about the Temple is true, then," Anakin mused.

"That it holds secret treasure? Hardly," Obi-Wan said. "These were drawn from a joint account in the Galactic Capital Bank. Many in the galaxy lend their resources to support the Jedi."

"I didn't know that," Anakin said, a little downcast.

"This represents a few percent of that account. Not that we are going to spend it foolishly. Vergere carried a similar amount with her. It is rumored that this is sufficient to purchase a Sekotan vessel. Let's hope the rumors are correct."

"But Vergere—maybe she's already bought a ship," Anakin said.

"It may be necessary for us to be completely ignorant of Vergere," Obi-Wan said.

"Oh . . . right."

Obi-Wan rolled up the ingots and tied the cord, then handed it to Anakin. "Keep it with you at all times."

"Wizard!" Anakin enthused. "No one'd suspect a boy would carry this much cash. I could buy a YZ-1000 with this—a *hundred* YZ-1000s!"

"What would you do with a hundred old star scows?" Obi-Wan asked with innocent curiosity.

"I'd rebuild them. I know how to make them go twice as fast as they do now—and they're plenty fast!"

"And then?"

"I'd race them!"

"How much time would that leave for your training?"

"Not much," Anakin admitted blithely. His eyes danced.

Obi-Wan pursed his lips in disapproval.

"Got you!" Anakin cried, grinning, and grabbed the packet. He stuffed it into his tunic and strapped it close to his body with the long remainder of cord. "I'll guard your old money," he said. "Who wants to be rich, anyway?"

Obi-Wan lifted an eyebrow. "To lose it would be unfortunate," he cautioned.

Even from thirty thousand kilometers, Zonama Sekot was an odd-looking planet.

A spot of pearl white at the northern polar region was surrounded by an entire hemisphere of rich mottled green. Below the equator, the southern hemisphere was covered with impenetrable silvery cloud. Along the equator, a thin patch of darker gray and brown was broken by what looked like lengths of river and narrow lakes or seas. The edge of the southern overcast curled in elegant wisps, and the wisps broke free to form spinning storms.

While they waited for the planet's answer to their landing request, Charza was involved in a birthing in another part of the ship.

Anakin sat in the small side seat on the bridge with his elbows propped on his knees, watching Zonama Sekot. He had performed his first set of exercises for the day, and his thoughts were particularly clear. It seemed sometimes, when his mind was settled, when he had tamed his turbulence for the moment, that he was no longer a boy or even a human. His perspective seemed crystalline and universal, and he felt as if he could see all his life laid out before him, filled with accomplishment and heroism— selfless heroism, of course, as befitted a Jedi. Somewhere in that life would be a woman, though Jedi did not often marry. He imagined the woman to be like Queen Amidala of Naboo, a powerful personality in her own right, lovely and dignified, yet sad and shouldered with great burdens—which Anakin would help lift.

He had not spoken with Amidala in years, nor of course with his mother, Shmi, but in his present frame of disciplined consciousness, their memory acted on him like a distant and ineffable music.

He shook his head and drew his eyes up, turning his feelings outward, focusing them until they seemed to make a bright point between his eyes, and concentrated on Zonama Sekot, to see what he could *see* . . .

Many paths to many futures flowed from any single moment, and yet, by being in tune with the Force, an adept could chart the most likely path for his awareness to follow. It seemed contradictory that one could prepare a path into a future, without knowing what that future would hold—yet that is what ultimately happened, and that is what a Jedi Master could do.

Obi-Wan was not yet so lofty in his accomplishments, he had told Anakin, but there had been hints that before any mission, any disciplined Jedi—even a mere Padawan—could also do a kind of looking forward.

Anakin was sure he was doing something like that now. It felt as if the cells in his body were tuned to a severely faded signal from the future, a voice, large and heavy, as if weighed down, unlike any voice he had ever heard . . .

His eyes slowly grew wide as he stared at the planet.

The boy, Anakin Skywalker of Tatooine, son of Shmi, Jedi Padawan, only twelve standard years of age, refocused all of his attention on Zonama Sekot. His body shuddered. One eye closed slightly, and his head tilted to one side. Then he quickly closed both eyes and shuddered again. The spell was broken. The moment had lasted perhaps three seconds.

Anakin tried to remember something large and beautiful, an emotion or a state of mind he had just touched upon, but all he could conjure was the face of Shmi, smiling at him sadly and proudly, like a protective scrim over any other memory.

His mother, still so important and so far away.

He could never see the face of a father.

Obi-Wan sloshed past the fall into the pilothouse. "Charza is done with his younglings," he said. "They're in training now to tend the ship."

"So fast?" Anakin said.

"Life is short for some of Charza's kin," Obi-Wan said. "You look thoughtful."

"I'm allowed, aren't I?" Anakin asked.

"As long as you don't brood," Obi-Wan said. The look on his master's face was both irritated and concerned. Anakin suddenly jumped out of his chair and hugged his master with a fierceness that took Obi-Wan by surprise.

Obi-Wan held the boy gently and let the moment flow into its own shape. Some Padawans were like quiet pools, their minds like simple texts. Only in training did they acquire the depth and complexity that showed maturity. Anakin had been a deep and complex mystery from the first day they met, and yet Obi-Wan had never felt such a strength of connection with any other being—not even Qui-Gon Jinn.

Anakin drew back and looked up at his master. "I think we're going to face real trouble down there," he said.

"Think?" Obi-Wan asked.

Anakin made a face. "I can *feel* it. I don't know what it is, but . . . I did some forwarding. Feeling ahead. It's trouble, all right."

"I've suspected as much," Obi-Wan agreed. "Even when Thracia Cho Leem was—"

The bridge was suddenly filled with a crowd of fresh, young, bright pink food-kin, all clattering and clacking with enthusiasm as they took their stations. Charza pushed through the shallow water onto the bridge with great dignity and weariness, as if he had accomplished something both satisfying and exhausting.

"Life goes on," he chuffed to Anakin as he took his seat. "Now . . . let us see if there has been an answer from the planet."

Raith Sienar entered the observation deck of his flagship, the *Admiral Korvin,* and stepped up on the commander's platform. He looked over the weapons arrayed within the circular assembly bay of the former Trade Federation heavy munitions cruiser, an antiquated hulk. He was both critical at the selection and dismayed that he was expected to coordinate this ragtag force.

To make matters worse, there was not a single craft of his own manufacture on board, a serious oversight, he believed, and perhaps a treacherous one.

Tarkin had either not described the force accurately, or he had remembered it with blind optimism.

Sienar flipped up the weapons list. E-5 droids . . . His lips curled.

The cruiser carried three landing craft, one hundred Trade Federation troops, and over three thousand droids. Three smaller and decidedly less useful vessels completed the squadron that Tarkin was now handing over to him.

It was not inconceivable that one could conquer a planet with these ships: a backwater planet, in the dark ages of technology . . .

But nothing more advanced than that. And conquer, but not then control.

"You are not impressed," Tarkin said dryly, joining him on the platform.

"I have never believed in droids as frontline fighters," Sienar told him. "Not even these new ones. Naboo was lost even though the forces deployed by the Trade Federation were hundreds of times larger than this."

"As I told you, these droids have been altered to be capable of independence, and they are considerably more rugged than earlier models," Tarkin said with some irritation.

"Would you trust them to carry out a complicated battle plan on their own?"

"I might," Tarkin said, sucking in his cheeks as he stared down the ranks of weapons and delivery vehicles. "I must say, Raith, I don't prize complete independence as much as you seem to. The Neimoidians gave central control a bad name. The controllers on this ship are quite competent and flexible. Zonama Sekot is only lightly populated, as you well know. It is mostly forest. These should be more than sufficient."

"Be honest with me," Sienar said, stepping closer to his old classmate. "For both our sakes. If Zonama Sekot were a pushover, as planets go, we could make do with a small expeditionary force. This squadron seems at once too much and perhaps too little, and that worries me."

"It is the best I can put together. The Trade Federation squadrons are being handed over to Republic control day by day, and this is all that they could hold aside."

"Perhaps it is the best *you* can persuade them to send, with your rank and the quality of your contacts," Sienar said.

Tarkin gave him a surprised, mock-hurt look, and then chuckled. "Perhaps you're right," he said. "When did a military man ever have everything his way? It's what you do with what you have that wins wars. We would both have preferred to design and build our own force, using more imaginative strategic thinking. But the Trade Federation has suffered from this economic downturn as much as the Republic has. A veritable swarm of petty villains have moved in with their old freighters to run the most lucrative goods illegally between systems. Fighting them and reclaiming trade routes and privileges was a matter of life and death for the Trade Federation. Now the Republic will have to police the trade lanes. And the Republic's armaments are, if anything, even sorrier. Frankly, I was lucky to procure even this."

"Spare me the weepy details," Sienar said coldly. "You have put me in charge rather than go yourself, though you are the more experienced in battle tactics. Failure of this mission will taint the commander—will taint *me*—irrevocably."

"Now who is engaging in weepy details?" Tarkin asked, even more coldly. "Raith, for a decade you have sequestered yourself with your collections, executing small contracts, trying to promote a strategy of small, elegant weapon design long out of fashion, complaining bitterly about lost opportunities and unimaginative buyers. During that time, I have been working my way up a very long ladder. We must make do with what we have. I chose you . . . because you are nearly my equal in tactics, and you will understand Zonama Sekot's factories better than I ever could."

Sienar regarded Tarkin narrowly. The two were breathing slightly faster, as if they might go after each other with fingernails and fists at any moment.

But that was not likely. They were gentlemen of military bearing and training, of the old school. Their dignity, at least, would not crumble under this pressure, even if other dustings of honor had long since been swept away.

"I swear, you've pushed me into this deliberately," Sienar said quietly, breaking their gaze in a way that showed such a contest was beneath him. "Looking at this equipment, I'm not at all sure of your motives."

"There you go again," Tarkin said, trying for a tone of amusement. "You have a large-capacity and heavily armored flagship with three landers, and three utility vessels—a *Taxon*-class probe ship, a fleet diplomatic boat that can double as a decoy, and a mobile astromech repair station. Battle droids, sky mines . . . Your squadron is more than sufficient to accomplish our mission."

"And you'll be in just the right place to repair any damage my failure might cause?" Sienar asked.

"I am staying on Coruscant to support the effort politically. That is likely to be far more difficult than conquering a jungle planet." Tarkin shook his head. "We both of us have far to go up the ladders of this new way of life that is coming. You, my friend, need opportunities to shine. So I give this job to you, not without ulterior motives, to be sure. I am certain you will not fail. Now." He drew himself up. "I must return to Coruscant. Ah, here is Captain Kett."

The captain of the *Admiral Korvin* approached Sienar and bowed his head quickly before speaking. "We are to leave orbit in twenty minutes, Commander. There is one last load of weapons to take aboard. Droid starfighters, I believe. They will be stowed in ten minutes." The adjutant glanced at Tarkin with a flicker of recognition.

"There, Raith," Tarkin said. "More than I hoped for. If you can't win this planet with droid starfighters . . . Well."

Sienar acknowledged Kett's message with a curt twist of his head. "Allow me to escort you to the transport deck," he said to Tarkin.

"No need," Tarkin said.

"I insist," Sienar told him. "It is the way things are done . . . on my ship."

And it would also insure that Tarkin had no time to make last personal arrangements with any secret cadre inside the cruiser. Suspecting as much was churlish, to be sure, but this was rapidly becoming an age of churls.

Sienar felt very much out of place in this age, and on his own flagship.

He would have to do something about that, and quickly.

Your ship is recognized," the voice of orbital control from Zonama Sekot said—masculine and probably human, Obi-Wan judged. "You have registered as an authorized client transport vessel. Yet the account of your last delivered client is in doubt."

Charza Kwinn seemed to be cleaning his bristles before he spoke. He drew himself up to the full height of the cabin bulkhead, and a shower of food-kin spilled off him. Anakin shielded his face as they clattered and leapt around the cabin.

Obi-Wan did not shield his face and received a fair-size pink shell square across the lips.

"Apologies," Charza murmured. Then he switched on the return link. "This is Charza Kwinn, registered owner of *Star Sea Flower*. I do not recall personally guaranteeing client accounts."

"No," the controller admitted, "but we prefer our client transports to bring us reliable customers."

"I will return my previous client to her homeworld, if she so desires, for free, and at no cost to you," Charza said innocently. "Where is she?"

There was a lengthy pause. "That will not be necessary," the controller said. "Landing permission granted. Use the northern plateau. Coordinates have not changed."

"Wastes fuel," Charza huffed. He switched off the link. "An equatorial landing site would be much better."

Obi-Wan watched the surface of Zonama Sekot roll by beneath. "Odd. I've never seen such a perfectly divided weather system."

"It has not changed since we were last here," Charza said.

The *Star Sea Flower* flashed its sublight drives for a few thousandths of a second and began the quick drop from orbit. Just as they entered the upper atmosphere, Obi-Wan thought he spotted an anomalous brown desert or rift in the wide, deep green, but it quickly passed out of view.

Atmospheric shields protected them from the buffet, and a beautiful plume of ionized air flared around the ship, blocking his view for a few seconds. When the glow cleared, the landscape below, a smooth carpet of green from orbit, quickly acquired mottled detail. Mountain ranges sparsely dotted with huge reddish boras, and valleys filled with thick green growth, stood out in shaded relief against the glancing light of a westering sun.

"Dextrorotation," Anakin observed. "Very little axial tilt. It looks normal enough, except for the southern weather."

Obi-Wan nodded. Vergere had provided them with so few details that all this was new information. "Temperature at the landing point?"

"Last time, it was above freshwater freezing," Charza said. "But only a little. The landing point is near the pole, a slender flat plateau surrounded by ice-covered seas."

"Are the seas salty?" Anakin asked.

"I do not know," Charza said. "Anything I do up here, such

as sending a laser beam down for spectrum analysis, becomes known to the planet's managers. They do not appreciate prying."

"Curious," Obi-Wan said.

"They love their secrets," Charza said.

The northern plateau where they had been cleared to land was easily a thousand kilometers long and narrow as a finger, covered with broken blocks of snow and ice. The top of the plateau showed little relief, and the square field, beside a small cluster of hemispherical buildings, was nothing more than smooth rock cleared of snow.

Charza swung the *Star Sea Flower* around in a graceful arc, relying on atmospheric propulsion jets, and brought it down gently in the middle of the field. Two other ships—atmospheric transports, not spacecraft—were parked in the open at the edge of the field, both lightly dusted with snow.

Snow was falling in large rainbow-hued flakes outside the craft as Charza dropped the ramp. Food-kin retreated from the draft of frigid air. Anakin drew up his robes, slipped out of his waterproof overboots at the top of the ramp, and walked to the bottom. Obi-Wan tossed him their kits and removed his own boots.

Charza watched them, bristles and spikes knocking together in the cold.

Anakin descended the ramp, with Obi-Wan a few steps behind. He saw a single figure, heavily bundled, standing away from the overhang of the ship: their lone reception.

Charza brought the ramp up behind them, and the ship lifted a meter or so and moved slowly to its berth beside the other two vessels.

"Welcome to Zonama Sekot," a woman's voice said through

the red face filter of a snow mask. Her midnight blue eyes were barely visible above the thick heat trap. She held up her hand in brief greeting, turned before they were even close, and walked toward the nearest dome.

Anakin and Obi-Wan looked at each other, shrugged, and followed.

Anakin was disappointed by both the reception and his first glimpse of life on Zonama Sekot. He had hoped for scale, spectacle, something to fit the vivid preconceptions of a twelve-year-old boy. What they saw, entering the first dome, was an empty shell, its interior so cold their breath clouded.

Obi-Wan, however, had carefully kept preconceptions from taking hold. He was open to anything, and thus found the reception and the spare quarters—if quarters they were—interesting. These people did not feel the need to impress.

The woman removed her helmet and mask and shook out a thick fall of gray-white hair. The hair quickly arranged itself into a neat spiral that hung with a springlike flex down the back of her suit. Despite the color of her hair, her face was free of wrinkles. Obi-Wan would have thought her younger than he, except for the cast of wary resentment in her deep blue eyes. She seemed very experienced, and tired.

"Rich, are we, and bored?" she asked curtly. "Is this your son?" She pointed to Anakin.

"This is my student," Obi-Wan said. "I am a professional teacher."

She shot off another question. "What do you hope to teach him here?"

Obi-Wan smiled. "Whether or not we are rich, we have money to buy a ship. What the boy learns here will begin with your gentle answers to *our* questions."

Anakin tipped his head in her direction, showing respect, but unable to hide his disappointment.

The woman looked them over with no change in expression. "Bankrolled by somebody else, or a consortium, too locked in luxury to come by themselves?"

"We are given funds by an organization to which we owe our education and our philosophical stance," Obi-Wan told her.

The woman snorted in derision. "We do not provide ships for delivery to research groups. Go home, *academics*."

Obi-Wan decided against any mind tricks. The woman's attitude interested him. Contempt often veiled bruised ideals.

"We've come quite a long way," Obi-Wan said, undaunted.

"From the center of the galaxy, I know," the woman said. "That's where the money is. Did they tell you—the traitors who do most of our *essential* advertising—that you must prove yourself before you come away with whatever prize Zonama Sekot will offer? No visitors are allowed to stay more than sixty days. And we have only resumed accepting customers in the last month." She flung her hand out at them. "We've seen all the tactics here! *Customers* . . . a necessary evil. I do not have to like it!"

"Whatever our origins, we would hope to be treated with hospitality," Obi-Wan said calmly. He was about to try a subtle bit of Jedi persuasion when the woman's whole aspect changed.

Her features softened, and she looked as if she might have suddenly seen the face of a long-lost friend.

She stared over their shoulders.

Anakin turned his head to look. The three of them were alone in the shelter.

"What did you do?" he whispered to Obi-Wan.

Obi-Wan shook his head. "Pardon me," he said to the woman.

She looked down from a vague distance and focused on Obi-Wan again. "The Magister tells me you are to go south," she said. "Your ship can remain for four more days."

The abrupt turnaround caught even Obi-Wan by surprise. She did not seem to be equipped with an ear-receiver. Some other comlink was concealed in her clothing, he surmised.

"This way, please," she said, and gestured for them to go through a small hatch on the opposite side of the empty dome. There, they found themselves again outside, in the middle of a biting, almost horizontal blast of snow.

Obi-Wan looked up at a ghostly shadow descending through the storm. Though the woman showed no concern, his hand slipped automatically through his jacket to his lightsaber.

What had alerted him? What stray bit of clue from the future had made him feel threatened by the expected arrival of a transport, of all things?

Not for the first time, he regretted this mission and its possible impact on his Padawan. The danger he felt came from no specific source but from all around—not threat of physical harm, but of a possible imbalance in the Force so drastic it overshadowed anything he had ever imagined.

Anakin Skywalker was not so much at risk as he was a possible cause of this imbalance.

For the first time since the death of Qui-Gon Jinn, Obi-Wan felt fear, and he quickly drew up the discipline instilled by long Jedi training to control and then quash it.

He reached out to grip Anakin's shoulder. The boy looked up at him with a brave grin.

"Your ride south," the woman announced over the wind as a broad, flat, disk-shaped transport landed in the blowing drifts of snow.

Obi-Wan lifted his own small comlink and opened a channel with the *Star Sea Flower*. "We are leaving the plateau," he told Charza Kwinn. "Stay here as long as they allow, and after that . . . maintain a position nearby."

Given that Obi-Wan felt he could trust no one, flexibility was essential.

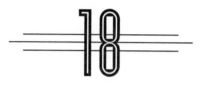

It should have been among the proudest moments of Raith Sienar's life. He had been given the rank of commander, in charge of a squadron, putting to use training he had once thought forgotten. The squadron of four ships was preparing to enter that most entrancing of places, hyperspace—entrancing for an engineer, if not a tactician—and yet he felt nothing but a cold, seedy dread in his viscera.

This was not what he wanted, and it was certainly not what he had imagined when he had purchased the Sekotan ship two years before.

Even learning the probable location of Zonama Sekot seemed a hollow triumph, since he had to share the knowledge. Sienar rarely liked sharing anything, especially with old friends. Most especially, now, with Tarkin.

Sienar was a competitive fellow, had recognized this since boyhood, but it had been a fragile knowledge, as he had realized over and over again, that his competitive nature had its limits. He had had to focus his efforts to win, and after a while, he had never failed to choose arenas in which his talents were most suited, and avoid those where they were not.

It was disheartening to be shown how much he had come to overestimate his greed, and to underestimate the infinite ambition of others. Of Tarkin.

But there was little time for ruing his precarious position. The adjutants, impatient and less than obsequious toward their new commander, had arrayed themselves on the command deck of the *Admiral Korvin,* and they expected dispatch.

He had to give the order for coordinated entry into hyperspace.

It was the final commitment he dreaded, leaving the system, in which he had pooled most of his armor, most of his political cronies and contacts, and all of his wealth.

Leaving home.

There had not been five seconds strung together in the last six hours since he had seen Tarkin off the ship in which he had been free enough to *think things through.* No time for arranging backup plans, escape plans. Instead, he had been involved in the minutiae of command: system checks, drills, and the inevitable, infuriating delays of old equipment breaking down.

Tarkin had from the very beginning herded him down a narrow chute like an animal in a slaughterhouse.

No time for self-pity, either. Sienar was not without resources. But getting his reflexes back into shape was going to take some time. He had built up considerable mental flab on Coruscant in the last decade, giving in to discouragement at the decline of the economy, embittered by the increasing corruption of the aristocracy that had been his mother even more than his real mother had.

He had put on a hard face and found that the expression was comfortable, and not entirely false. It seemed natural for his uniform, which he had chosen the day before—that of an old-line Trade Defense officer, black and gray and red with opalescent striping.

He now had at least the illusion of control over these ships, these men. Might as well use that as a beginning, a stable ground on which to regain his footing and test how much power and independence he actually had.

"Are the squadron cores in synchrony, Captain?" he asked.

"They are, Commander," Kett responded. Kett wore a merchant's uniform, a holdover from the Trade Federation, no doubt something he was used to, and less formal than Sienar's. Rumpled, actually.

We are all of us little better than pirates, but we choose our images carefully, Sienar thought. "Then let's blow the stardust off our tails," he said, hoping that language was not too antiquated.

"Yes, sir." Kett made a small, secret smile.

Sienar stared through the forward ports, hands gripping the railing of his command pulpit. Kett, half a level below him, stood at bridge-rest position, hands folded behind his back, knees slightly bent, as the order was carried through to the linked squadron droid navigation system.

"Departure, Commander," Kett murmured to Sienar as the forward view skewed and fanned outward, then drew in to a brilliant point. "We are entering hyperspace."

"Thank you, Captain Kett," Sienar said.

"Estimated journey time, three standard days," Kett said.

"Let's use that time to examine and do more drills on defensive systems," Sienar said. That would serve as a good distraction for the flagship crew while he did other tasks. "And present me with the service records of every command officer in the squadron. The *complete* records, Captain Kett."

That sounded better.

"I'll prepare a plan and submit the records within the hour, sir," Kett said.

Much better. It felt right, a good beginning to a complicated mission.

Sienar drew up his shoulders and set his jaw firmly, staring with steely determination at the potentially nauseating and twisting view outside the ship until the port covers closed all the way.

He then stepped aside and climbed down. A slender, pipe-frame, dark blue navigational droid mounted the pulpit to perform its essential and quite boring duties.

Anakin squirmed on the cramped transport, unable to see through the small ports placed inconveniently behind the seats. All he could see was a flash of sky and a lumpy green horizon. As the transport flew south, they were moving in and out of the terminator, and the cabin grew light and dark alternately until the transport veered to the west and they flew toward the youth of the day.

The transport offered only the most basic comfort on their trip: four seats, narrow and slung beneath a low ceiling, and a closed cabin door between them and the pilot. Obi-Wan could sense a human behind the door and nothing more. The transport was a familiar enough model, a light expeditionary vehicle often carried inside larger vessels for close-in exploration. Nothing exotic here.

"This is no way to run a planet," Anakin said.

Obi-Wan agreed. "They behave as if they have recently suffered problems."

"With Vergere?"

Obi-Wan smiled. "Vergere was given no instructions to disrupt. Perhaps with the unknown visitors she was sent to investigate."

"I don't feel anything like that around here," Anakin said. "I can feel the Force in this entire planet, and in the settlers, but . . ." He grimaced and shook his head.

"Nor do I feel anything unexpected," Obi-Wan said.

"I didn't say I couldn't feel anything unexpected."

Obi-Wan leaned his head to one side and looked at his Padawan. "What, then?"

"I don't expect what I feel. That's all." The boy shrugged.

Obi-Wan knew that Anakin was often much more tuned to small variations in the Force. "And what do you sense?"

"Something . . . large. Not a lot of little curls or waves, but one big wave, a really big change that's already happened or is coming. I don't know how else to describe it."

"I do not yet feel such a combined surge," Obi-Wan said.

"That's okay," Anakin said. "Maybe it's an illusion. Maybe something's wrong with me."

"I doubt that," Obi-Wan said.

Anakin held his hands behind his neck and sighed. "How much longer?"

The transport landed with a shudder an hour later, and the hatch instantly swung down with a harsh squeal and banged against hard ground. Warm, thick air flowed into the cabin, scented with something at once floral and rich, like a freshly baked dessert.

Anakin found the smell appetizing. Maybe they had fixed food for the visitors—breakfast or lunch.

But as they bent low to climb out of the craft, no tables spread with food awaited them. Instead they found themselves on a broad platform suspended between four huge dark trunks, the middle portions of boras thick and squat as barrels, each over a dozen meters in diameter. Overhead, bright sun filtered through rank upon rank of layered foliage, many meshed canopies of growth that shaded their surroundings and made it seem as if they walked in deep twilight. Obi-Wan helped Anakin down the ramp, eyes darting right and left. They both straightened and faced a tall, strong-looking human male in long black robes decorated with brilliant green medallions. He stood well over two meters in height, much taller than Obi-Wan, and his face was pale and blue as Tatooine milk.

"You're on Zonama Sekot," he said. "A planet of considerable beauty and firm tradition. My name is Gann."

"A pleasure to meet you," Obi-Wan said as he and Anakin approached the tall man. Judging by his color and bearing, he was native to one of the inner Ferro systems, reclusive and not always compliant with the laws of the Republic. Ferroans were a proud and independent people who seldom welcomed outsiders and almost never traveled far from home.

"Where are your ships, the really fast ones?" Anakin asked, bored by this adult show and his enthusiasm getting the better of him.

"This is my student, Anakin Skywalker of Tatooine," Obi-Wan introduced. "I am Obi-Wan Kenobi."

Gann looked down on Anakin and his expression softened. "I, too, have a son," he said. "A special student. Many sons and daughters. That is what we call our students here. Whoever they are born to, we are all mothers and fathers and teachers. I'm afraid you will not see one of our ships for some days, young Anakin." He returned his attention to Obi-Wan. He swung out his arm. "We are at what we call the Middle Distance, our first home on Zonama Sekot, where we settled twenty Ferroan years ago. Sixty standard years. Not that time means the same here as on any of the Ferroan worlds, or on Coruscant."

"Our accents give us away?" Obi-Wan asked.

"Even a few months on the capital world imparts a distinctive speech," Gann said. "Zonama Sekot has its own approach to letting time pass. I feel as if I have spent my entire life here, and yet, it might have been only a year, a month, a week . . ."

Obi-Wan gently interrupted this reverie. "We wish to purchase a ship," he said. "We have the money, and we are ready to engage in the tests and the training."

Gann dramatically drew up his thin black eyebrows. "Ritual first. Answers and tests much later."

The Ferroan turned at some vagary of the wind, a brief whistling sound through the canopies high above. "The view from here is not the best," he said. "Come with me. I need to introduce you to Sekot."

Obi-Wan and Anakin followed Gann to a gap between two of the huge trunks that enclosed and supported the platform. He opened a small gate thickly woven from reedlike stalks and gestured for them to pass through. Walking between the trunks, master and apprentice stepped out onto an exterior platform bathed in sunlight and overlooking a scene even more spectacular than that which Charza Kwinn had shown them aboard the *Star Sea Flower*.

Gann folded his arms and smiled proudly. Morning mists were rising from a wandering river valley, its depths still lost in shadow fully two kilometers below the platform. Along the upper walls of the valley, tier upon tier of dwellings and platforms covered the bare rock faces, held in place by great brown and green vines. The vines hung from great-rooted boras straddling knife-sharp ridges, topped with more brilliant purple and green canopies. Several airships navigated the calm morning currents between the ridges. These were made up of clusters of rigid tube-shaped bone-white balloons strapped side by side and stabilized by more outrigger balloons. The airships followed lengths of cable strung across the valley, supported at hundred-meter intervals by trunks thrust up from the sides. Even now, an airship was threading its way through the circular crown of foliage at the top of a support.

"The planet is named Zonama," Gann said. "The living world that covers it is named Sekot. This is a small part of Sekot, as are the boras around and behind us, and, we believe, as are we who live here. To be worthy to fly a piece of Sekot, one of our ships, you must tune yourself to our way. You must acknowledge the Magister and his role in our life and history, and you must acknowledge union with Sekot. It's not an easy course—and there are real dangers. The power of Sekot is awesome. Do you accept?"

Obi-Wan's expression did not change. Anakin looked up at Gann with a questioning squint.

"We accept," Obi-Wan said.

"Follow me, please, and I will show you where you will stay."

"**W**hy don't you just go and ask about Vergere?" Anakin said to Obi-Wan as they settled into their rooms for a night in the clients' quarters of Middle Distance.

"I get the impression we must be patient," Obi-Wan answered as he opened a pair of shutters and looked down over the valley. "We must learn more about this Magister, whoever he is."

The airship ride to the training district, near a particularly expansive rise in the eastern ridge, had been routine enough, but still beautiful—and to Anakin, very exciting. All of his odd sensations and premonitions had faded in the glory of bright sun and open air—rare enough on Coruscant, impossible aboard the *Star Sea Flower.*

"It's different here," Anakin said. "Not like Tatooine . . . but I still feel at home."

"Yes," Obi-Wan said ruefully. "So do I. And that concerns me. The air is rich with many substances. Perhaps some of them affect humans."

"It smells *great,*" Anakin said, leaning out the window and staring down into the shadows at the river coursing far below. "It smells *alive.*"

"I wonder what Sekot would be saying if we could understand these odors," Obi-Wan mused, and tugged his Padawan back in before he leaned too far. "Keep a grip."

"I know," Anakin said brightly. He artificially deepened his voice. *"Things are not what they seem."*

"What else do you sense?" Obi-Wan asked, the very question Anakin had hoped to avoid. He made a sour face.

"I don't want to sense anything now. I just want to enjoy the daylight and the air. Charza's ship was wet and cramped, and I've never liked space travel. It always feels cold to me, out there in the middle of nowhere. I prefer being in the middle of living things. Even Coruscant. But this . . ." Anakin looked up at Obi-Wan. "I'm yakking my head off, aren't I?"

Obi-Wan grinned and touched Anakin's shoulder. "Cheer is a useful emotion at times, if it does not mask carelessness." Obi-Wan thought of Qui-Gon, and of Mace Windu—he had seen both of them almost ebullient even in difficult situations requiring deep concentration.

A talent he had not yet mastered.

"Are you ever cheerful, Master?" Anakin asked.

"I will have time to be cheerful when you tell me what you sense. I need a baseline against which I can measure my own perceptions."

Anakin sighed and pulled up a tall stool with four slender legs. His fingers felt the dark green substance of the piece of furniture, and he suddenly dropped it, letting it thump to the floor. "It's still *alive!*" he said in wonder, then bent to set it upright again.

"They call their building material lamina," Obi-Wan said. "It is not necessary to kill to make their homes and furniture. All the furniture is still alive, and the dwelling itself. Extend your feelings for a moment, and see what is there, rather than what you wish to be there."

"Right," Anakin said. But almost immediately, his mind wandered back to the curiosity of the moment. "How does it stay alive, this . . . lamina? What does it eat, how does it—"

"Padawan," Obi-Wan said, without a hint of sternness, but in a distinct tone that Anakin had long since come to recognize, and instantly react to.

"Yes." The boy pushed the stool aside and stood still in the middle of the room. His arms remained at his sides, but his fingers splayed out. He became intensely outward-alert.

A few minutes passed. Obi-Wan stood a pace away from Anakin, all of his own feelings neutralized, senses withdrawn, to give the boy greater range.

"It's an immensity, a unity," Anakin said finally. "Not a lot of little voices."

"The life-forms here are all naturally symbiotic," Obi-Wan agreed. "Not the usual pattern of competition and predation. It's part of what you felt before—the sense of one fate, one destiny."

"Maybe, but I was feeling something outside, something about us."

"They may be intertwined."

Anakin thought this over with a frown. "I can feel the newcomers, the colonists, separately," he said. "I don't sense Vergere anywhere."

"She has gone," Obi-Wan agreed.

"So let's go ask where she went."

"In good time." Obi-Wan lifted his eyes. "Observe your stool."

Anakin looked down and saw that one foot had fastened to the floor. He bent and touched the connection, then looked up in wonder at Obi-Wan. "It's feeding!" he said. "The floor's alive, too!"

"We should be prepared early in the morning for the arrival of our hosts."

"I'll be ready," Anakin said, getting to his feet. "I'll be *charged!*"

The boy's emotional energy level was still too high for Obi-Wan's comfort. There was an interaction between Anakin and Sekot he could not yet understand, and what puzzled him was that this revealed as much about Anakin as it did about Sekot . . . and also revealed that Obi-Wan still knew very little about either.

It was the first day of client celebration that had been held for some time at Middle Distance, and the air was filled with many-colored balloon ships flying back and forth along their cables, loaded with officials, workers, and the curious. Anakin and Obi-Wan stood by the rail of the gondola of the large airship that carried them down the length of the valley. The oblong gondola featured a small cabin and a long, curved roof made of sheets of lamina and thickly woven tendrils, all still alive.

Gann accompanied them on this trip. About midway down the canyon, he grabbed a handrope and stepped forward around the cabin to the prow to confer with a tall Ferroan woman.

Wind carried snatches of string instruments and song from other airships. Obi-Wan listened to the musicians and singers with wonder. These ceremonies were important, but something else was in the air: a sense of renewal after a long ordeal.

He wondered whether Vergere had witnessed that ordeal. Had she left any messages for the Jedi who would follow? If so, Obi-Wan had not found them.

Anakin leaned out over the woven rail of the hanging gondola and peered down at the river, thin and white and roaring even from this height. He saw sleek, pale creatures as wide as a Gungan sub, and about the same shape, gliding back and forth above the river. Other, smaller shapes, dark and quick, veered around them.

"I'd love to ride a raft down there," Anakin said.

"It's too dangerous," the airship pilot warned. A young man of sixteen or seventeen standard years, barely an adult by the Ferroan measure, he stood behind three thick control levers aft of the cabin, steadying the airship's course.

"Nobody's tried it?" Anakin asked him.

"Nobody with half a brain." The pilot grinned. "We have better ways to take risks."

"Like what?"

"Wellll-llll"—the pilot drew out the word to some length— "on Uniting Day . . ." Gann returned from the narrow prow and gave the pilot a look. He was telling tales out of turn.

"Ten minutes before we arrive," Gann said. "You have all that is necessary?"

Obi-Wan looked to Anakin, who winked and patted his waist. "Yes," Obi-Wan answered. "But I'd be much more comfortable if we were more familiar with the procedures."

Gann nodded. "I'm sure you would," he said. "Everybody would. There is only one client this day, counting you and the boy as a partnered team. So you are alone in your time of choosing. Any more than that—" He glanced at the pilot. "—would be telling."

The young pilot nodded soberly.

The other passengers on the airship were Ferroans, as well, with pale blue and ghostly white skins, long jaws, and wide eyes.

The female Gann had been conversing with was larger and some-
what more heavily muscled than the males. She walked around
the cabin as they approached the high, vine-suspended landing,
and introduced herself to Obi-Wan and Anakin.

"I am Sheekla Farrs," she said, her voice strong and deep. "I
am a grower and daughter of Firsts. Gann gives you to me now
for the rest of this day."

"Sheekla," Gann said, bowing slightly and retreating a step.
Farrs leaned close and sniffed at Obi-Wan's face, then drew back
with a discerning squint. "You aren't afraid." She did the same
for Anakin, who glanced at Obi-Wan in some embarrassment.
"Neither are you," she concluded.

"I can't wait," Anakin said. "Are we going to see the ships?"

When Farrs laughed, her deep voice became high and quite
musical. "Today you meet your seed-partners. When that is
done, you design your ship. My husband, Shappa, will guide you
in that task."

The pilot unhooked the airship from its cable and turned
it into the shade of a ridge wall, then deftly strung it onto a
secondary cable and toward the landing. The basket wobbled
between a pair of heavy black dampers mounted on thick pilings.
The cable sang as the dampers pinched in and grabbed the basket, tugging it down slightly before the gate was opened by
attendants at the landing. A ramp was dropped, and Sheekla
Farrs indicated they should cross ahead of her.

"That was rugged," Anakin told Obi-Wan as they disem-
barked. "If there's some sort of airship race here, can we try it?"

"We?" Obi-Wan asked.

"Sure. You'd be great," Anakin said. "You learn fast. But . . ."
He waggled his shoulders. "You got to be more confident."

"I see," Obi-Wan said.

"We are now at Far Distance," Sheekla Farrs said. "This is where we join our seed-partners and the prospective clients. There is a ceremony, of course." She smiled at Anakin. "Very formal. You'll hate it."

Anakin wrinkled his nose.

"But you'll be meeting what could become your ship," she added.

Anakin brightened.

"And you'll undergo what the Magister experienced, so many years ago, when he alone saw Zonama and knew Sekot for the first time."

"Who's the Magister?" Anakin asked.

Sheekla Farrs gave Obi-Wan a glance then that he could not read, though it seemed to mingle both respect and warning. "He is our leader, our spiritual adviser, and the knower. His father was founder of Middle Distance and the pioneer for all we do here."

Gann made his farewells, promising to meet with them later, and Farrs led them across the bridge that connected the landing to a broad tunnel dug directly into the rock wall. Water dripped to either side of a long walkway elevated above the floor of the tunnel, its lamina surface damp with seep. Green tendrils crisscrossed the wet floor like a grid. Everything was very regular, very patterned, almost too tidy.

"The seed-partners emerge from a Potentium," Farrs told them as they approached the end of the tunnel.

Surprised by that word, *Potentium*, Obi-Wan reached back far into his memory, to conversations with Qui-Gon Jinn before the Jedi Master had taken him on as a Padawan.

Farrs pushed through the door and took them into a broad courtyard open to the sky. The trunks of smaller boras leaned over the courtyard on three sides. On the fourth side, the neatly paved stone floor ended abruptly at the abyss. They heard the sound of the river beyond, apparently rushing into a subterranean cavern. "If you fail, they will return to the Potentium. All is conserved. The seed-partners are very important here."

"I don't know that word," Anakin said to Obi-Wan. "What's a Potentium?"

Qui-Gon and Mace Windu had once dealt with group of apprentices who had shown promise, but had not been accepted as Jedi Knights. In disappointment and anger, one of them had tried to start his own version of the Jedi, enlisting "students" from aristocratic families on Coruscant and Alderaan. Qui-Gon had mentioned the Potentium, a controversial view of the Force.

The theory of the Potentium had long since been judged by the Council to be in error, and abandoned. It was no longer even mentioned to Padawans.

"I'll be curious to discover the meaning myself," Obi-Wan said. *And how and why it is being used here!*

The courtyard was filled with a brightly dressed crowd of celebrants, standing in clusters of five and six throughout, all silent. Anakin and Obi-Wan advanced slowly at the urging of Sheekla Farrs. A woman's low voice began singing—the same song they had heard coming from the other airships.

In Ferroans, maturity darkened the hair of males, but not females. Two older men with jet-black hair stepped forward, carrying sashes hung with bloodred, gourdlike fruits. The taller of the two slung a sash around Obi-Wan's neck, and the other slipped his over Anakin's head. Now all joined in the song, and the chorus of voices echoed from the courtyard's stone walls.

Farrs smiled broadly. "They like the way you look and smell. You aren't afraid."

The taller man backed away a step, walked in a circle, thrusting his chin at three points of the Zonama compass, and then turned back to Obi-Wan and held out his hands.

"Your offering to the Potentium," Farrs suggested.

At a gesture from Obi-Wan, Anakin slipped his hand through his loose tunic and drew out the pouched belt containing the bars of old Republic aurodium. He passed it to Obi-Wan, who passed it in turn to the elder, who accepted it with a smile and a slight bow.

"Now, we introduce you to Sekot," Farrs said, rewarding them with a beaming and most unmercenary smile. "I am so very, very optimistic!"

The lengthy journey through hyperspace was beginning to wear on Raith Sienar. He sat in a chair facing a blank bulkhead in the commander's quarters aboard the *Admiral Korvin*, shifting a small metal cylinder from hand to hand, lost in thought.

While the theory of hyperspace fascinated him—and while he was always interested in designing ships that could travel more and more swiftly by means of this mode of extradimensional travel—Sienar was much less interested in so testing himself. The routines of command held even less interest. He much preferred working alone and had always structured his life so that he spent most of his time by himself, to think.

Now, that tendency was just one more weakness.

There had been three inspections so far of the *Admiral Korvin* and the holds that carried the greater part of their armament. With some plan forming, as yet embryonic, he had ordered a personal and individual inspection of the various weapons systems—the *walking* droids, the *flying* droids, those that could both walk and fly, the *large* droids and the *small* droids, many no larger than his hand—so tedious, when he wanted little to do with these machines. He knew their limitations, whatever puff talk Tarkin had delivered.

He could not forget the droids that had stood around like sticks on Naboo, slow to think, slow to fire, centrally controlled by their organic idiot counterparts. The *droids* that had essentially brought down the Trade Federation.

However much Sienar tried to muster enthusiasm for his tools, he could not stop that intellectual itch that told him he was being set up. He just could not figure out *why* he was being set up. Who would benefit from the failure of this mission?

The time was approaching—if time could be called any such thing on a ship hurtling above time—when he would have to meet with his appointed "assistant," the Blood Carver, Ke Daiv. Ke Daiv gave him the creeps, but at least he seemed intelligent and, despite his failure against the Jedi, competent enough. Strangely, as Sienar got up from his chair and paced his spacious and well-appointed cabin, he was not disturbed by the possibility that Ke Daiv was the one assigned to execute him should he fail.

He needed more armor, and he needed an ally whose motives he understood and could at least partially trust.

He drew himself up. It was time to probe Ke Daiv's armor. He would do it ahead of schedule, and while they were still incommunicado in hyperspace.

That would require some preparation.

He pulled a small box from his locked and coded luggage case and examined it in a bright light that descended from the ceiling at the touch of a button. A small table and set of tools rose from the floor before the closed forward-facing port that filled most of a wall in the commander's sitting room.

The tools on the table he had requisitioned from ship's stores the day before. His fingers were less than steady, but the work of preparing the box was not exceptionally delicate.

One of the reasons he had little faith in droids was that he had long ago created ways to subvert them. For reasons of his own—and because he had always been convinced battle droids would fail on their own—he had never marketed these items.

Inside the box was a custom droid verbobrain of his own design, carrying his own programs.

He fingered a communications button, and an image of Captain Kett flickered to low-resolution "life" before him. He could see Kett, but Kett could not see him.

"Send me a Baktoid model E-5, fully operational and armed, to my quarters." Baktoid Combat Automata had designed and manufactured these heavy, unwieldy droids as Trade Federation replacements after Naboo, before assimilation into the Republic. He would have preferred a lighter model, but the E-5s had more than enough power and their motivators were quite good. They were, in Sienar's opinion, the best of a mediocre lot, their greatest weakness being their lack of intelligence. Their verbobrains were as slow as any tank's. But then, that is what Baktoid specialized in: transports and tanks.

Sienar knew the chief designer well. The dunderhead just *loved* tanks.

He opened the box, removed the verbobrain, and inserted a new programming cylinder into a vacant slot. Immediately, the spinner within the unit began to whir and seek data from its radiance of inputs.

With this, Sienar believed he could make an E-5 dance like a female Twi'lek.

And with the modified E-5 a fixture in his quarters, he would meet with Ke Daiv, and tell him a thing or two about the people— the *humans*—he was working for.

The crowd had parted in silence to let Obi-Wan and Anakin through. They walked across the courtyard alone. Sheekla Farrs held back and watched them approach the massive stone and lamina door. The door swung wide. Beyond lay a great, open spherical chamber, like the inside of a ball with its top cut away. Late-morning sun moved in a brilliant oblong across the rear of the chamber, which crawled with thousands of living things: spike-covered balls a little smaller than a human head.

Obi-Wan observed this motion with some concern. Anakin, however, looked upon the thousands of thorny spheroids with a smile.

"These will grow to become our ship," he whispered to Obi-Wan.

"We don't know that yet," Obi-Wan said.

"A Jedi can feel his destiny, can't he?" Anakin asked.

"A fully trained Jedi may rely on such feelings, but changes in the Force can deceive an apprentice."

Anakin ran ahead, and Obi-Wan broke into a trot to keep up. The boy held out his arms as if in welcome.

Across the wide chamber, every thorn-covered organism stopped its rustling motion. Except for a morning breeze lazing down from the opening to the sky, silence filled the room.

"They're seed-partners!" Anakin shouted.

The door behind them closed noiselessly. They were alone with the seed-partners, if that was what they were. Obi-Wan felt it best to keep an open mind, but it was obvious Anakin had no doubts whatsoever.

"What are you waiting for?" the boy shouted. His voice did not echo—the thick carpet of spikeballs absorbed all sound.

"We should let *them* take the initiative," Obi-Wan advised softly.

Anakin scowled impatiently. Suddenly, he was a twelve-year-old boy, nothing more. He showed nothing of the three years of training in the Temple. Obi-Wan placed his hand on Anakin's shoulders and felt the tension in the boy's body and limbs, like a young animal, totally impenetrable to suggestion.

The dropping away from his Padawan of every aspect of Obi-Wan's teaching dismayed him for a moment. It was as if he stood behind a totally different child than the one Qui-Gon had thought so special.

Anakin spoke, his words barely audible.

Then, louder, "I'm ready."

Only now did Obi-Wan catch on, and the hair on his neck bristled in a way it had not for years, since he had encountered and defeated, though just barely, the strange red-and-black Sith with the double-bladed red lightsaber, Darth Maul, the Sith who had mortally wounded Qui-Gon.

The boy had totally damped all extraneous personal vibrations. He had become quiet in the Force in a way Obi-Wan still found exceptionally difficult, though not impossible, and the boy had done this in fractions of a second.

With the swift and native genius of a child, Anakin had made himself into a quiet antenna listening to the creatures within the sphere.

And the spikeballs, in turn, equally quiet, listened to both of these potential new clients with all the openness of a different variety of childhood.

"They want something from us," Obi-Wan suggested.

Anakin shook his head. The apprentice was disagreeing with the master, not for the first time and, Obi-Wan suspected, not by a long shot for the last.

"We're not what they expected," Obi-Wan said.

Anakin nodded.

Two of the bristling spheres disengaged midway up the wall of the chamber and clambered over their companions until they came to the clearing on the bowl of the floor, the empty space surrounding the two humans. The spikeballs rolled slowly, in a wavering path, until they were just centimeters from the boy's feet.

More spikeballs disengaged and followed. In a few moments, Anakin and Obi-Wan were surrounded by ten of the milling seed-partners, each making small clicking noises and producing a rich, flowery smell.

"They approve," Anakin said, glancing at his master. "They sense we're not afraid." Within the boy's eyes, enthusiasm had been tempered by a new caution. "But . . . if they approve, it means a real commitment, doesn't it?"

"I presume," Obi-Wan said.

"For them, it's got to be *serious*."

"Perhaps."

The ten spikeballs drew back and stopped their restless motion. The air was rich with their scent, now tangy, like breeze from a salty sea.

"I wish Sheekla had told us more," Anakin said, his eyes darting around the chamber.

The atmosphere was thick and damp, as if a storm were near.

The spikeballs began to vibrate on the floor. Obi-Wan looked up to the rim of the chamber wall and saw many more descending. The purposeful descent quickly turned into frenzied dropping. The carpet of seed-partners unraveled as dozens, then hundreds of the thorny spheres broke free and fell to collide with their companions in the bottom of the bowl. The spikeballs bounced, whistled, clicked, and released a nose-cloying cloud of electric-flowery scent.

"They're *all* going to drop!" Anakin shouted, and turned, but there was nowhere to run. He stood straight, then crouched and reached for Obi-Wan. "This is going to be bad! *But whatever you do, don't be afraid!*"

Obi-Wan instinctively reached for his lightsaber, but that would have been useless. All they could do was stand back-to-back and cover their faces as every spikeball in the chamber poured down onto the floor in a thorny cascade. In seconds, Anakin and Obi-Wan were awash in the deluge, bumped and battered mercilessly. They pushed out with their hands to keep their faces clear. But the torrent pressed from all sides, rising over their heads and slamming the backs of their hands against their lips and noses. Fragments of spikeball shells flew into the air, and a cloud of dust rose from the churning heap.

They could not move.

In seconds, they could not even breathe.

I have great respect for the culture of the Blood Carvers," Raith Sienar told the tall, quiet, golden figure that stood in the anteroom to the commander's quarters. He could hear Ke Daiv's slow, soft breathing and the steady *click-click* of his long black nails on one hand, knocking together like wooden chimes in a breeze.

"Why did you bring me here?" Ke Daiv asked after a moment. "It is early in the mission."

"So insolent!"

"It is my way. I serve and obey, also in my way."

"I see. Please, make yourself comfortable." Raith stood back and gestured toward the sitting room.

Ke Daiv moved half a step, then hesitated and bowed slightly. "I am not worthy."

"If I say you are worthy, then you are worthy," Sienar told the young Blood Carver, with just the right measure of sternness.

Ke Daiv bowed again and walked into the viewing room. The port hatches were still closed. The navigator droid had predicted another four or five hours in hyperspace before they emerged into realspace.

"Please, *sit*," Sienar urged again. He wished to hold his command voice in reserve. He sensed Ke Daiv would be more susceptible in due time, after he learned a few things about his situation—and about Raith Sienar.

Ke Daiv gently bent his triple joints and knelt by the crystal-top table, rather than sit on the divan.

"Have you been treated well aboard the *Admiral Korvin?*" Sienar asked.

Ke Daiv said nothing.

"I am concerned with your well-being," Sienar said.

"I am fed and left alone in small quarters reserved for me. As I am not part of the crew, they stay away, and that is good."

"I see. Something of a *wall* there, hm?"

"No more so than on Coruscant. My people are few in that part of the galaxy. We have yet to make our mark."

"Of course. I, personally, admire your people, and I hope we can exchange information useful to both of us," Sienar said.

Ke Daiv turned his head, and his face formed that disconcerting blade shape as his wide nose flaps came together. He turned slowly to look at the E-5 droid hulking in one corner. The droid rotated its wide, flat head in their direction, jewel-red eyes glowing like coals, and adjusted its stance to face the Blood Carver directly.

"Do you believe all that you've been told about this mission?" Sienar said.

Ke Daiv shifted one eye toward him, but kept the other on the E-5. "I have been told little. I know that you do not trust me."

"We're equal in that regard," Sienar said. "And in no other. I am still commander. I am your leader."

"Why remind me if you are so certain?" Ke Daiv asked bluntly.

Sienar smiled and held out his hands in admiration. "Perhaps we are equal in other ways. You have doubts, and I have doubts. You know little or nothing about me, or what I hold in reserve."

Ke Daiv's joints cracked softly, and he looked away from the E-5. The droid did not frighten him. "What do you wish to know?"

"I understand you have a contract with Tarkin."

"You cannot understand what you do not know, and you cannot know this."

"A little respect," Sienar suggested in a soft rumble.

"Commander," Ke Daiv added with another cracking of his arm joints.

"Tell me about your arrangement."

"I do not mind dying. I am in disgrace with my family, and death is not feared."

"I have no intention of killing you, or of letting you die," Sienar said. "The droid is here in case you have instructions to kill *me*. It's completely under my control."

"Why would anybody wish to kill you? You are commander."

"Such insolence!" Sienar said with a *tsk-tsk*. "Almost admirable. Please, I'll ask, and you'll answer."

"You show weakness in your phrases."

"No, I show politeness, and that is *my* culture and my upbringing, and you show ignorance about me, and that is a *true* weakness, Ke Daiv."

Ke Daiv fell silent again and faced the closed port.

"You have other weaknesses. Your contract with Tarkin is all you deserve, because you failed to kill a Jedi."

"Two Jedi," Ke Daiv corrected.

"An understandable lapse, but still, a disgrace to your superiors and, I presume, your clan. Do you hope to make up for this disgrace by succeeding in this mission?"

"I always hope for success."

Sienar nodded. "Killing Jedi is a mug's game, Ke Daiv. They are strong and they have honor, and they respect all peoples and their ways. Why would you want to kill them?"

"I have no honor in my family, and that is all I may say," Ke Daiv told him.

"I did some research before I left, and discovered, in the Blood Carver genealogical registry on Coruscant, that you are listed as 'extended,' which means, I believe, a kind of extreme probation. Is this true?"

"It is true."

"Tell me how this happened. That is an order."

"I am constrained," Ke Daiv said.

"If you disobey my order, I can have you executed . . . under the Trade Federation rules these officers still believe in and follow. That would remove you from any chance of redeeming yourself and put you on the list of permanent exclusion from the Art Beyond Dying. That is the finale of life within the Blood Carver belief system, a glorious conception of the afterlife, with which I, personally, would hate to interfere."

Ke Daiv's head bowed slightly, as if under some weight.

"You have contacted my clan," he said. "You bring me shame beyond my ability to erase."

"No, I haven't contacted your clan," Sienar said. "And I intend you no shame. I respect the Blood Carvers and their ways, and you are in enough trouble already. But I ask you listen closely to what I have to tell you."

Ke Daiv lifted his head and brought his nose flaps submissively back against his cheeks.

"You followed your quarry to the bottom of the Wicko refuse pit, and remarkably, you survived the garbage worms there. You climbed back against all the odds and reported your failure. That is bravery befitting any clan warrior, and a commitment to duty beyond anything I've heard about on Coruscant for decades. Yet there is a rumor going around that . . ."

Sienar hesitated for effect and shook his head incredulously.

"There is a rumor going around that in the future of the Republic, there may be no room for your people. No room for any race but humans. I, personally, will not support such a scheme. Will you?"

Ke Daiv glared at Raith Sienar. "This is true?"

"It is what I have been told, by an old friend and classmate who seems to know."

"Tarkin?"

Sienar nodded and, using his most persuasive voice, trained by years of speaking with armament and ship agents and fleet buyers, said, "Examine your memory of Tarkin and disagree with me if you must."

Ke Daiv closed his eyes, opened them, said nothing.

"Let us talk some more," Sienar said, "and see if there are plans on which we can agree."

Sienar, of course, did most of the talking.

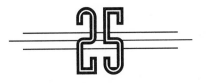

The great stone and lamina doors swung open again, as quietly as the little hush of current that crept down the open bowl of the room beyond. The celebratory crowd had pulled back to the periphery of the great room, leaving only Sheekla Farrs near the door. She was now joined by Gann.

They peered curiously into the big round chamber. The spikeballs once more covering the walls were as still as the stone to which they clung. At the bottom of the bowl, a slight descent from the big doors, a pile of debris rose two meters above the stone floor.

A sigh came from the crowd.

Farrs called out two names.

Obi-Wan Kenobi got to his feet first and touched himself with quick gestures. Three spikeballs clung to him, one on each arm and one on his chest. Their grip was tenacious, and he did not try to dislodge them, much as he wanted to. He looked around the piles of shed spikes and shells littering the bottom of the bowl, the detritus of the terrifying cascade, and saw an arm poking from the thickest mound. He stepped over with a grunt and grabbed Anakin's hand and pulled him up.

Anakin, from head to foot, was cluttered with spikeballs, twelve of them. His pulse was strong, but he had gone inward to conserve oxygen and avoid the shock that might come with physical injury, and his eyes were closed.

"Great skies!" Farrs cried. "Is he all right? We've never seen such a—"

Gann ran down the dip to the bottom of the chamber and helped Obi-Wan carry the encumbered and unwieldy boy through the doors. They laid him out on a cushion brought by two young female attendants. All were careful not to dislodge the seed-partners. Once again, seeing the clients, the crowd let out a breath, some muttering little strings of words as if in prayer.

"Great is the Potentium, great the life of Sekot."

"All serve and are served, and all join the Potentium."

Obi-Wan held his anger and concern in tight check, lest he reveal his lightsaber and ask more than a few tough questions. "Did you know this would happen?" he asked Sheekla Farrs through clenched teeth.

Her face was heavy with dismay. "No! Is he alive?"

"He's alive. Do they take sustenance from us?" He reached down to touch the spikeball on his chest. It had pushed a spike through his tunic and coat to reach the skin beneath, but he felt no wound there, merely an uncomfortable adhesion.

"No," Gann said, kneeling beside Anakin. "They don't suck your blood. So many! The most partners we've ever seen on a client—"

"Three is normal," Farrs interrupted and finished for him. "You have the normal number. Your student must be an extraordinary young man!"

"What made them do it?" Gann wondered.

Anakin's eyes fluttered, then opened, and the boy stared up at Obi-Wan from the depths of an utter calm. Somehow, he had maintained that inner stillness even when confronted with extreme danger.

"You're not injured," Obi-Wan told him. "They cling but do not wound."

"I know," Anakin said. "They're friendly. So many wanted to join us . . . all at once!"

Obi-Wan turned to Farrs. "You avoid a truth," he said.

Gann looked suddenly guilty, but Farrs shook her head and told the attendants to carry the boy into the postpartnering room. The two females, little older than Anakin, helped him to his feet, avoiding the spikeballs, and the group walked toward a narrow door near a corner. Anakin gave the girls a shy grin.

The crowd's heads turned as one until they were through the door.

The stone walls of the low-ceilinged and smaller room beyond had one opening, a narrow window that showed a scut of sky and the green and purple of the outside growth.

"I need to verify something . . ." Farrs murmured. She guided them toward a low table illuminated by a broad lamp.

Farrs and Gann took brass and steel instruments from a cupboard and measured Anakin's spikeballs first, then pinched the clinging spikes until they released their grips with small sighs. Each spikeball was placed in a lamina box, and the attendants labeled the boxes with a circle. They then removed Obi-Wan's seed-partners and placed them in boxes marked with a square.

"There *will* be a ship, a very dense and marvelous ship, I think," Farrs murmured as she checked her measurements against a chart on a scroll mounted on one end of the table. She conferred in whispers with Gann for a moment.

"Three of these seed-partners have chosen a client before," Farrs said when they stopped their whispering. "One of them chose you, Obi-Wan, this time. Two chose you, Anakin."

"Who did they belong to before?" Obi-Wan asked.

"We do not reveal the names of our clients," Gann said.

"That is right," Farrs said. "We did not want to deceive, but . . ."

"This client did not stay with us long enough to grow a ship," Gann said, and exchanged another look with Farrs. "The seed-partners returned to the Potentium."

"Pardon us," Sheekla Farrs said. "We need to confer again, in private. Please, rest, relax. The attendants will bring food and drink."

"All right," Anakin said. He lifted his arms and clasped his hands behind his head. The boy grinned once more, even more broadly, as Farrs and Gann left through the narrow door. The girls stepped back, their faces solemn.

"I see you're amused," Obi-Wan said.

"I'm glad to be alive," Anakin explained. "And I got more than you," he added. "More even than Vergere!"

Obi-Wan pressed his finger to Anakin's lips—enough about Vergere. "We do not know the other was her."

"It had to be!" Anakin said. "Who else?"

Obi-Wan let this pass. He suspected the boy was right. "At any rate, how do we know more is *better?*" he cautioned.

"It always is," Anakin said.

They ate in the cool silence of the room: thin brown cakes served on carved stone platters, cool water in sweating ceramic pitchers. Their cups were made of green- and red-streaked lamina, and the water tasted pure and slightly sweet. Anakin seemed happy, even ebullient. He looked at Obi-Wan as if he expected his master to burst this particular bubble at any moment.

Obi-Wan withheld his judgment for the time being as to how well they were doing, and whether they had made any progress.

After ten minutes, Gann returned alone. Anakin's face fell on seeing the older Ferroan's dour expression.

"There's a difficulty," Gann told them. "The Magister thinks we should not proceed to the designing and forging until he meets with you."

"Is that good or bad?" Anakin asked. "Do we get to make the ship?"

"I don't know," Gann said. "He rarely meets with anybody."

"When will he come?" Obi-Wan asked.

"You will go to *him*," Gann said tersely, eyes rolling, as if that should be obvious. "And you will go at the Magister's convenience." He peered at them from under thick, merged brows. "We will keep your seed-partners ready, and when you return, if all is well, we will begin the design, and the conversion, and proceed to the annealing and the shaping."

Captain Kett greeted the commander with civility as he mounted the navigation deck of the *Admiral Korvin*. "We are nearing emergence," he told Sienar.

Sienar nodded abstractedly.

The port covers slid aside, and Sienar turned half away from the twisted, star-streaming view.

"Reversion at mark," he muttered.

"So ordered, sir," Kett acknowledged.

"How good are the ship's duplication facilities, Captain Kett?" Sienar asked.

"Our astromech complement is adequate to conduct many major repairs in transit," Kett reported.

The E-5 was doing quite well with its new capabilities. And the Blood Carver was reacting favorably to his new perspective. So far, so good, but there was so much farther to go.

Sienar held out a small box of data cards. "I would like to have these programs loaded into the ship's manufactory and placed in all the battle droids. The programming will be duplicated from these data cards and activated in each unit, to replace all previous programming. *All,* Captain Kett. And, of course, I will perform authentication tests."

Kett's polite expression froze. "That is not authorized, sir. It's against Trade Federation policy."

Sienar smiled at this slip into old ways. "When we return, all our weapons will be handed over to the Republic. This programming meets Republic standards and the droid will answer to Republic control."

"It is still not in my brief," Kett said.

"I have my own instructions, from Tarkin himself, and they are explicit," Sienar said calmly. He knew that as commander, and with Tarkin's backing, his command would be sufficient—now that he had at least some influence over Ke Daiv.

Now that he would not meet an unfortunate accident if he did something unexpected and out of turn.

The Baktoid E-5 droid strode with a surprisingly light tread out of the turbolift and onto the bridge of the flagship. It stood just below the navigation deck, clearly visible to all on the bridge. No threat was implied, merely a demonstration of the new way of things. Normally, this droid would not have been activated until battle.

Kett watched with obvious misgivings. "Understood, sir," he said.

"And show me the astromech reports when the job is completed," Sienar said, sucking his teeth.

Kett watched him for a couple of seconds, barely hiding his distaste.

Sienar ignored him and glared at the port.

"Reversion," the hyperdrive control officer announced.

"Realspace!" Captain Kett shouted as the stars whisked back

into proper perspective, and space and time returned to their familiar dominance.

"About time," Sienar said with a sigh. He pushed a lever, and the navigation deck rolled on its track toward the large port until the view filled his field of vision.

He would have reveled in any normal pattern of stars whatsoever, but what he saw now was impressive, very impressive. The outward-spiraling ribbon of the red giant and white dwarf components filled his eyes with a dreamlike, fiery light. Such a sight was a rare privilege.

With some assurance of subtlety and Sienar-bred creativity in his weapons systems, he could actually enjoy the view.

"Our destination planet is in sight, and we are locked on to a holding orbit around the planet's yellow sun," Kett said. "We will not approach any closer until so ordered by you, Commander." Kett, still mulling over his options, was reluctant to leave the bridge.

Sienar did not mind independent thought, so long as it did not become *too* independent.

"You may carry out your instructions . . . now." Sienar pointed aft.

"Yes, sir." Kett hurried to the turbolift, the deep-set and jewel-like eyes of the E-5 droid firmly and balefully fixed on the space between his shoulder blades.

The Sekotan air transport took them south over some of the strangest terrain Obi-Wan Kenobi had ever seen. Flying at an altitude of less than a thousand meters, the small, flat craft dodged with dizzying speed over tall, thick-trunked boras with bloated balloonlike leaves that spun and wobbled in their wake.

"I think the settlers use those leaves to make their airships," Anakin said, looking aft through the windscreen that curved almost completely around the transport.

Obi-Wan nodded, lost in thought. If seed-partners preferred Jedi, then some research was called for. Only organisms strong in the Force could detect Jedi. It was becoming more and more apparent that the life-forms of this world—Sekot, as Gann called the living totality—were special, and that his Padawan strongly attracted them.

"This is really beautiful," Anakin said. "The air smells great, and the jungle is wizard."

"Don't grow too attached," Obi-Wan warned.

"I've never been to a place like this."

"Remember your earlier feelings about Sekot."

"I do," Anakin said.

"You mentioned a single wave, something happening now or in the future."

"Yeah," Anakin said. He nodded his head forward, to the door that hid the pilot from them.

Obi-Wan held up his hand. "He is oblivious to our talk. It's important we analyze what's happening before we get drawn in further."

"It comes and goes, this sensation of a single wave. I might have made a mistake."

"You made no mistake. I feel it myself now. Something coming toward us rapidly, something dangerous."

Anakin shook his head sadly. "I hope nothing happens before we get our ship made."

Obi-Wan narrowed his eyes in disapproval. "I am concerned you are losing your perspective."

"We came here to get a ship!" Anakin said, his voice breaking. "And to find out about Vergere. She didn't get her ship, so it's even more important for us. That's all." He folded his arms.

Obi-Wan let these words sit between them for some seconds before asking, blandly enough, "What does the ship mean to you?"

"A ship that tunes itself to a need for speed . . . Wow!" Anakin said. "For me, that would be the perfect friend."

"That's what I thought," Obi-Wan said.

"But it won't distract me from my training," Anakin assured him.

Once again, Obi-Wan felt he was losing control of the situation. Before Anakin had been Obi-Wan's apprentice, Qui-Gon had encouraged behavior in the boy that Obi-Wan had disapproved of. And now, the Council and Thracia Cho Leem, sending them to this world, were once more tempting Anakin in ways that made Obi-Wan uncomfortable.

"We're going where the Force sends us," Anakin said quietly, anticipating the direction of his master's thoughts. "I don't know what else we can do but observe and accept."

"And then act," Obi-Wan said. "We must be prepared for the course laid out for us and receptive to the unexpected. The Force is never a nursemaid."

"I'll know when something is about to happen," Anakin said with quiet confidence. "I like this planet. And the living things here like *me*. And you. Don't you feel it—something is watching out for us?"

Obi-Wan did in fact feel that—but the sensation gave him no comfort. He did not know who or what could extend such an influence over them, and especially over his Padawan.

The journey continued for another hour. Anakin looked east and pointed out a huge brown scar on the landscape, stretching over the horizon. Obi-Wan had seen this, or something like this, briefly from space—but Charza Kwinn had brought them down before completing a full orbit of Zonama Sekot. The scar had dug clear through to bedrock. Iron-rich red crust opened like the edges of a wound over dark tumbled chunks of basalt.

"What made that?" Anakin asked.

"It looks no more than a few months old," Obi-Wan said. Thin white threads of waterfalls slipped over the red cliff sides into the gouge. "It resembles a battle scar."

The craft now turned and headed due south, flying between and through the tops of the unbroken deck of cloud. A seemingly endless scape of billows and whorls puffed and streamed beneath them.

Anakin turned in his seat. "Look," he said excitedly, and

pointed to their right. They were veering southwest toward a jagged reddish black mountain that pushed up through the clouds, its sloping flanks almost bare of Sekotan growth and its leveled summit capped with snow. It looked like an old, weather-worn volcano.

"We will be at the Magister's home in three minutes," the pilot said. "I hope you've had a nice nap."

Anakin smiled at Obi-Wan. "Well rested!" he said.

They crouched low once more to exit the transport, and stood on a level field of crushed lava. A few meters away a flat stone pathway led to a magnificent, fortresslike palace of skewed blocks stacked around a squat central tower. Beyond the palace, four volcanic terraces spilled orange-tinted water over broad, multicolored falls. The air smelled of Zonama's depths—hydrogen sulfide—alternating with fresh breezes blowing from the south.

Each of the blocks around the tower was over ten meters high and fifty meters wide, its walls lined with windows that gleamed like rainbows in the sunset light. The promontory supported only a few tendrils, barely as thick as an arm, nestled haphazardly between the rocks and around the mineral-spring terraces like lines of red and green thread.

"The Magister lives far from his subjects," Obi-Wan observed, rubbing his hands on the hem of his tunic, then holding them out palm up and dropping his chin. His eyes swept the horizon shrewdly. "And he makes do with very few attendants." Looking at the torn wisps of clouds passing overhead, and the darker masses visible to the south, Obi-Wan estimated they were a thousand kilometers below the equator. "Peculiar customs.

They seem to prefer their clients be misinformed and kept off balance."

"At least they haven't checked us for weapons," Anakin said.

"Oh, but they think they have," Obi-Wan said.

"You did that . . . without my knowing?" Anakin asked.

Obi-Wan smiled.

"You surprise me all the time, Master," Anakin said with a touch of awe. "But that's what an apprentice should expect from his teacher."

Obi-Wan lifted one brow.

"We make a great team, don't we?" the boy said with a sudden grin. His face colored with the expectation of adventure.

"We do," Obi-Wan agreed.

"I'm glad you're here. I'm glad you're my master, Obi-Wan," Anakin said. He gave a small shiver, then he, also, rubbed his palms on his tunic, held them out, and looked around. Obi-Wan had learned years ago that Anakin could become both expressive and imitative whenever he felt excited or ill at ease.

The boy looked up at the glowing pinwheel of plasma unwinding from the distant double-star system, obscured by rips and shreds of thin, high clouds. Zonama's own sun perched on the horizon, turning the sky above into a flaming tapestry easily the match of the astronomical spectacle beyond. "It's out there now. It's closing in."

"Do you see its shape more clearly?"

"It's a time of trial. For me."

"Do you fear it?" Obi-Wan asked.

Anakin shook his head but kept staring up at the red and orange sky. "I fear my reaction. What if I'm not good enough?"

"I have trust in you."

"What if the Magister turns us down?"

"That . . . seems a separate issue, don't you think?"

"Yeah." Anakin said, but persisted with boyish stubbornness, focused on what seemed to him, for the moment, the most crucial of their many problems. "But what if the Magister doesn't want us to get a ship?"

"Then we'll learn something new," Obi-Wan said patiently. The title *Magister* implied someone of accomplishment, of dignity and bearing, and for all his searching the landscape, Obi-Wan received no signs of any impressive human personality.

It was possible the Zonamans could conceal themselves. Jedi Masters could hide from detection, even at close range. Sometimes Obi-Wan could manage to conceal his presence from someone as perceptive as Mace Windu, but never with complete confidence.

Did that imply that whoever lived here could deceive a Jedi for minutes at a time?

Glow lights mounted beside the pathway switched on and illuminated the way to the lowest and closest block of the Magister's dwelling. A small figure appeared at the end of the path and walked toward them with arms folded.

It was a girl, taller than Anakin but no older, and she wore a long green Sekotan robe of the kind they had become familiar with. It draped to her ankles with its own restless motion.

Anakin stepped back as she approached.

"Welcome! My name is Wind," she said. The girl had long hair as dark as the stone on the walkway and of roughly the same hue. The pupils of her eyes were black, set in golden sclera. She scrutinized Obi-Wan with mild approval, and he returned her gentle dip of the chin. Anakin she seemed to find unworthy of much notice. This caused the boy to ball up his hands, then relax them. Anakin never liked being ignored.

"My father is bored and welcomes any distraction," the girl said. "Would you follow me, please?"

The daughter watched them from the entrance to the Magister's small workroom. Here, he kept only a small central desk and chair.

"I have four daughters and three sons. My sons and two of my daughters are in training around Zonama. They are concerned with defense. Who better to help us than Jedi?"

The Magister was a small man, wiry in build, with a long, narrow face and large eyes as black as those of his daughter. His hair, however, was of a pale shade of gray-blue more typical of a Ferroan. He did not wear Sekotan garments, just a simple pair of pants woven from plain beige Republic broadcloth and a loose-knit white shirt.

He had met them in the hall of the uppermost of three levels in this branch of the palace. The interiors of the three rooms they had seen thus far were plain to the point of austerity, though the furniture was well designed and comfortable, apparently made off Zonama. Obi-Wan was not familiar with Ferroan styles, but he judged that all the furniture here was from the Magister's birth world and had been carried here by the original settlers.

"My assistants at Middle Distance tell me you paid in aurodiums," the Magister said. "That was a tip-off. And then . . . your experience with the seed-partners confirmed my suspicions."

The last of the sunset glanced from golden clouds down into the room through a spherical skylight, shading golden-orange the top of the desk and a pile of extracts and readers.

The room smelled of ashes, and also of the eternal sulfide of the springs.

"We did not intend deception," Obi-Wan said.

"You did not announce yourselves as Jedi," the Magister said. His fingers moved restlessly, rubbing against each other. "Well, there was never a need for deceit. I have nothing against the Jedi. In fact, I owe them a great deal. I have nothing against the Republic they serve, and I have nothing to hide . . . except an entire planet. My home." He chuckled. "That's all I'm protecting."

Anakin stood relaxed and ready, assuming nothing, as he had been trained. With the barest of signals, at the appearance of the Magister, Obi-Wan had alerted his Padawan that they were now acting as Jedi, representatives of the order and the Temple, but in a covertly defensive mode.

Something was not right. Something was incomplete.

"We've come here for another reason," Obi-Wan said. "We're looking for a—"

The air seemed to shimmer inside the large room. Obi-Wan shook his head. He had been about to ask a question, and it had fled from the tip of his tongue, leaving no trace.

"Our way of life is precious to me," the Magister said calmly. "As you can see, we have something unique on Zonama Sekot. Customers, clients, come and go with only a vague notion as to where they've been." He smiled. "Not that our little tricks will work against Jedi. And of course, we *do* have to trust those who deliver our clients to us."

A second girl walked from a door on the opposite side of the room. She was identical in appearance to the first, of the same age and size, and wore the same long green Sekotan dress.

Anakin stared at the second girl with a puzzled expression. Obi-Wan's critical faculties were fully engaged. *Something is being playful*, he thought. *Or testing us. Something hidden.*

"Still, I'm pleased you've come," the Magister continued. "I wanted . . . needed to meet with you personally. You appear to be the genuine article—a Master and an apprentice."

"You've studied the Jedi?"

"No," the Magister said, grimacing as if at an unpleasant memory. "I was a promising student. There were difficulties, not entirely of my own making . . . Misperceptions. But that was fifty years ago."

Obi-Wan judged the man before him to be no more than forty. But then, deeper still, a question: *What man? His facial expressions are subtly false. Like a marionette.*

The Magister lifted his hands. "Sekot seems to have taken a liking to you! All is explained. Sekot is sensitive, and it favors Jedi . . . Very well. I accept you as clients. You may proceed. Please excuse me. There's so much work to do. I trust you'll be comfortable on your way back to Middle Distance."

The Magister smiled warmly at Anakin and left the room.

"That's it?" Anakin asked, eyebrows arched. "He's not going to, like, put us through a test or something? We're home free?"

Obi-Wan pressed his temples with finger and thumb, trying to clear his mind, but he could not penetrate whatever illusion surrounded them.

The second daughter escorted them from the block-shaped building and across the stone pathway, now black in the late twilight gloom. She said nothing and barely glanced at them.

Obi-Wan was tempted to reach out and touch her, but controlled the impulse. No need to reveal his suspicions at this point.

The double star and the brightest coil of the spiral lay below the horizon. Scattered stars and faint spills and streaks of nebular gas showed between thin veils of swiftly moving clouds.

The evening breeze passed cool and sweet over them as the Magister's daughter left them by the transport. She turned and walked with an even gait back to the darkened silhouette of the Magister's dwelling.

It had been one of the strangest meetings in Obi-Wan's experience. Strange, unsatisfying, and unrevealing. They knew little more than when they had arrived. Obi-Wan tried to remember the meeting in detail. He had not even bothered trying to persuade the humbly dressed man to tell them more about himself, about Vergere, because he was not sure the figure they saw *could* tell them more.

The man and his daughters were not real. Yet the illusion had been powerful and almost completely convincing. In Obi-Wan's experience, no single being—not even a Jedi Master—could delude two Jedi at once. Hide, yes—that had certainly been done by Qui-Gon and others. Yet the Council had long suspected that the Sith knew how to disguise themselves and pass undetected by Jedi.

Obi-Wan was positive, however, that this was no Sith conspiracy. Even with time to ponder the experience, what they had actually witnessed was not at all clear to him.

"Maybe now we know why they call him Magister," Anakin said in a low voice as they boarded the transport. "Maybe nobody really gets to meet him, and that's how he protects himself."

Obi-Wan again held his finger to his lips. Persuading the pilot not to listen was insufficient. The transport itself, as part of Sekot, was now suspect, and Obi-Wan doubted he could effectively use Jedi persuasion and deception on the living tissue, the biosphere, of an entire world.

The transport lifted away from the promontory and flew them north and east again, back to Middle Distance.

We've met our match, Obi-Wan thought grimly. *Perhaps that is what happened to Vergere, and she is hidden . . . completely hidden from us.*

Then he faced his Padawan across the space between the seats. He moved his lips without sound:

The planet's recent past is closed to us. Observe the path of the transport—the weather is calm, the way is unobstructed, yet we fly a zigzag course. We may be avoiding other evidence of the battle—if there was a battle. We cannot avoid passing over the one scar—it was too large to miss.

Anakin agreed. *Someone is hiding something. But why give us a chance to see the gouge?*

The Magister may assume we saw it from orbit. He just doesn't want to make things too obvious. "No," Obi-Wan whispered, his eyes half-closed. *He believes he has nothing to fear from Jedi. But he may be ashamed, perhaps, of a past weakness. A near-defeat. I am speculating now.*

And how! Anakin said with a slight chop of one hand. He faced forward. *At least we're going to be allowed to make the ship.*

Obi-Wan found no comfort at all in that. *The weak lie to survive. What would make an entire planet feel weak . . . out here, isolated, on the edge of nowhere?*

Anakin shook his head. It was outside the range of his experience. The boy sighed. *I'll bet it all has to do with Vergere and why she came here in the first place.*

The mood at Middle Distance was much subdued, a contrast to the festival that had begun the ceremony of choosing. People went about their business on the terraces as if this were a time like any other. From their apartment parapet, Obi-Wan watched the late-night lanterns flicker across the canyon and listened to the distant voices while his three seed-partners clung to him like a long-lost parent.

Anakin slept very little that night. His bed was crowded and busy with twelve molting seed-partners. The seeds were not used to being separated from a client after the choosing, and had suffered some distress, though nothing, Sheekla Farrs told them, they would not soon forget. They crawled about on his thin covers, mewling plaintively, and occasionally fell to the floor with soft plops, then cried to be picked up.

The seeds were splitting along one side, showing firm white flesh covered by a thick and downy fuzz. The spikes on each had twisted into three thick stiff feet on one side, and along the seam of the sloughing shell, the spikes were curling up and withering away.

* * *

In the morning, now that he and Obi-Wan had passed inspection by the Magister, or so Gann thought, they were given the keys to Middle Distance. Gann delivered client robes to them, red and black, conspicuous amid all the green, and they were allowed access to the valley's small library, housed above the rim in the trunk of a huge and ancient bora.

Not that there would be much time to visit the library, or travel much of anywhere else around Middle Distance. The design phase was about to begin. Sheekla Farrs told them that her husband, Shappa, would guide them in this.

Later, the seeds would be combined and sent off to those mysterious Sekotan manufactories called Jentari, of which they were being told very little. Only one ship would be made by the Jentari, Gann informed them, but he thought it was likely to be a special ship, indeed, coming from fifteen seeds. "The normal complement is three or four," he said with subtle disapproval. He was a man of strong convictions, a believer in traditions.

Anakin put up with the mewling, the shedding of spikes, the restless wandering of his uneasy companions, knowing that he was closer to his goal of flying the fastest ship in the galaxy.

Even if it had meant getting no sleep at all.

Obi-Wan emerged from his room, trailing his three seed-partners, looking just as rumpled and distracted as the boy felt. The master greeted his Padawan with a grunt as a special breakfast was served on the veranda outside.

They sat in comfortable lamina chairs and drank a sweet juice neither of them could identify, and soon, Obi-Wan sniffed the air and said, "We smell different."

"They're preparing us for the next step," Anakin said. "If we're going to guide the seed-partners, we have to smell right."

Obi-Wan was not happy at having his internal chemistry altered, but Anakin's reaction concerned him more. "I wish there were less mystery here," he said.

Anakin grinned. Obi-Wan knew the boy was restraining himself from saying, "You *would!*" Instead, Anakin said, "I bet the smell is temporary."

The seed-partners now found them irresistible and tried to stay even closer, if that was possible. Some of them had shed their old shells completely and emerged as pale, oblate balls with two thick, wide-spaced front legs, two black dots for eyes in between, and two smaller legs at the rear. All the legs were equipped with three-hook graspers that could give quite a pinch.

By the early afternoon, when Gann and Sheekla Farrs came for them, the situation was almost unmanageable. The seed-partners scrambled madly about the quarters and hung from the walls and ceiling and raced back to hook and hug Anakin or Obi-Wan, making tiny little shrieks of distress when another seed-partner blocked the way, which was often.

Farrs smiled at the commotion like a mother entering a nursery. Gann looked on the situation with some concern, for he was planning the next step of the process and wondering how to transport so many seed-partners in the ritually accepted fashion.

Farrs pish-poshed his stodginess. "The ritual must bend," she said. "We'll use a bigger airship."

"But the colors—!" Gann protested.

"Everyone will know, and everyone will understand."

Gann did not find this reassuring. In the end, he called ahead on a small comlink and arranged for a bigger gondola to be hung from the red-and-black airship balloon.

Anakin managed to hook and carry all of his partners, though a few fell off as they passed through the doorway. They trotted after him, mewling and whickering. Obi-Wan, with only three, had fewer problems, though they scrambled unceasingly around his clothes, climbing his pants and tunic, pausing on his shoulders or head, clamping their hooks painfully around his ears, to peer with their tiny eye-spots.

Obi-Wan had gained insight, watching Jedi youngsters play with their pets, into how the children would behave around others later in life. He had never seen his Padawan happier. Anakin, he thought, would be loving and patient, a real contrast to the often harum-scarum youth he was now.

The boy spoke soothingly to his seed-partners, and finally, following his example, Obi-Wan managed to calm his, as well. There would be one more separation, Sheekla told them, before they boarded the airship.

The ship's architect, Sheekla's husband, Shappa, had cleared an appointment for them this morning. "We'll go there now," she said. "He thinks his time is very valuable, and to keep the peace, I humor him."

"Let me guess," Anakin said, eyes sparkling. "He spends most of the day thinking about ships!"

"Not thinking," Sheekla said with a sniff. "Dreaming. They're his life. The Magister made him a happy man with this job."

Obi-Wan and Anakin walked along a narrow walkway outside the broad windows of Shappa Farrs's office. They pushed through a lamina and glass door and entered the small, cramped design room, perched on the edge of a terrace overlooking the canyon and flooded with light from the midmorning sun.

Shappa Farrs sat on a tall stool in the center of a half-circle drafting table, his head enveloped in a drafting helmet, ascribing broad arcs with a repliscribe clenched in his left hand—the only hand he had, since his right arm was missing. Anakin noted that the hand sported only two fingers and a thumb.

"Working with Jentari must be dangerous," Anakin whispered to Obi-Wan. Shappa looked up and surveyed the room for a moment, though blinded by the helmet, as if searching for whoever had spoken. He grinned toothily and removed the helmet.

"Not the Jentari," he said with a quick, melodic laugh. "It's forging and shaping can knock a few limbs away. The forgers and shapers never did teach me how to handle their tools. So here I stay now. They won't let me come near the pits, lest I lose a leg or my head." He stood and bowed deeply. "Welcome to my domain. Shall we fashion something unique and beautiful today?"

Shappa Farrs was a small, slender man, immaculately dressed. His face was narrow and flat, his nose barely projecting from between prominent cheekbones, and his hair was almost black with age. He stood up from his stool, stepped from behind the desk, and looked the Jedi over with a wide-eyed, amused expression.

He saw Sheekla lurking beyond the door, talking with Gann, and bent forward suddenly, neck outthrust. He flapped his arm and made a sharp squawking noise. "Lurking, my dearest?"

"Stop that," Sheekla said with a wry face, entering the room. "They'll think you're crazy. He is, you know. Completely crazy."

Gann followed reluctantly, as if entering a shop full of feminine undergarments.

"She knows me, yet she *loves* me," Shappa said smugly. "I'm twice any other man in brain and body, in her heart, even when mangled. As for Gann . . . my liaison with all that is practical on Zonama Sekot! So timid! So fearful of the dark secrets of Sekotan life! Like looking back into the womb, for him."

Gann's face grew longer, but he kept his silence.

"Come in, all," Shappa crowed. "All are welcome."

The desk was piled with broad stacks of flimsiplast and ancient information disks, not seen on Coruscant for centuries except in museums. Shappa turned to Anakin, then glanced at Obi-Wan.

"You pay, he flies, is that it?" he asked Obi-Wan.

"We're buying the spacecraft together," Obi-Wan said. "And he will fly."

"I'll bet your seed-partners are chewing up the upholstery in my waiting room right now," Shappa said. "Can't let them in here. They love to eat flimsi, throw disks. But we won't keep you more than a couple of hours." He focused on Anakin once more. "Would you like to see what's possible?"

Anakin's face glowed with enthusiasm. "It's why I'm here," he said quietly.

"Possible, I mean, in ships, young man, ships only," Shappa added, drawing back a little at the boy's response. "The boy has an appetite. Very well, let's feed. Here!" He flung out his hand and grabbed a broad, crackling sheet of change flimsiplast. "Hold this," he told Gann. Gann held one edge, and Shappa unrolled it with deft, fast fingers.

On the flimsi was precisely sketched in red and brown lines a lovely starship, all compound curves and gentle swellings, the engines nestled within graceful fairings, the surface shaded with marvelous artistry to look smooth and taut as the skin on a crisp shellava. Judging from the scale, the length was thirty meters, the beam or wingspan—the wings were indistinguishable from the fuselage—over three times that.

"I've wanted to make a ship like this for some time, but it was only a dream," Shappa said. "No seed wants to get this complicated, and clients bring me only three or four seeds. But for you . . ." He smiled and swept his fingers over the drawing. At his prompting, the flimsi produced different perspectives, each new sketch stored in the porous surface and emerging at the artist's command.

Anakin whistled. "This is *ferocious*," he commented.

"High praise indeed," Obi-Wan translated for a puzzled Shappa.

"Yes. You bring me fifteen seeds, the largest complement ever for a ship."

"Can you work with so many?" Gann asked.

"Can I?" Shappa said, and his body twitched with energy. "Just watch! The best Sekotan ship ever made. A marvel."

"He says that to everyone," Sheekla warned them.

"This time, I mean it." Shappa handed Obi-Wan the edge of the change flimsi and tapped Anakin on the shoulder. "Can you draft?" he said. "I have a second helmet. And a third. Come, clients. I'm sure you have your own ideas."

"I'm sure," Obi-Wan said, with a nod to Anakin.

"Let's knock heads and helmets and wield our scribers as if they were . . . lightsabers, no? Let's dream in the air. It will all come out on the change flimsi. New designs will replace the old. It will be like magic, young Anakin Skywalker."

"I don't need magic," Anakin said solemnly.

Shappa laughed a little nervously. "Neither do you, I bet," he said to Obi-Wan. Obi-Wan smiled.

"I forgot. You're Jedi. No magic, then. But of mystery there will be plenty. I doubt the shapers and forgers will reveal all their secrets, even to you, dear Jedi."

He handed Obi-Wan and Anakin drafting helmets pulled from a drawer, and pulled up stools around the periphery of the table. As they sat, he perched on his own, taller stool, clapped his hand on the table in front of him, and said, "Your turn!"

"A solid, sturdy design is what we're after," Obi-Wan reminded Anakin. Anakin wrinkled his nose.

Shappa held his own helmet above his head and regarded them each in turn for several seconds, face blank. Then he twitched his lips, said, "It's all in the mind of the owners. Sometimes we just have to find out who we truly are, and the ships, the beautiful ships, will just be there, like visions of a lost love."

"You have no lost love," Sheekla said, amused. "Just me. We were married when we were very young," she said to Obi-Wan.

"A figure of speech," Shappa said. "Allow me my enthusiasms."

The rest of the morning passed quickly. Obi-Wan found himself deeply absorbed in the design process, as absorbed as his Padawan, whose involvement was intense. He also found himself more and more impressed by the architect. Beneath Shappa's blithe surface lurked a powerful personality. He had seen this several times in his life, strong artists who in some sense seemed to gather the Force around them, collaborating on a deep and instinctive level.

Yoda had said, once, in a training session with Qui-Gon and Obi-Wan, "An *artist* the Force is. Not to be happy about that— look what artists do! Unpredictable they are, like children."

Under the skilled, though eccentric, guidance of Zonama Sekot's master architect, Obi-Wan's own sense of freedom and boyhood came back, and he found himself alternating between the inner structure of the beautiful craft coming together in the space accessed by their three helmets, and the space of his own memory.

A memory of a time before he was apprenticed to Qui-Gon. Youth: painful, awkward, brighter than a thousand suns. A youth filled with dreams of travel and fast ships and endless glory, an infinite futurity of challenge and mastery and, all in good time, knowledge, wisdom.

No different from Anakin Skywalker.

Not in anything that truly mattered.

If only I could believe that! Obi-Wan thought.

The Blood Carver made his report to Raith Sienar on a catwalk overlooking the bay that contained most of the squadron's battle droids. They were still too far from Zonama Sekot to make detailed observations, so Sienar had sent Ke Daiv down in a fleet two-passenger spy ship with banked engine flares, part of *Admiral Korvin*'s complement of small craft. Ke Daiv had gone in with a pilot Sienar had picked from the most experienced of the Trade Federation personnel.

"We made our way in, and returned, without being scanned," Ke Daiv said. "The planet is half covered with clouds."

"You made no attempt to see below the clouds?"

"We looked at what was immediately visible, and nothing more," Ke Daiv confirmed.

Sienar nodded. "Good. From what I've been told, the whole planet is sensitive."

"There is little detail visible in the southern hemisphere," the Blood Carver continued. "A single mountain pushes through the clouds, an ancient volcano—nothing more."

"Yes," Sienar said. He nodded as if this was familiar to him.

"The northern hemisphere is comparatively cloud-free, though storms migrate from south to north, dropping great quantities of rain and some snow."

"Naturally," Sienar said, lip curling.

Ke Daiv paused indignantly, as if concerned he might be boring the commander, but Sienar lifted his hand. "Go on."

"There are signs of a recent struggle. At least fifteen deep slashes in the crust, over three kilometers wide, not natural. They are mostly hidden by the southern clouds, but I saw long, straight dips in the clouds along the equator, signifying clefts many kilometers deep. Perhaps these are the effects of large orbital weapons, though of a power and type unfamiliar to me."

Sienar's face went blank. He was thinking. "Are you sure they're not an excavation? Some massive construction project?"

"No," Ke Daiv said. "In the slash visible above the equator, there are jagged edges, scorch marks, jumbled terrain. But there were many large elevations in the northern hemisphere, rectangular in shape, and far from the inhabited regions. All these elevations are uniform in size, four hundred kilometers by two hundred, and densely covered with growth."

Sienar cocked his head to one side and poked his thumb into his chin. He waggled hand and thumb, as if trying to find something behind his jawbone. "Did you see the factory valley?"

"Yes," Ke Daiv said. "Although at this point, we thought it best to return, to avoid being observed."

"Good. Tell me about the valley."

"It is a thousand kilometers long, three kilometers deep, and lined on both sides by huge growths, much larger than anything else we could see."

"Jentari," Sienar breathed. "What I would not give to have that valley installed on another world, some more practical location," he said wistfully. "Did you see any ships?"

"No. The valley was engaged in some manufacture of large objects, not ships, but like pieces of ships, or equipment. Some were being carried to the southern end of the valley, where it debouches on a wide river. Transports were waiting there, some already laden. And then—without warning—the valley was covered by huge limbs, growths, hiding it from view. I believe we were not observed, but this concerned me enough that I decided we should return."

"Excellent, excellent," Sienar said.

Ke Daiv did not react. Among Blood Carvers, compliments and insults were very little different—either one could lead to a duel. He had placed Sienar in a special category, however, outside normal Blood Carver etiquette.

"Now for the next step, and this one is crucial. We must move quickly. Tarkin informed you we would attempt to capture a ship, did he not?"

"Yes."

"He didn't have the slightest notion how difficult that might be—his kind believes might is quicker than reason. He's far too used to money to realize how useful it can be."

"Might," Ke Daiv repeated.

"*Forget* might for now. I will reveal another part of my not-so-little secret to you, because you are such an excellent and efficient fellow."

Ke Daiv stood like a piece of stone on the catwalk. Below, droids were being activated and preprogrammed. The noise of thousands of tiny motors whirring and clanking made it difficult to hear, even on the catwalk, but the Blood Carver's nose flaps functioned as gatherers of sound, as well. He leaned forward to catch Sienar's words.

"We have with us a very elegant little starship, in its own bay on this flagship. Not part of the normal complement. One of my private vessels, obviously the craft of a well-to-do individual. Scrubbed of identity but waiting for a new owner." He smiled at the thought of getting Tarkin to approve this addition. He had tried to suggest, with a semblance of childish pique, that being without any of his toys would make him less effective as a leader. Tarkin had agreed with a barely concealed new freshet of contempt for his former classmate. "A rich and well-bred owner," Sienar continued, "who has stumbled across one of the approved pilots and sales representatives of Zonama Sekot, and convinced him—or *it*—of his wealth and legitimate interest in the art of spacecraft design. A connoisseur. That would be *you*. I did my research well on Coruscant—you come from an influential family."

"Powerful, not wealthy," Ke Daiv corrected with a slight hiss. Even when placed in a protected category, this human could push him near the edge.

"Yes, indeed, the concentration of resources being a sin of sorts among your kind. Well, now you have ample sin to work with—over six billion credits at your disposal, in untraceable Republic bonds. Quite sufficient to buy a Sekotan ship."

Ke Daiv's eyes grew smaller and sank deeper into his skull. Though he was constitutionally incapable of being impressed by money, he knew how much six billion credits was, and how much it would impress others. "How do you know all this about Zonama Sekot?"

"Not your concern," Sienar said lightly. He really did enjoy

Ke Daiv's reactions—the constant sense of treading in dangerous territory was stimulating.

Without showing the least anxiety, as if working with a spooked animal and knowing when to turn his back and when not to, Sienar looked down over the railing toward the Xi Char weapons. The elegant and powerful droid starfighters were stored on long rolling racks, their claw nacelles collapsed and pulled inboard. The racks were being pushed by astromechs from one side of the bay to their streamlined, dull gray, stealth-cloaked landing ships.

The *Admiral Korvin* contained three landing ships, each of which carried ten of the versatile starfighters. With slender nacelles that could split, rotate, and become legs, these droids were flexible, ingenious, and powerfully armed. They were perhaps the best of the centrally controlled Trade Federation weapons systems.

Inside the broad mouths of the lander weapons pods, loading drums spun about with hollow ratcheting sounds. The starfighters were attached quickly to broad, flat drums for rapid-fire deployment just above the planet's atmosphere. The drums were mounted in turn on vertical rotors. When the starfighters were launched they would emerge from the pods like bullets out of a spinning cylinder. When a drum was empty, it would be ejected into space, and the next would move forward on the rotor.

Sienar admired the Xi Char engineers that had designed and built the starfighters, but he doubted the droids would be decisive.

A ferocious battle had just recently been decided, apparently in favor of the locals. Whatever had left those hideous marks on the surface of the planet was no longer in evidence.

"I would like to introduce you to your sponsor on Zonama Sekot, the authorized representative, in my quarters, in one hour," Sienar told the Blood Carver.

Ke Daiv may have felt curiosity—emotions or impulses were hard to read on the face of the highborn Blood Carver—but he simply bowed his head and narrowed his nose flaps, forming once again that disconcerting hatchet that denoted respect and compliance, as well as—with certain color changes—anger, rage, and intent to kill.

The black and red ritual airship carried them beyond the last dwellings of Middle Distance and along a narrowing in the canyon. This far north and west, the rocky walls were wet and slippery but almost devoid of Sekotan growth. Boras could not gain purchase here. Streamers of cloud dropped into the canyon and left the air around the gondola thick with moisture.

Anakin stood in the prow, foot propped in a heroic pose on a forward cleat. His seed-partners clustered around him, quiet for once, peering over the rail with their small, intent black eyes as if looking into their future.

Obi-Wan stood two steps behind Anakin, letting the boy enjoy this moment. There would be little enough joy in the next few days, he suspected. What Anakin had detected days before—and called a "single wave"—now left the space around them charged with a feeling of imminent and massive change in the Force, which Obi-Wan could only describe as a *void*. Neither Qui-Gon nor any other Jedi Master had ever hinted at such things. That the change was coming from beyond Zonama Sekot, however, was not as apparent to Obi-Wan as it had been to Anakin. *I sense something very close, triggered by something from without. But Anakin is correct—it will be a trial.*

The airship's guiding ropes flexed under the pressure of winds rising out of the deep gorge and the rushing waters below. The pilot was having some difficulty keeping the airship from exerting too much strain and parting the ropes. The airship would not last more than a couple of minutes in these winds, in such close quarters, before being smashed against the sheer, slick stone walls—an ignominious end for a party of clients!

That kind of danger Obi-Wan appreciated: immediate, manageable, if one trusted the conveyance and its pilot—and the young woman seemed experienced enough. None of the other passengers—not Gann, nor Sheekla Farrs, nor the three attendants—showed alarm. In fact, they seemed to feel the same exhilaration he did.

Anakin looked back and grinned at his master. "The seeds are trembling—feel them? They know something big is happening!"

Gann hooked two hands to the rail and sidled closer to Obi-Wan. "The boy's a natural," he said over the roar of wind. "There can be only one pilot. Have you decided which of you it will be?"

"The boy will be pilot," Obi-Wan said. He could never hope to match Anakin's skill in that area.

Gann nodded approval. "He's obviously the one," he said. "But he has so many partners! We've never joined that many together." He shook his head in some dismay. "I have no idea how you'll control them. I'll be most interested to see what Shappa Farrs has to say."

The canyon walls spread farther apart, and the airship moved closer to the eastern rim. Its cable guides depended from long, leafless limbs pushed out by the gnarled boras that lined the edge of the precipice. The pilot deftly kept a uniform strain on the cables.

The river's roar subsided with the broadening of the canyon, and the wind quieted, as well. The gondola rocked gently.

Anakin's partners grew more agitated as the airship glided above some of the most spectacular congregations of Sekotan creatures they had yet seen. With more purchase available on the canyon walls, boras and other organisms had carved out terraces similar to those that supported the houses at Middle Distance. In their natural state, the terraces supported dense jungles. Like acrobats, large, long-limbed climbers slowly lifted themselves up and over the canopy with slender, vine-clinging claws. Avians with translucent carapaces flitted over broad flowers spread wide in the sun. Minutes later, the flowers folded their spectacular petals, broke loose from the boras, and inched up hanging tendrils to higher, more brightly lit terraces.

Anakin whispered soothingly to his seed-partners as he absorbed Sekot's variety.

A young woman emerged from the small gondola cabin and walked past Obi-Wan with a polite smile. Her attention was on Anakin, and she paused beside him in the bow. Obi-Wan observed her with interest, not least because she was the spitting image of the Magister's illusory twin daughters.

This girl, however, was solid and real.

A seed slipped down Anakin's arm in small jerks and clamped its hooks painfully into his flesh. Anakin grimaced, turned to lift the seed back onto his shoulder, and saw the girl. His eyes widened.

"Have we met?" she asked him, with a pretty frown of inquiry.

"You look familiar," Anakin said.

"Oh, then maybe it was one of Father's things," she said, nodding as if that explained everything. "He puts holograms of me in different places at different times. Like arranging flower pots. It's aggravating."

"How does he do that?" Anakin asked, but the girl decided not to answer.

"Sheekla told me to explain the different kinds of boras here."

"Finally! Everything is so mysterious."

"Trade secrets—I know," the girl said. "Sometimes it's a bore. What's your name? Father forgets that when I'm not really there, I don't actually *meet* people."

Anakin was at a loss for a moment and looked past her at Obi-Wan. She, too, looked over her shoulder. "Is he your father?"

"No," Anakin said. "He's my teacher. Didn't your father tell you?"

"There's a lot my father doesn't tell me, and a lot you don't know about my father. I actually haven't seen him in months—not since . . ." Her eyes lost their focus for a moment, then brightened once more.

"I am Anakin Skywalker, and this is Obi-Wan Kenobi."

"I live in Middle Distance with my mother and my younger brother, but he's just a baby. Father sends us messages now and then. Anyway, I can't explain everything to you now. Maybe later. I'm supposed to tell you about boras, and where they come from, and what they do when they're forged and annealed. You can listen, too," she said, glancing back at Obi-Wan.

"Thank you," Obi-Wan said.

"By the way, my name is—"

"Wind," Anakin said.

She laughed. "Wrong! That's one of Father's jokes. My *real* name is Jabitha. Father knows all about Jedi training," Jabitha said solemnly. "He told me a year ago that it's very hard to become a Jedi Knight. So you must be special." She patted a seed. "They seem to think so. You're popular." She took a deep breath. "Seeds are where the boras begin. Each bora creates seeds in the middle of our summer, when the storms whirl out of the south and bring rain. Most of the seeds creep off into the growth, the tampasi, in the old Ferroan language. *Boras* means *trees,* and *tampasi* means *forest,* but they're not really trees *or* forests."

"All right," Anakin said. The vibrating seeds were a real distraction now. His head was starting to hurt from their jostling.

Jabitha patted a few of his restless seeds, and they made little drum sounds. Her touch seemed to soothe them for the moment. "The seeds take root in a nursery protected by the oldest boras. Then they go through the forging. That's really something to see! The boras drop dead limbs and old dry leaves and these special little pellets all over the nursery, until the entire open area is covered. The seeds just dig around and eat and eat and eat for hours, growing all the time. When the seeds are big enough, the oldest boras call down lightning from the sky—just call it down, with uplifted branches. The branches actually have iron tips! The lightning forks down and sets what's left of the nursery heap ablaze, and the seeds kind of cook inside, though they aren't killed. Something changes and they split open. The seeds have a way of expanding outward, almost exploding, making these puffed-out bubbles, shapes with thin walls of tissue— like the lamina, only even more malleable and alive.

"Other boras called annealers have these long spadelike shaping arms that sculpt the exploded seeds. The air is thick with this perfumey smell, like cakes in an oven . . . It's very complicated, but when they're done, the seeds become different kinds of boras, and they can move out of the nursery and take up their places in the tampasi."

"When did the settlers learn to control the shaping?" Obi-Wan asked.

"Before I was born," Jabitha said. "My grandfather was the first Magister. He and my grandmother studied the boras and made friends with them—that's a *really* long story—and they were allowed to watch the changes in a tampasi nursery. After a while, the boras invited them in as shapers—but it took them twenty years to learn the craft. They taught it to my father. A few years later, the rest of the settlers came from Ferro."

"The image we saw of you in the Magister's house was not a hologram," Obi-Wan said. "It was a mental image, projected by some extraordinary will."

Jabitha looked uncomfortable. "I guess that's my father, then," she said. She turned and looked over the basket's railing. "Those are wild-type boras," she said. "We call them rogues. They don't have any nursery affiliations. They scavenge off the communal fields."

Anakin again saw white triangular flying shapes, as well as many-legged creeping cylinders, bigger than a human, moving in and out of caves in the walls of the valley. Small avians twinkled in the valley shadow like night wisps on Tatooine. Dark tentacles lashed out from the shadows beneath overhangs to snatch at them.

This part of the valley seemed engaged in a much more familiar planetary life cycle—eating and being eaten.

"Do they ever rejoin with the communal boras?" Anakin asked.

"No. They're called lost ones," Jabitha said. "Father thinks some of them escape from the burning nurseries and get shaped elsewhere, maybe by other rogues. But they're useful. I think they keep the communes on their toes. Sometimes they fly in and snatch seeds, to eat or to raise as their own. I've even seen clouds of smaller wild-types come in during the forging, before the lightning is called down, and snatch up the branches and scraps and pellets intended for the seeds. There aren't many rogues overall. This part of the valley is pretty thick with them, however."

"Have you ever shaped anything?" Anakin asked.

"I helped my mother make our house a couple of years ago. We had three seed-partners Mother had bonded with, and I helped her use the carvers and prods . . . but that's getting ahead of things!"

Anakin shook his head. "It all sounds terrific. But I still don't see how you can turn seeds into spacecraft."

"You have to be patient," Jabitha said petulantly. She looked at Obi-Wan. "My father made the first spacecraft when he was a boy. They used the engines from their original colony ship. That was just after my grandfather went looking for more settlers. We wanted all types of people here."

"We have met only Ferroans," Obi-Wan said.

"There *are* others. Quite a few now. They work in the factory valley."

"Why did your father decide to sell these spacecraft?"

Jabitha ignored Obi-Wan's question. "Look! We're getting close."

Sheekla Farrs stepped forward as the airship was pulled into a docking chute and tied down. Jabitha leapt over the railing onto the landing and helped Anakin out of the gondola. Obi-Wan she left to his own devices. Anakin seemed very interested in everything she had to say.

Jabitha could become a distraction for Anakin, but likely a

welcome one, Obi-Wan decided. She would take his mind off ships and help him come to a better understanding of social relationships. Anakin's social upbringing, with the exception of his times spent with the other affiliates and auxiliaries, had been piecemeal at best. A few normal encounters with people his own age could be very helpful—and this girl seemed refreshingly normal. *When she is actually physically present!*

But Obi-Wan was still concerned about so many unanswered questions. They were still no closer to understanding what had happened to Vergere.

The night before, while Anakin slept, Obi-Wan had visited the library, trying to keep his seed-partners from chewing on the texts. The library had told him nothing he needed to know.

Obi-Wan Kenobi hated knots, puzzles, and conundrums. As Anakin—and Qui-Gon—had reminded him so often, he was a linear kind of guy. But he understood something very well.

The Force was *never* a nursemaid.

Though at times a very patient man, Raith Sienar itched to get on with his mission. Instinct told him time was of the essence, that such an open world, with such a valuable secret, was like a ripe carcass under a sky full of winged scavengers.

Not that he had ever contended with winged scavengers. Sienar preferred the high-tech comforts of a well-developed planet, whose wilderness had long since been tamed. But he was an educated man and he knew a scavenger when he saw one.

He felt like a scavenger himself, right now.

The first of many.

He looked down on the small image of Kett that flickered to bluish life on his command table. "Yes, Captain?"

Kett seemed uncomfortable. "I have complied with your orders and released the Blood Carver in your ship, Commander."

"All went well?" Sienar had introduced Ke Daiv to his sponsoring "pilot" in the small shuttle docking bay where the private starship had been loaded. Ke Daiv had seemed uncomfortable working with a droid. Sienar had not bothered to explain how he had come by this droid, or how the droid had become a sponsor of clients for Zonama Sekot. Some secrets were best kept.

"Yes, sir."

"And he is well away, heading toward Zonama Sekot?"

"Yes, Commander."

"And no one on the planet has detected our squadron, this far out in the system?"

"No, Commander."

Sienar breathed a sigh of relief. "Then we will await word from Ke Daiv before we make our next move. You seem unhappy, Captain Kett."

"May I speak freely, Commander?"

"Indeed, please do."

"None of this is in accord with our original orders, as outlined by Tarkin."

"And so?"

"I hope to be blunt without causing offense. This is a delicate time, Commander. My ships were once part of an honorable and effective defense force assigned to protect ships belonging to members of the Trade Federation. Our record goes back centuries, with never a blot."

"A record to be proud of, Captain."

"I do not know how we will be treated as part of the Republic defense forces. I hope the integration will be smooth, and that I may continue my honorable career."

Honor, Sienar thought, *is much overstated in that record. You took part in the worst of the Trade Federation transgressions. You personally held planetary systems at blasterpoint, forced concessions, escorted contraband drugs and machines, and transported immigrants whose bodies were laced with time-delay biological weapons . . . You will be lucky if people like Tarkin can divert the attention of the senatorial arm of justice and save you from a summary trade-crimes trial.* But he maintained a sympathetic face for the captain.

"I do not trust this Blood Carver, sir. His people are notorious for fiery tempers and dirty deeds."

"He was handpicked by Tarkin. You have in your orders that he is to be accorded complete cooperation in whatever he might do."

Including assassination of your commander should things go wrong.

"I am aware of that, sir."

"Then what is your point, Captain Kett?"

"I wish to communicate my unease, sir."

"So noted. I hope you will maintain your vigilance."

"Yes, sir."

Sienar disconnected, and the image blipped into nothing.

Using the Blood Carver as a client was not a brilliant stratagem, but it would serve. Judging from all he had learned from the pilot of the ruined Sekotan craft now in his deep-city hangar, before that pilot had died . . .

Things Sienar had not revealed to Tarkin—he'd even lied to Tarkin about how he obtained the ship. Facts that he had learned long before Tarkin had in his slippery way tried to involve Sienar in this overblown and all-too-obvious scheme.

From the Gensang pilot's dying words, encouraged by subtle Agrilat drugs, Sienar had concluded that Zonama Sekot's settlers were hungry for something, or just plain greedy—that they had found a treasure of incredible proportions, and instead of arranging for a well-orchestrated exploitation, with bidding wars conducted between members of the Trade Federation, they had taken a decidedly risky path, catering to the galaxy's spoiled little rich boys, and engaging in a remarkable but ultimately futile quest to hide themselves.

The settlers needed capital to buy things. Expensive things. They needed it quickly and quietly, and as soon as possible.

The pilot, a newly wealthy Gensang spice thief whose forebears had smuggled for over a thousand generations with no great success, had picked up a curious sort of compact protocol droid in a gambling palace on Serpine.

That droid had been lost to the Gensang by a reckless and exceedingly wealthy young Rodian in a life-or-death, total-forfeit game. Life had not been the young Rodian's fate. Instead, he had rolled a fist-sized ruby joom-ball along the classic spiral chute, the joom-ball had fallen into the mouth of a cranky and venom-drooling old Passar, the Passar had blurted in its disgusting and bubbling voice a prophecy insulting to the extremely superstitious emperor-governor of Serpine, and the Rodian had been cut to pieces by outraged palace guards. Everything in his possession, including his spacecraft hold full of credit bonds, had been handed over to the Gensang, who had reveled in his run of luck.

The small droid that had come with this booty had told its new master a fantastic tale. The droid claimed it was fully qualified to take customers to a mysterious world that made the fastest starships etc. etc. etc., a journey that the Rodian had not lived long enough to make.

The Gensang had been intrigued. He had passed a puzzling social-psychological test conducted by the droid, showed the droid part of his cache of bonds, more than sufficient, and had been warned he would experience the adventure of a lifetime on an exotic world, some details of which he would soon after almost completely forget.

It had been the Gensang's misfortune to buy his Sekotan ship and run afoul of thieves. They had taken the Gensang and the droid and the disintegrating remains of the ship and sold them to Sienar's agents for a tidy sum. Sienar's agents had then killed the thieves.

Such was the endless roil of greed and money. Perhaps the Blood Carver's people were right to hold such disdain for wealth.

Sienar lay on his stomach by the long sitting room window, now open to the stars, with Zonama Sekot eternally in view. Before his communication with Kett, he had finished a light repast of biscuits and steamed Alderaan wine, one of the few tastes he shared with Tarkin.

Generally Sienar was unimpressed by food and drink, and almost never was he tempted by other fleshly pursuits. What got his blood going was power. The power to design and build extraordinary things. The power to make one's old friends sorry they had ever tried a clumsy double cross.

I, who have built ships for the galaxy's most powerful . . . I, of all people, manipulated by a second-rate military student, deceiving himself that he sees more clearly than his intellectual superior the shape of a new order!

The very thought made his lips curl and his eyes narrow to dark slashes.

Sienar had let the protocol droid perform its tests on the Blood Carver. As he had suspected, the Blood Carver had passed handily—elegance, education, good family, and the sight of so many credits piled on the floor of the commander's cabin had tripped all the droid's little circuits.

Foolish leaders on a lost world, trusting such judgments to a protocol droid!

Now the droid was flying with Ke Daiv in Sienar's personal starcraft to Zonama Sekot. If Ke Daiv brought back one of the planet's wondrous ships, Sienar was ready with all the surgical and mindwipe tools necessary to turn the Blood Carver into his own personal chauffeur. He would analyze the living Sekotan craft, learn its secrets, and reverse Tarkin's game with such stunning speed that his old friend would never recover.

And that could give Sienar the power and influence necessary to cut his own deals with any emerging political power.

Delicious. Absolutely delicious. Much better than even the choicest of Alderaan wines, warmed in the finest gold-flecked crystal over a muskwood fire.

Sienar gave another great sigh. The game was truly interesting now. *Dear Captain Kett,* he thought, *my honor is no purer than your own. But I at least am not a hypocrite.*

Reaching the docking ramp, it turned out, was just the beginning of a new leg of their journey. Anakin, Obi-Wan, Jabitha, and Gann descended the carven steps of a steeply slanting volcanic tube to a low-ceilinged cavern set with dimly glowing lanterns.

They could hear the sound of rushing water.

"An underground river," Anakin said. Jabitha nodded, reached up, and touched the top of his head. He flinched, and she smiled.

"It's just a way of saying how smart you are! But we have to go some distance before we reach the river."

Obi-Wan had never enjoyed being deep underground. He much preferred the openness of space to the depths of a planet, though he had never admitted this to anyone.

After another twenty minutes, they emerged from the end of the tube into a wide round chamber carved out of the basalt. A stone slab jutted into swift water that flowed around the slab with a guttural rumble. Regular and frequent splashes darkened the rough surface of the rock. A slender boat floated in a calm spot in the slab's shadow. Ahead, they could dimly make out a mouth leading even deeper into the planet's crust.

They boarded the slender boat, and two male attendants pushed them away from the dock. Gann then poled the boat out of the calm, into the swift water. The river rushed them down the broad, dark channel.

The seed-partners were still. Anakin was concerned that they might be sick or even dead. Jabitha reassured them this was not the case. "They know we're going to see the forgers and shapers. It's a serious moment for a seed."

"How do they know?" Anakin asked.

"This river feeds the factory valley," she said. "It's carried seeds for millions of years. They just recognize it."

"What are the Jentari?" Obi-Wan asked.

"Grandfather trained them first. Trained them, or made them, or both! They're very large shapers that work for us and with us. You'll see." She sounded very proud.

As their eyes adjusted, they spotted long red lines glowing on the tunnel ceiling, well above the water. Gann played a torch beam on the rock, revealing unbroken, close-bundled tendrils of red and green. "Sekot sends these through the rivers and tunnels and caverns," he said reverently. "All parts of the planet are connected."

"Except for the south," Jabitha said quietly.

"And why not there?" Obi-Wan asked.

"I don't know," she said. "Father said it was all finished down there."

"That's where his house is," Anakin said.

Gann broke in. "The south died of a disease just a few months ago, the entire hemisphere," he murmured. His face appeared ashen, features wavering in the moving lights from the boat lantern and his torch.

His hands are shaking, Obi-Wan observed.

"Was it a war?" Anakin asked.

Gann tightened his jaw muscles and shook his head. "No," he said. "Just a disease."

"You shouldn't talk any more about that," Jabitha said. "Even I don't know what happened down there."

"Does your father know?" Obi-Wan asked.

She gave him a veiled look that held no small amount of anger. Best not to pursue the matter.

The river journey lasted several hours. Anakin and Jabitha sat on the bench at the bow, talking. Obi-Wan allowed his eyes to linger on the tendrils that glowed like tracer shells frozen in flight.

Wherever their destination was, a Sekotan air transport could have easily carried them there in a few minutes. The settlers were hoping to keep a few secrets from their clients. Or perhaps they understood the value of ritual.

Personally Obi-Wan found ritual a bore. Jedi training was remarkably free from it—only the greatest moments were so marked.

When conversation with Anakin lagged, Jabitha worked intricate geometric puzzles from a small lamina box she carried in her cloak. When she placed the box on the bench of the boat, Anakin noticed that a corner of the box fastened to the lamina of the bench. And when she finished a puzzle, the pieces re-formed into new shapes. She would never have to work the same puzzle twice.

Communication, coordination, constant touch—these people

had harnessed a marvelous network of living creatures that seemed, all of them, intimately related, like a huge family.

How much more disturbing it must have been, then, for literally half the family to die of disease! Or to face the destruction caused by whatever energies had gouged the planet to bedrock along the equator.

Perhaps this journey was devious not because of a misplaced sense of ritual, but because of fear.

33

"Your ship has arrived at the northern plateau," Captain Kett told Sienar. "We've received a laser beacon signal from Ke Daiv himself. The protocol droid has established its credentials and presented him. He is awaiting transport to Middle Distance."

Kett preceded the commander down the bright corridor leading to the *Admiral Korvin*'s shuttle bay.

Sienar nodded absently at the news. He was about to inspect the squadron. If Ke Daiv failed to buy a Sekotan ship, the next step would be all too Tarkinish: a show of power diplomacy at close quarters.

Sienar briefly gave in to a vision where he traded one Republic Dreadnought for all the ships in his squadron. *Not like you to prefer the large and impressive. Tarkin's thinking getting to you? Not sure Ke Daiv will succeed? Subtlety will win this day. You have what you need.*

He was confident he could make what he had seem a very tangible threat, under the circumstances. *Something has burned them already. Once burned, perhaps twice cowed.*

Unless they've faced an even greater threat . . . and prevailed.

But he could not see how that was possible. The planet was only very lightly developed and sparsely settled. It was practically virgin territory. Who would bother to mount a planet-scarring invasion?

They walked up the short ramp into the diminutive shuttle.

Kett absorbed the long pause philosophically. He was growing accustomed to this commander's style, though he did not like it. Sienar pulled back his long coat and sat in the central chair, with a good view of the slowly precessing star field beyond the shuttle's long, sloping nose. "Anything more on those gouges?"

"No, sir."

"Battle scars?" he mused. They had reminded him of snips made along puckered flesh by an expert surgeon.

"I believe they will prove to be geological anomalies," Kett said.

"Maintain squadron distance and keep all intership communication to a minimum," Sienar said. "I want *no one* scanning that planet. *We are not here.* Send a specific directive to all ships reminding them of that."

"Yes, sir."

"We're very close," Sienar said, rubbing his hands on his elbows. They were unaccountably damp with sweat. "I will not tolerate any mistakes."

A dim green light dropped like thick syrup from the end of the tunnel. The river had settled into a smooth, gently roiling flow as the cavern widened. Gann guided the boat with a few sure, deft stabs of the pole. They glided behind a natural ledge festooned with green and red tendrils. An open space atop the ledge had been kept clear, and Gann and the two attendants slipped ropes to two older Ferroans in black and gray.

The boat was snugged in and bobbed against the dock's buffers like an animal nuzzling up an old friendship.

Obi-Wan walked forward and saw that his Padawan had fallen asleep. The long, restless night had finally taken its toll on him. Anakin lay in deep slumber, surrounded by his seed-partners, all still. His face was beautifully blank, brows straight, lips parted in slow and shallow breath, a simple and profound work of living art. Jabitha sat near his head, her hand brushing at the boy's silky hair, and looked up at Obi-Wan, with her lower lip between her teeth.

"He's very pretty," she said. "Should we just let him sleep? There's time."

Anakin slept like a baby in the girl's presence. That was significant. Obi-Wan was well aware of the boy's frequent nightmares. He seemed much younger, asleep. Obi-Wan could easily bring back in memory the nine-year-old who had become his apprentice, now grown two hand spans taller—the same pleasant broad features, the nose a little larger.

He misses the female. Thracia Cho Leem knew that.

Obi-Wan reached out, then hesitated. He felt a strong urge not to wake the boy, to let him sleep like this forever, to forever anticipate a great adventure, forever dream of personal triumph and joy. This feeling held too much sentiment and weakness to be allowed, but he allowed it nevertheless. *This must be how a father feels, looking down on his son, worried about an uncertain future,* Obi-Wan thought. *I would hate to see him fail. But I would hate far more to lose this boy. I would almost rather freeze time here, and freeze myself with it, than face that.*

Someone familiar seemed to stand at his shoulder, and lost in this un-Jedi emotion, self-critically, wonderingly, Obi-Wan murmured, "He is no more special than any other child, is he?"

Like a whisper, in reply, "To you, he is. And now *you know.*"

Obi-Wan swung about and saw Gann approaching. The voice had not been Gann's.

"Time to move on," Gann said, searching Obi-Wan's drawn and startled face. "Something wrong?"

"No." With a small shiver, Obi-Wan gripped Anakin's shoulder and gave him a single gentle shake. Anakin, as always, came from deep sleep to instant alertness. His seed-partners stirred and reattached themselves to his tunic and pants.

Obi-Wan's seeds crawled up to his shoulders and chest, and together, master and apprentice climbed out of the long boat. Gann and Jabitha followed.

"I dreamed I was with Qui-Gon," Anakin said. "He was teaching me something . . . I forget what." The boy smiled and stretched his arms. "He said to tell you hello. He said you're so hard to talk to." Anakin ran for the ramp and stepped up onto the ledge of stone.

Obi-Wan stood as if stunned by a blow, then set his jaw and followed his Padawan.

Drums and the music of plucked strings drifted down the shaft. Behind this music came a number of deep male voices engaged in a strong, grunting chant.

"They're waiting," Gann said anxiously. "The forging is about to begin!"

Jabitha walked in step beside Anakin. "Are you excited?" she said.

"Why should I be?" he asked with bravado.

"Because you're the youngest client ever," she said. "And because if you succeed, your ship may be the best ever made."

"All right," Anakin said, taking a deep breath. "That's pretty exciting."

Jabitha gave him a broad smile and put her arm around his shoulders. Anakin's face stiffened in youthful dignity, and Obi-Wan detected a flush on his cheeks, even in the dim light. As they climbed, they passed two choruses of Ferroan men, all holding small drums and stringed allutas. Lit by electric torches, they chanted, their voices following the party of four all the way to the top of the shaft.

"Aren't they grand?" Jabitha said.

"If you think so," Anakin said.

This is the head of the factory valley," Gann said as they reached the top of the last long flight of steps. Anakin's extra brace of seed-partners felt particularly heavy after the climb. Jabitha had run ahead, reaching the top before they did, and now rejoined them, her face wreathed in a smile.

Anakin looked up at the high, arching branches of boras densely interlaced over a hundred meters overhead, forming the roof of an immense hall. Sunlight filtered through the thick canopy, casting a dreamlike, green-tinted light over a causeway of stones. The causeway extended for several kilometers between straight walls comprised of long, close-packed, octagonal columns of lava.

Tumbled brown boulders had been caught in these walls before they solidified, interrupting the regular fence-post arrangements. Some of the boulders, as big as Anakin's room in the Temple, had cracked open, revealing hollows in which brilliant orange and green crystals were packed as tight as needles in Shmi's knitting cushion. All along the walls, thick black tendrils striped with red thrust up between the regular, octagonal basalt paving stones of the causeway, pushing them aside, and reaching for dozens of meters to join with the trunks of the boras. Smaller green-striped tendrils forked from the big ones and curled within the hollow boulders, as if resting before some final effort.

The air beneath the canopy was dense and moist, blood-temperature, not easy to breathe. It was filled with thick, sweet smells—flowers and cakes, wine and ale, and an intense under-tone of soil.

"The stones were here before we arrived," Jabitha said, face solemn in the green-cast gloom. "And the boras were here, as well. Just last year, Father made a new rule: When the factory be-gins its work, the boras hide what we're making, in case anyone should catch us by surprise."

"Your father is a brilliant man," Gann said solemnly. Obi-Wan again noted Gann's pallor when they talked about the re-cent past.

A sound like giant horns blew down between the stone walls, followed by great warm blasts of thicker, moister air. Above, the massive trunks of the boras twisted and shivered, and the arching branches stirred and rustled with a sound like many hissing voices. Fragments of cast-off boras skin showered down upon the causeway.

Their seed-partners shivered violently.

"They can't wait much longer," Gann said.

Anakin could not believe he was actually here. Had he dreamed this place, that it seemed so familiar? With every step, he felt as if he were two people, one who had been here before, who knew all this so well, and a young boy born on another world far, far away. He was not sure from moment to moment who was foremost, who did his walking and thinking. He looked at Obi-Wan and for a moment could not remember who the man was, walking beside Gann, wearing a Sekotan ritual robe.

But Anakin bore down and drew these selves together, using Jedi discipline to sharpen and unify his consciousness, and to unify and bring to order all those ranks of thought below consciousness.

All but the lowest and most private layer, on the edge of non-self. It was here that this other lurked with its vague, dark, and separate memories.

Anakin decided that now was no time to report this anomaly to his master. But he was interrupted. What looked like large red, black, and green insects marched along the causeway toward them. Their bodies were wide and flat, with three legs on each side and a seventh, central leg front and center. Two long, gray, thornlike spurs thrust up from beside the central leg. They seemed to have been born to carry heavy cargo.

On each of these creatures a stocky, soot-smudged man rode between the spurs, gripping them with hands covered with thick black gloves.

"Are those Jentari?" Anakin asked Jabitha.

"No," she said, laughing lightly. "They're carapods. The men riding them are forgers."

"Are the carapods alive?"

"Mostly. Some of them are part machine." She stared straight ahead at the many-legged creatures.

Gann looked down at Anakin. "We leave you here with the forgers. They will prepare your seeds and take you to the shapers and the Jentari." He looked sad and a little resentful. "I have never been beyond this point. It is the Magister's will."

"Good luck!" Jabitha said. "I'll catch up with you on the other end!" She returned to the steps with Gann and gave Anakin one last glance over her shoulder, eyes bright, lips pressed tightly together. Then she quickly descended.

"I grow weary of ceremony and mystery," Obi-Wan said. "And I tire of being passed hand to hand like old clothes."

"I think it's *wizard,*" Anakin said. And he did. It was exciting, and it helped him in some way he could not put into words— helped him to visualize the task ahead. Still, he knew Obi-Wan was suspicious, and with good cause. Anakin frowned. "I'm so excited, and yet I'm a little afraid. Master, why do I feel that way?"

"The seeds are talking to us," Obi-Wan said. "Some of them have been here before, perhaps with Vergere. You're hearing their enthusiasm and responding to their memories."

"Of course," Anakin said. "The seeds! Why didn't I think of that?"

"Because you carry so many they're flooding you," Obi-Wan said. "I wish I had the equipment to measure their midi-chlorian levels." A funny, introspective look came over his face.

"They'd be very strong," Anakin said, giving Obi-Wan's arm a light poke, as a teacher might rouse an inattentive student.

Obi-Wan lifted an eyebrow. "But not, I think, as strong as you," he said, and shook his head. "Listen to them, but control your connection with the Force, Padawan. Do not forget who and what you are."

"No," Anakin said, a little chastened.

The carapods were now within a few dozen meters of where they waited, alone, under the high, restless, arched canopy of the boras. Anakin wiped dust from his eyes and folded his hands in front of him, as if holding a practice lightsaber.

Each carapod stood as high as a man at the main joint of each leg. Glints of metal shone here and there on their bodies, as if the living organisms of Sekot had been melded with steel.

The expression on his master's face had grown more and more peculiar. "Something's distracting *you*, Master!" Anakin said.

The carapods drew up around them, yet Obi-Wan paid them no attention. "Vergere," he finally said. "In the seeds . . . she's left a message . . ."

He drew himself up and composed his features just as one of the riders clambered down from his mount and approached them with a dark and determined expression.

"What does she say?" Anakin asked, in a whisper.

"She's left Zonama Sekot, to pursue an even greater mystery."

"What?"

"The message is not clear. Something about beings from beyond the boundaries, unknown to the Jedi. She had to move very quickly."

The rider's thick-skinned, heavily wrinkled face looked squashed and sunburned, and his eyes were a reddish hazel, as if filled with fire. "Clients?" the rider asked in the thickest-accented Galactic Basic they had yet heard on Zonama Sekot.

"Yes," Anakin said, stepping forward and thrusting out his chin, as if to protect Obi-Wan.

"Magister's folks leave you here?"

"Yes."

"Get on," the rider said gruffly, smirking and pointing to the steplike first joint of his carapod's center leg. "You're late! We're getting our last load!"

The rider looked up as Anakin and Obi-Wan climbed to the back of the stable mount, and his eyes widened. "We are your forgers. Team, in line!" he shouted. The carapods and their riders formed a tight single line.

Dozens of riderless carapods ran at top speed from the rim of the valley down ramps flanking the staircase shaft down to the river. They must have traveled from the tampasi, and on their broad flat backs they carried heaps of boras foliage, shattered stalks, branches, deflated leaf-balloons, scraps dried and rustling and held down by upthrust side legs.

The tinder-laden carapods rushed past with a staccato cacophony of drumlike calls, jostling their fellows in the tight line.

At the same time, overhead, other creatures, obviously related to the carapods but with different arrangements of grasping limbs, clambered along the underside of the arched canopy of boras, transporting more scraps in pendulous baskets.

"Forging fuel," the forger said as he took his place between the carapod's spurs. "That's the last load! Let's go and get our seeds in before they start up with more big ones!"

The carapods spun about and followed the herd at a remarkably smooth and comfortable gallop, legs thudding with hypnotic rhythm against the floor of the stone causeway.

Anakin looked once more at Obi-Wan. His master seemed to be in control again, face firm. The boy listened to the voices of his own seeds. With enthusiasm and joy, they were promising unmatched friendship and vital beauty beyond compare.

But Anakin realized, *They don't know what they're going to make!*

The carapods trotted to where the stone columns ended, and the shapers brought them to a halt. Here, beyond the basalt causeway, the factory valley broadened out onto a plain covered with tightly coiled tendrils arranged like markers on a game board. The fuel-laden carapods ran ahead between immense pillars of water-sculpted rock, each hundreds of meters high, acting as supports for the green vault of boras.

It was the biggest enclosed space Anakin had ever seen. Clouds bunched up around the tops of the pillars, and in the distance, kilometers away, a thick layer of mist below the interwoven canopy was actually condensing out as rain.

"We keep the forging pits here," the red-faced forger told them. He dropped down from the carapod and pointed to where thick billows of smoke boiled up from red-lit pits near the overgrown valley walls. He looked up to count their seed-partners, his lips moving as he jabbed his finger. "You have a lot of 'em, boy. What do they say to you? Hear them?"

Anakin nodded.

"Well? Tell your forger."

"They say they're eager."

"That's what I like to hear. Give 'em to me and follow."

Anakin took his twelve seeds and gently plucked them from his clothes. Each made a tiny squeak but did not attempt to hang on. He passed them to the forger, who tossed them to the back of the carapod.

"They ride, you walk," the forger announced, and then took Obi-Wan's complement of three. "The most and the least," he added with a sniff. "Make 'em as one for the clients they hand over to us, that's the way! Good thing you got *me* rather than them." He flung his thumb back over his shoulder at the other forgers, who laughed. He hooted and laughed back. "They're all *amateurs* compared to me. I can easily forge fifteen and persuade 'em to join!"

"Don't listen to the braggart," another forger called out.

"You'll be lucky to end up with a handcart!"

"Ah, they're giving you the complete *experience*," their forger growled. "Never mind. We're buds, us all." He squinted at them and rubbed his arms, knocking off shed bits of white shell from many seed-partners. The bits drifted down around him like flakes of snow. "The old Magister split us into the valley folks upland and down. We're down, and we know this end of the run better than anyone. He picked us out by hand and told us to make families, the Ferroans upland, the Langhesi down. We know our places. He did right."

Anakin had learned about a small and ancient world called Langhesa, read about it in the Temple map room on Coruscant. It had been overrun a hundred years before by Tsinimals, who had enslaved the Langhesi natives, forcing huge migrations to other parts of the galaxy. They had specialized in farming and the vital arts, learning how to mold the elements of life into new and novel forms. For many centuries, they had supplied exotic pets to rich families throughout the Republic.

The Tsinimals, graceful and intolerant, had regarded the Langhesi's vital arts as a sin against their gods. Piracy and galaxy-wide conquest, however, had not bothered the Tsinimal gods in the least.

"But never mind the details. You'll get your ship, and then the uplanders will bring on a forgetting! Still, you'll have the complete experience. You'll remember the forging pits. And—" He leered, making a grotesque, ruddy mask of his face. "—my name is Vagno. You'll remember *me!*"

There appears to be a difficulty on Zonama Sekot," Captain Kett said. He climbed to the navigation bridge and handed Sienar a decoded message from Ke Daiv. Sienar read the message with a blank expression, then, abruptly, his brow furrowed and he looked at Kett as if he might be to blame.

Kett's eyes narrowed defensively.

"He's been rejected," Sienar said. "Something about seed-partners taking a dislike to him. Chewing off all his clothes."

Kett did not have to feign ignorance.

"We cannot rely on Ke Daiv," Sienar concluded.

"I also have a message from Tarkin," Kett said with a twitch of his lips. He gave Sienar the second small cylinder, and the commander read the brief message on the secure rollout.

"He's getting nervous. He wants an update," Sienar said, pursing his lips.

"Shall we move into a diplomatic orbit, or a negotiation orbit?" Kett asked. "All systems and droids are ready. Taking action immediately could be the best foundation for a reply."

"It would be, if I were Tarkin," Sienar said, regarding the captain shrewdly. "But I am not here to play political games. There isn't time. Ke Daiv still has his instructions, and I will give him another day." Sienar wondered himself if that was a smart move, betting everything on a Blood Carver. But he had no choice! Something told him massive action on their part would be a mistake.

"Sir, we risk being discovered by even the most primitive sensors if we do not act soon. The element of surprise—"

"Have we detected any weapons systems on Zonama Sekot with our passive sensors?"

"No, sir, but I have never depended upon passive sensing alone. It is a shallow—"

"The planet has relied on stealth for decades. Maybe they're complacent." *But don't count on it,* he told himself.

"Sir, I have been thinking about those signs of battle damage on the planet's surface—"

"As have I, Captain Kett. And what have you concluded?"

"They could not have been produced by any weapons known to me, sir. The signature of turbolasers and proton weapons leaves very different residues in rocky targets. These gouges may have been made by neutron dissemblers, which in theory would leave the residues we detect, yet no one in the known galaxy has learned how to harness such weapons."

Sienar listened to this as if he were being lectured by a grade-school child, but then looked away in frustrated silence, and his brow furrowed deeper. He tapped his fingers on the railing, his long nails making distinct rhythmic ticks. "Do you think they conceal such weapons, and have recently fought a war?" he asked, barely hiding his satisfaction.

"No, sir. The pattern is more like that of a preemptive strike, or a dramatic show of force, with no discernible follow-up. I can't imagine a state of apparent peace, and a total absence of visible weapons, if the political forces on the planet have recently undergone such a challenge. We have been listening to communications from the planet since we arrived, and there is total silence. All comm systems are secure and efficiently channeled. All I can conclude with confidence is that there is too much we don't know."

Sienar was no fool. Hearing his own conclusions stated by another gave him no comfort, but if he was to survive this mission with status and reputation intact, comfort was the least of his concerns.

He keyed a quick reply into the secure datapad and handed it back to Kett.

Kett lingered as if he might be made privy to what was on the message. Sienar turned away, and Kett departed from the navigation bridge.

On the datapad, he had written, *Your operative has tried to assassinate me and failed. I gave him a suicide mission-of-honor. Have discovered something unexpected and quite marvelous. Am proceeding with my own plans. Do not require assistance.*

Sienar smiled. That would undoubtedly bring Tarkin running with the biggest force he could assemble, but it would be days before he arrived, and by then, Sienar would have tried all his plans and engaged all the forces at his own disposal.

And there was always Ke Daiv's backup plan.

If that succeeded, they would have an intact Sekotan ship, a living—and very frightened—pilot, and perhaps even two Jedi, though Sienar hoped to avoid having to deal with them.

He knew what Jedi were capable of.

With deep misgivings, Anakin watched Vagno toss their seed-partners into the same deep pit. Night had fallen over the arched canopy, and the only light came from torches carried by the shapers' assistants or hung from poles stuck into the cindery ground, and from the fires scattered at some distance around the valley.

"Some of the pits are huge," Anakin said to Obi-Wan. "I wonder what they make there?"

"I don't think they make anything while clients are around," Obi-Wan said. Their forger had said, "before they start up with more big ones." Big what?

Vagno's assistants gathered at the edge of their pit, which was about twenty meters across. Each assistant in the crew carried a long, razor-sharp, scythelike blade on the end of a metal pole.

Carapods dumped their loads of fuel—the detritus of the upper tampasi—on top of the seed-partners, and Vagno directed his crew to even out the piles and push aside holes with their long blades. He then inspected the pit, looked back at Anakin and

Obi-Wan from the center, gave them a thumbs-up and a toothy grin, and deftly clambered along the top of the debris. "We need pellets here, and here," he told his men, and baskets of small red pellets, each round and smooth as a protanut case, were poured into the holes.

"Your seeds are quiet," Vagno said thoughtfully. "Moment of destiny."

"How many survive?" Anakin asked, his throat dry. He could still feel the separate flavors or voices of the seeds in his mind, lingering traces of their need, their affection.

"Most. Don't worry. We keep the heat distributed. It's better here than out in the tampasi. And remember—it's the way of Sekot."

Anakin had hoped Vagno would say "All." The boy hunkered down beside Obi-Wan and played with a bit of dry stick. Vagno walked toward him, stared down, and pointed for the stick to be tossed into the pit. "It's our way," he said. "The ground must be clean."

Scattered around the valley, other clients—Anakin counted three, each half a kilometer or more from the others—watched their own partners be heaped with fuel.

"How many new clients?" Anakin asked.

"Three, apparently," Obi-Wan said. "I see three other active pits."

"Right," Anakin said. "I feel so nervous!"

"The connection with the seeds," Obi-Wan said. "Beware."

"Of what?"

"They are about to be transformed. No one here knows what that feels like to them—but you and I, perhaps, will learn."

"Oh," Anakin said. He swallowed a lump in his throat and stood, brushing off his pants and the edge of his tunic.

Vagno finished his inspection. He shone his torch beam up, and Anakin saw a circular shape, like a thick hoop, descend from the canopy. Carapods there were lowering it on heavy tendrils. As it descended over the pit, limbs unfolded from the underside and displayed a variety of implements, some apparently natural, others made of metal.

Anakin knew many cultures that had combined organic forms with technology. The Gungans were masters at that—but they had never built interstellar ships. Still, most of those procedures were kept secret—and now he was going to witness, if not understand, how the Zonamans worked to achieve even more startling results. He would have felt proud if he had remained the boy Qui-Gon had freed on Tatooine. Jedi training had, at the very least, taught him the perils of pride. Instead, he felt an intense curiosity.

Curiosity was the deepest expression, for Anakin, of a connection with the living Force.

He looked to his master. Obi-Wan wore an expression of both concern and curiosity. Anakin could feel the banked flame of his master's controlled spirit, and at its core, though more ordered, it was not so different from his own.

The descending circle of shaper tools stopped, and valves popped open between the hanging limbs, which all folded or retracted, making the hoop shiver. Vagno let out a shout, and his crew reached up and tapped the hoop simultaneously, all around the pit, with the flats of their long blades.

From the open valves descended an aromatic fluid that made Anakin's nose smart. He drew back just as Vagno planted his feet firmly in front of them. From his thick belt Vagno produced a wick and a flint, and with one chop of the flint, the wick caught fire. "Just in case," he said. "This can be tricky."

The hoop quickly ascended.

With a chant in Langhesan, the crew held out their blades and peered up. A hole about a hundred meters wide had opened in the overgrowth. Above the hole roiled thick, heavy black clouds.

Anakin saw long tendrils rise from the circumference of the hole, their tips glinting. Across the factory valley, other holes opened over other pits. The air smelled electric.

"The tampasi controls the weather," he whispered to Obi-Wan.

"A fair conclusion," Obi-Wan agreed.

Vagno's face wrinkled, and he drew his arm back in anticipation. He turned his head away and, with one hand, motioned for Anakin and Obi-Wan to do the same.

His crew raised their blades, and they, too, squinted and looked away from the pit.

The tension in the air became unbearable. Anakin's hair crackled and his clothes clung to his skin, writhing as if alive. His eyeballs felt as if they would dance out over his cheeks. It was an awful sensation and he wanted to cry out.

Simultaneously, sun-hot orange bolts of lightning tumbled from the thick, pillowing clouds, danced along the upraised, iron-tipped tendrils, and fell with sizzling rage to the pits below. The bolts raced around the upraised tools of Vagno's forgers, quicker than the eye could follow, flinging the lances back though the men held on with all the strength in their massive arms.

The crew sang out as one and pushed the lances forward, and the bolts converged on the pit.

Vagno cackled with glee and tossed the flaming wick aside, not needed. "It's a sky fire!" he shouted. "The best there can be!"

The burst of flame where the bolts struck was intense. The accelerant from the hoop spread the ignition in less than a second, and the entire heap of fuel and pellets blazed up against the smoky darkness. In just seconds, the pyre poured flame into the sky to a height of at least forty meters, illuminating the underside of the canopy and all the scuttling creatures and creature-machines there. The entire canopy seemed alive with movement.

Anakin felt as if he were inside a gigantic colony of myrmins.

Then he felt the voices of the seeds. *They are afraid. The heat is baking them. Their shells are crisping.*

Most of the heat rose in rippling sheets of air, but as the fuel blazed and embers settled out, the seeds were being roasted like sugar hulls in a campfire.

Perversely, Anakin shivered as if with cold.

Obi-Wan put an arm around his shoulders. Anakin saw that his master's face was beaded with sweat. He, too, could feel the seeds in the fire.

"Something wrong?" Vagno asked, his face glinting and flowing in the yellow light from fire, as if he were part of the blaze, a stray ember given human shape. He walked around them critically.

"We're fine," Obi-Wan said.

But Anakin did not feel fine. He wanted to curl up and hide, or run, but he knew the seeds no longer had legs, no way of escaping, even if they wanted to.

"I've never lost a client. No fear, no fear," Vagno said.

The seeds were afraid but did not move under their burden of embers and flame. Theirs was courage, and also an awareness of fate or destiny.

The seeds were not nearly as intelligent as a human—they did not really think for themselves—but inside of each was the potential for awareness and intelligence. The fire was bringing that awareness to the fore.

This will happen to you.

Anakin gasped. He was not dreaming.

This is your destiny, your fate.

Obi-Wan had said nothing. Anakin knew where the voice was coming from, whom it belonged to, but could not believe what he knew.

There will be heat and death and resurrection. A seed will quicken. Will it burn or shine? Will it think and create or be ruled by fear and destroy?

And then the voice fell silent.

Obi-Wan's arm tightened around Anakin, as if he would protect the boy. "The wave is not what we expected," he said.

Anakin stared into the flames, his inmost self suddenly calm. The seeds were changing. They were no longer afraid.

"They'll pop like bombs! Stand back!" Vagno pushed Obi-Wan and Anakin back just as the first explosion sent a cloud of embers high into the air. Sparks showered around them, crisping little holes in their robes. For a moment, Anakin looked like a devil, his hair sending out tendrils of smoke. Obi-Wan extinguished the little fires with quick, light slaps of his hand.

One, two, three . . . suddenly, there were many explosions, too many to keep track of. But Anakin knew that all the seeds had survived, and all had been quickened by the flames.

"It's going to be a fabulous ship!" he enthused, slapping his knees. "It's going to be the greatest ship ever made!"

"Not yet," Vagno said, grimacing critically. "They have to be gathered, annealed, and shaped—we'll teach them ways of the outer worlds! Come. Let the ashes be stirred." He herded Anakin and Obi-Wan back with his hands until they stood beside an empty carapod. "And stand back! Some of the seeds explode twice."

Obi-Wan felt woozy, a little ill. He had never experienced such a strange twist in his awareness of the living Force. That the twist was centered on Anakin was evident, but something about where they were—about the planet itself—gave the effect a peculiar focus and intensity.

He could almost convince himself that had Mace Windu or Yoda or any other Jedi Master been on Zonama Sekot, the twist—the shape of this strange wave of destiny—would have surprised them, as well.

And perhaps these unprecedented circumstances explained his repeated sensing of the presence of Qui-Gon.

Obi-Wan had seen his Master impaled on the glowing, singing lightsaber of Darth Maul. The Force had not been gentle or supportive then. Qui-Gon's body had not vanished; it had shown the truth of death, of the severing of all connections with the flesh.

And that was as it should be. The Force had a shape, and death was an inevitable part of that shape. Perhaps Obi-Wan was not yet mature enough to let go of all sentiment and all love for his Master, to say good-bye to him forever.

Vagno and his crew stirred the ashes from the perimeter of the pit. The dependent hoop of limbs and tools dropped lower with the subsidence of the flames, and thick, blackened paddles dropped to help them mix the embers. Smoke and ash swirled high into the darkness, and flecks of red ember blinked like feral eyes.

Elsewhere under the broad canopy, in the factory valley, new fires burst forth. Obi-Wan could see, kilometers away, hidden by low hills in the terrain, that the canopy itself glowed brilliant with much larger forges than theirs. New seeds were being forged, far too many to satisfy just a few clients from offworld. The valley was filled with such forges, dozens, even hundreds of them.

The big ones are being made now, even as we watch, Obi-Wan thought.

Vagno put on heavier boots and fireproof waders and jumped into the pit. He flung up clouds of hot ash and laughed as he poked forth something large, maybe twenty times bigger than a seed. He exchanged his tool for a flat-bladed shovel and scooped into the ash, then flipped out a broad, flat, fringed disk, immobile, sooty, and gray. He wiped off some of the ash and revealed a palm-swipe of pearly white. His crew grabbed the disk by its fringe and flung it callously onto the back of a carapod. Vagno probed, discovered, and laughed once more, flipped out another disk, and again the crew grabbed and stacked.

Anakin looked to Obi-Wan, his eyes dancing with joy. The seeds had been forged. All fifteen seeds had survived. Each had exploded in the heat, puffed out into the fringed disks now loaded on the carapod behind them.

Then the boy's face fell. "I don't feel them," Anakin said. "Are they still alive?"

Obi-Wan had no answer. He was almost punch-drunk with what he had experienced. He felt like a boy himself now, lost in shock and wonder and an irritating tickle of fear.

At last you know the spirit of adventure!

Obi-Wan closed his eyes tightly, as if to ward off the voice. He missed his Master intensely, but he would not let a vagrant fantasy besmirch Qui-Gon's memory.

"Adventure," Anakin said. The boy rode beside Obi-Wan on the carapod. Vagno was taking them across the valley, around several of the tall, river-carved pillars, toward a narrower and darker cleft on the southern side. "Is adventure the same as danger?"

"Yes," Obi-Wan said, a little too sharply. "Adventure is lack of planning, failure of training."

"Qui-Gon didn't think so. He said adventure is growth, surprise is the gift of awareness of limits."

For an instant, Obi-Wan wanted to lash out at the boy, strike him across the face for his blasphemy. That would have been the end of their relationship as Master and apprentice. He *wanted* it to end. He did not want the responsibility, or in truth to be near one so sensitive, so capable of blithely echoing what lay deepest inside him.

Qui-Gon had once told Obi-Wan these very things, and he had since forgotten them.

Anakin stared at his master intently. "Do you hear him?" he asked.

Obi-Wan shook his head. "It is not Qui-Gon," he said stiffly.

"Yes, it is," Anakin said.

"Masters do not return from death."

"Are you sure?" Anakin asked.

Obi-Wan looked south into the dark maw of the cleft. There were no fires there, no forges. Instead, a cold blue light flickered across the wet stone walls, and long tendrils crawled like snakes over the walls and the sandy, rock-strewn floor.

"Clients never return!" Vagno shouted at them as he marched alongside the carapod, his stumpy legs pounding the ground. He capered and poked his blade into the air. "They don't remember, and if they did remember, they'd be too afraid! But me and my crew, we *live* here! We're the bravest in all the universe!"

Obi-Wan, at this moment, could not have agreed more.

Vagno gruffly introduced them to the chief of the shaping team, a tall, wiry man named Vidge. Where Vagno was squat and red, Vidge seemed more like a tall wisp of night fog—pale, with large, wet eyes. Even his clothes were wet and sprinkled with bits of glowing slime that made him look like a creature hauled forth from the depths of an ocean.

"You've brought so many," he complained in a sepulchral tone as he counted the disks stacked on the three carapods. "What are we to do with fifteen?"

Vagno shrugged expressively. Vidge turned to gloomily survey Anakin, then glanced over at Obi-Wan. "Did you pay more to the uplanders, to get so many seeds?"

"No questions!" Vagno cried out. "It's time to paint and shape!"

Vidge raised his hands in mock surrender and turned to his own team, all tall and damp and insubstantial. They wielded different tools, long heavy brushes and rough-edged paddles. Behind them rose a tall warehouse made of roughly assembled sheets of lamina, sagging and corroded from years of rough use. Vidge grabbed the carapod closest to him by its center leg and pulled it toward the warehouse. It hung back reluctantly, as did the other two, who were urged forward by Vidge's crew.

Vagno stood back. "Not my place," he said, suddenly humble. "Here's a different art." He waved them to follow Vidge.

The warehouse echoed with hollow bubbling and sighing. Tendrils crept in from around the edges and spread wide and flat, and at their tips grew broad fruits unlike any they had seen elsewhere: swollen, translucent, and filled with a sparkling, thick fluid that swirled slowly within, churned by screw-shaped organs at the core of each fruit.

Anakin and Obi-Wan helped Vidge's crew unload the seed-disks and arrange them upright in racks near the shaping platform. Here, on a riser about ten meters wide, Vidge and two assistants lifted a long knife and harvested one of the fruits, slicing it along a lateral line with three swift whacks. The glowing clear fluid within oozed forth and writhed slowly along the platform, filled with a haze of flexible white needles.

From a door at the back of the warehouse, a large carapod crawled out of the shadows. On its back it balanced a metal and plastic frame, apparently a form for their spacecraft.

"A ready-made frame, sent here by Shappa Farrs," Vidge said sorrowfully, as if announcing the death of a dear friend. "The shaping brings it alive."

Another carapod, protected by thick metal plates woven into a fabric shield, carried objects Anakin recognized immediately: two Haor Chall type-seven *Silver*-class light starship engines, as well as a very expensive hyperdrive core unit. Anakin saw that on both the engines and on the core unit, some parts were oddly missing, and other parts had been modified.

And yet a third carapod, much smaller—barely as large as Anakin himself—walked with jaunty steps forward into the greenish light emanating from the warehouse walls. This one carried a delicate crystalline structure Anakin did not recognize.

Obi-Wan, however, did. Organoform circuits had been rumored for hundreds of years, and supposedly had been developed on the more advanced Rim worlds that had continued to resist involvement with both the Republic and the Trade Federation. Rumors only . . . until now.

"What's that?" Anakin asked, fascinated by the glittering curves and continually active circuitry.

"I think it's the device that will integrate our ship," Obi-Wan said. "The interface between the living and the machine."

The first thing Vidge did was cut away and scoop up a thick glob of fluid from the fruit. He spun the glob about, tossed it in the air, and caught it with his long spade, forming it into a ball. He then dropped it deftly onto the back of the smallest carapod, where, with a hiss, it settled over the organoform circuit. Cutting loose more globs, he spread them on the edges of each of the white seed-disks as his assistants carried them past. Where the gel touched, the disks turned a dark purple, and the edges began to curl and stretch forth sinuous, questing pseudopods.

Next, the shaper critically analyzed the frame atop the largest carapod. "Not enough," he grumbled. "Shappa never tells us what we need to know." To his crew, he said, "Get a second frame."

His crew conferred doubtfully among themselves. Vidge shouted out, "Fifteen forged plates, too many for one frame! We need two frames!"

"Are they going to make two ships?" Anakin asked Obi-Wan.

"I don't think so," Obi-Wan said. But he was in no position to be certain.

"Now, we move fast," Vidge called out, his tone as slow and tomb-haunted as before. "To the Jentari!"

Anakin and Obi-Wan climbed up beside the large carapod just as a second frame was loaded beside the first.

Vidge gave them their instructions. From this point on, they would ride inside the frames, sitting on thick flat beams between the oval-shaped main members, surrounded by a flexible weave of struts and cross braces. "It's the way it's done."

Anakin took his position within one frame. Obi-Wan sat in the other. The frames creaked and rattled on the back of the carapod.

The entire warehouse smelled of flowers and baking bread, and of other things less pleasant, odors that made Anakin dizzy. He felt as if the dream had become too much for him, too strong. His stomach was doing flip-flops.

Obi-Wan felt the same incipient nausea, but kept his attention on the slow, deliberate walk of Vidge beside the three carapods conveying the components of the Sekotan ship. The carapods exited through the back of the warehouse, back into the sea-gleam shadows of the cleft. Darker shadows like giants rose on each side, backs pressed against the walls of the cleft, with more giants on their broad shoulders, climbing hundreds of meters to a canopied ribbon of night, a few lonely stars gleaming through the interlaced branches.

Anakin felt like an insect about to be squashed. Even with the shapers running and walking alongside, he had lost his confidence. Not even the memory of Qui-Gon's words—if they had come from Qui-Gon and not from his fertile imagination—could reassure him now. This was unsettling, disturbing—were there actually giants on either side? Maybe the air was drugged. Maybe it was all an illusion and something dreadful was about to happen to him and to his master. He felt his throat closing down and tucked his chin into his chest, drawing from the exercises he had learned two years ago: control of the body's fear, control of animal chemistry and hormonal rhythms.

The mind's fear—his worst enemy, the deepest and darkest failing of Anakin Skywalker—was another problem, one he was not sure he would ever overcome.

Obi-Wan could feel the faltering of his Padawan's heretofore almost boundless confidence. Strangely, he, himself, was now calm. The smells bothered him, but were no worse than some very unsavory places where he had stood beside Qui-Gon and calmly carried out his duties.

Anakin felt the frame lurch forward as the carapod was brought to a halt by Vidge's crew. Vidge climbed up slowly and gracefully beside them and waved his flat-bladed instrument over his head, letting the fumes of the gelatinous interior of the swollen fruit drift away in dim purple sweeps.

Vidge's assistants played bright torch beams along the shadows of the giants, and Anakin saw not arms and legs, but thick green and purple trunks, gleams of metal, glints of other artificial substances, supplements, add-ons to the natural makers of the boras and the tampasi.

The purple vapors rose between the giants. Limbs stirred, joints creaked.

"Stay here inside the frame, no matter what," Vidge said, and handed Anakin and Obi-Wan breather masks similar to the Jedi issue they carried concealed in their robes. "We're loading up the engines and core and organoform circuitry now. They will be conveyed alongside the frames, until the time comes for their placement. The ships will be made around you. The seeds will make you part of their dreams of growth. They will ask you *questions.*" Vidge leaned forward to examine Anakin closely. "They will make demands. This is crucial. The ship will not be made if you fail to give the necessary guidance."

"I won't fail," Anakin said.

Vidge's crew transferred the engines and core and circuitry to smaller Jentari. Large limbs lifted them high, like giant cranes in a starship maintenance yard.

"And you?" Vidge queried Obi-Wan. "You, too?"

"We will not fail," Obi-Wan said.

"There will only be one ship, unless I've guessed wrong," Vidge said softly. "And I've never guessed wrong before." He drew back. Great grasping limbs dropped from the sides of the cleft and lifted the frames high above the ground, above the cara-pods and shapers.

"The Jentari!" Vidge shouted. All the shapers waved their blades in unison. "The makers of Sekot!"

"Hang on!" Obi-Wan shouted. It was their turn now. The limbs dropped, lifted them along with the frames, and passed them from one Jentari to the next, along with stacks of forged and painted seed-disks. Other limbs slapped the disks around the frames, almost jolting the passengers loose. Instantly, the seeds began to join and grow, to mold and shape.

The two frames were jammed together. Engines were slipped into their fairings. Seed-disks slipped purple-edged tissues on the joints, and sparks flew as the points of lasers darted all around.

Their journey began.

They were passed limb to limb down the cleft, the frames groaning, the fluid tissues of the seeds and the treatment juices flopping and slopping around them, deeper into the realm of the Jentari. Their eyes could hardly follow the process.

Every second, a thousand moves and assemblies were carried

out on the joined frames. Around Obi-Wan and Anakin, the ship began to take shape as if by magic. The giants flung them even more quickly from limb to limb, hand to hand as it were, making sounds like hundreds of voices singing deep geological chants.

"The Jentari are composites! Cybernetic organisms!" Obi-Wan shouted. "The Magisters must have bred them, made them, and put them here to work for them!"

Anakin was lost to any rational explanation. His seed-disks, the former seed-partners, were asking him what he wanted. They offered him up Shappa's catalog of designs, plans for past ships, dreams of what future ships might be like in a century of more development and learning. Shappa's design was not final; Sekot would have its input, as well.

Anakin Skywalker was in a very special heaven. After a while, in his own time and in his own way, Obi-Wan joined him, and together they listened to the seed-disks, to the Jentari.

In the blur of speed and questions, they lost all sense of time.

The frame and the new ship-owners sped down the cleft, surrounded by sparks and vapors and flying tissues and trimmed bits of metal and plastic.

Within less than ten minutes, they were over twenty kilometers from the warehouse and the shapers, and the finishing was upon them.

The passage through the Jentari slowed.

Their numbness passed. Perception slowly returned.

"Wow!" Anakin said when he could breathe again. "That was *unbelievably* rugged!"

"Wow," Obi-Wan agreed.

Anakin was filled with an unadulterated, primal delight. He could think of nothing but the Sekotan ship. Obi-Wan could see it in the boy's eyes as they roamed over the smooth, iridescent lines of the ship's interior. Green and blue and red, gleaming like a coat of ruby and emerald mineral enamel, yet not just a dead brilliance, but a pulsing quality of light that signified youth and life.

"Ferocious!" Anakin cried out in approval. "It's here! I can't believe it's really here."

"It doesn't look quite finished," Obi-Wan observed.

Anakin's face wrinkled into a brief frown. "Some little stuff, that's all," he said. "Then it will fly. And did you see that hyperdrive core? I can't wait to find out what they did to it—how they modified it!"

Raith Sienar's first foreboding came with a mechanical shiver of his E-5. The battle droid sentinel loomed large in one corner of the commander's cabin, its senses tuned to all the cabin's ports of entry.

He entered the viewing area in a tight-cinched sleep gown, wondering what the subdued whirring and clinking was all about.

"Stand down," he commanded the droid when he saw it was having difficulty. The droid dropped to a position of rest, relieving some tension from its vibrating limbs. Still, the droid remained a sad, shivering hulk.

He returned to his personal effects in their cases in the sleeping quarters and brought out a small holo-analyzer. The device could find nothing wrong with the droid's external mechanisms. Still, whenever the E-5 tried to return to an active posture, it clanked like an old iron wind chime in a stiff breeze.

"Self-analysis," he commanded. "What's wrong?"

The droid returned a series of beeps and whines, too high-pitched and too fast for Sienar's instrument to understand. "Again, reanalyze."

The droid responded and the analyzer once again failed. It was as if the droid were speaking another set of languages entirely—a near impossibility. No one else had tampered with it—and he had programmed this droid himself. Sienar was very knowledgeable about such things and adept at small engineering tasks.

He also had a sixth sense about ships, and the sudden small series of vibrations he felt through the soles of his slippers felt distinctive and *wrong*. Before he could demand a report from the bridge, Captain Kett's image appeared in the middle of the viewing room, full-sized and tinted alarm red.

"Commander, five battle droids have unexpectedly departed from the weapons bay. Did you order a drill . . . without my knowledge?"

"I've ordered no such thing."

Kett seemed to listen to someone. He turned to Sienar—whom he could still not see—Sienar had his room projectors covered for the evening—and said, his voice shaking with anger, "Sir, passive detection reports—we have a visual sighting, actually—that five starfighter droids have exited through the *Admiral Korvin*'s starboard loading hatch and are flying directly toward Zonama Sekot. I have already locked down all other droids and sent my personal ship's engineers into the weapons bay. No more will escape."

Sienar absorbed this as if Kett had just announced there would be a change in tomorrow's meal plan. Without replying, leaving Kett's image to hang and flicker above the floor of the cabin, he slowly turned back to the E-5.

"Did you install my program in all of the starfighters?" Sienar asked the captain.

"I followed your orders to the letter, Commander."

Sienar's lips curled in a brief and silent curse. He had underestimated Tarkin. No doubt Tarkin had customized the droids—all the droids—with hidden subcode blocks containing contingency programs. Sienar had not bothered to look. He had taken some things at face value.

So who was the fool now?

"Destroy the starfighters," he said, trying to keep calm.

"That will reveal our presence, Commander."

"If we do not destroy them, they will reveal our presence for us. I do not want rogue units in action out there."

"Yes, sir." Kett made a slashing motion with one hand. Another vibration came through the ship's hull—turbolasers reaching out with short-range settings.

"We have intercepted one of the five," Kett said. "The others are out of range. I will dispatch—"

"No. Hold. Sweep this entire system with active sensors, Captain Kett. Let me know the results immediately."

"Yes, sir."

Sienar took out his laser pistol and approached the shivering E-5 with some trepidation. He wondered if Tarkin's subcodes included orders to assassinate. In truth, however, he could not be sure such subcodes even existed—and he needed to learn quickly.

"Drop your armor integrity. Deactivate and shut down all energy sources, damp them completely," he ordered, and flashed an authorization code from his analyzer. The droid complied with his instructions—which meant that any subcode programs did not completely wrest control from the main intelligence.

As the E-5 slumped with a weary little howl, Sienar slipped on a breather mask and applied his laser to the droid's outer shell. In minutes, he had filled the commander's cabin with dense smoke, setting off alarms which he grimly ignored.

Workers at the end of the factory valley helped Anakin and Obi-Wan out of the new-made Sekotan starship and guided them to a platform that surrounded the finishing station. It was early morning, and darkness still covered the valley, though they were now above the canopy. The blaze of stars and glowing gases, and the ubiquitous red and purple pinwheel, cast vague colored shadows on the dimly lit platform.

Their new ship lay in a cradle of Jentari tendrils, rocking gently from its brisk creation, or—Anakin could not help thinking—quivering with its own youthful energy.

Anakin had never seen a prettier ship. The hull of the little starship glowed faintly from within, and pools of deep-sea luminosity seemed to come and go under its shiny green skin. He walked around it on the platform, with Obi-Wan at his side, and together, they surveyed the ship in whose creation they had played such a substantial role.

"I wonder if it's lonely," Anakin said.

"It can stand to be apart from us for a few minutes," Obi-Wan said. "Besides, they need to put in the last—"

"I know," Anakin said. "I was just wondering." His Master's inability to understand what he meant irritated him. The ship filled his eyes and it filled his heart, it seemed so much a part of him.

The workers and artisans at this end of the valley were once again Ferroans, dressed in long black robes with edges of nebular blue. They walked over the lamina platform in the near dark, their slippered feet making tiny padding noises, and younger assistants—most no older than Anakin—directed the spots of tiny electric torches on the parts of the new ship they wished to examine.

This end of the valley was crowded with stone pillars. Houses, administration buildings, engineering sheds, and warehouses occupied other pillars nearby, and a dense network of bridges made of living tendrils and lamina connected them.

A transport flew over the platform and came to rest on a rock pillar some fifty meters away.

Obi-Wan patted Anakin's shoulder in reassurance that he was not without feeling, that he did understand, and looked west to see if he could make sense of all the other activity they had seen in the factory valley.

Some hidden and massive project was under way, of that he was sure—something that probably involved all of Zonama Sekot. The Magisters had long ago harnessed the peculiarly ordered and interconnected organisms of the planet to do their bidding. Was it possible that now, Sekot and the settlers of Zonama had some mutual interest that demanded even more extensive cooperation, even more construction?

Anakin was dead on his feet. He had never felt so tired, even after racing, and so it was with relief that he joined Obi-Wan on a long couch as the chief of artisans at this end of the factory valley brought them a tray of cold drinks and a sheaf of plans.

"My name is Fitch," the Ferroan introduced himself. He was shorter than the others, and stouter, and his hair was dense black. His face shone with ghostly pallor in the starlight. "You've got an extraordinary vessel," Fitch added with his own share of pride. "My people will finish her in the next couple of hours. The Jentari's work was well done—no seams, no filling, very little patching inside. Just the usual non-Sekotan instrumentation to bring the ship up to Republic standards."

"Where did you get the hyperdrive core?" Anakin asked after he had drained his glass of sweet water. "Did you make it here? I've never seen another like it."

"We have our sources," Fitch said with a smile. "The ship's speed lies in part in those cores, but also in how we connect them with the ship's heart—and with you. The next couple of days will be spent learning the ship. You'll be quartered here. You won't go far from the ship—not for the next forty-eight hours. If you did, the ship would die—she would rot from the inside out, just as if I would pluck your own brain from its pan."

"But I'm not the ship's brain," Anakin said. "I can feel it— *her* thinking for herself. All the seed-partners have joined together and are thinking for themselves, aren't they?"

Fitch looked at Obi-Wan. "Smart lad. He's going to be the pilot?"

"He'll be the pilot," Obi-Wan confirmed.

"No," Fitch said. "You're not the brain, young owner, not in literal truth. The ship does think for herself, after a fashion, but she needs you while she's still young, and while she's being finished, or she gets, let's say, confused. Like a baby. You're her guardians now." Fitch stood and walked back across the platform to the cradle, which had now lifted the new ship higher for inspection of her underside. Artisans scrambled in through the hatch, carrying bits of equipment familiar to both of the Jedi: subspace communications, compact instruction boxes for coordinating with non-Sekotan repair droids, remote slaving and control systems required for arrival in orbit around the more crowded planets, transponders and emergency signaling, hyperdrive governors, control panels, two more acceleration couches for passengers, dozens of little bits and pieces apparently not relegated to the seed-partners and the Jentari.

With the ship lifted so high, they could now see all of her at once—and Obi-Wan was as lost in admiration as his Padawan was.

In his youth, Obi-Wan had been almost as fascinated with machinery as Anakin was. He, too, had built flying models of ships and dreamed of becoming a pilot, but with time and age, and under the guidance of Qui-Gon, he had integrated these impulses into a larger vision of duty and self.

But he had never truly lost the dream. His own twelve-year-old self, so long restrained by the rigors of being a Jedi Knight, joined Anakin on that platform, and together, master and Padawan walked around the Sekotan ship—their ship—and spoke in low, admiring tones.

"Isn't she the most beautiful thing ever?" Anakin murmured, his eyes wide.

"She's beyond any doubt the sleekest," Obi-Wan said.

The hull was broad and low in the cradle, with three major lobes, like three smooth oval skipping stones joined and molded together. The leading edge of the hull was sharp as a knife, and the ship's internal glow still concentrated here, making the edge fluoresce in the evening air. The trailing edges were less sharp, and were divided along the two rear lobes by engine ports, heat exchangers, and shield ducts. There were no weapons. She measured about thirty meters across the beam and twenty-five from stem to stern, and seen from the front, her two rear lobes made a dihedral of about fifteen degrees.

As they completed their circuit, two wide viewing ports dilated, like slit eyes set in the forward lobe. A technician peered at them through one port and smiled at the new owners, lifting a thumb in approval.

"Think where we can go in this!" Anakin said.

"If the Temple lets us go anywhere," Obi-Wan said.

"They will. They'll want us to let her out and see what she does. I *know* they will."

Obi-Wan was less sure, but now was not the time. He had finished his inspection—the wondering part, at any rate—and stood directly before the Sekotan ship with arms folded. He tuned all his senses and let the Force resume its ascendancy.

"Anakin," he said quietly.

His Padawan turned to face him, expression suddenly serious. "I know," he said. "I feel it."

"The middle of the wave," Obi-Wan said. "Your trial, I believe."

The color drained from the Padawan's face. "Couldn't it wait . . . until we fly the ship?"

Obi-Wan did not answer. Anakin looked down at his hands, folding into fists, and relaxed them. "All right," he said. "It is the way, and I accept it."

"Do you, Padawan?" Obi-Wan asked gently.

"It is what we've prepared for."

"Do you feel that as truth or . . . say it just to placate me?"

"I never lie," Anakin said, looking him straight in the eye, color returning to his face.

"You have never lied to others. But even worse is to lie to oneself."

"But the ship . . . we're responsible for her! She's alive, Obi-Wan. She will die without us!"

A second transport passed low overhead and landed on a pillar nearby. As Fitch fussed about the new ship and conferred with his technicians, Obi-Wan saw Sheekla and Shappa Farrs, Gann, and Jabitha marching along a bridge to the platform.

Jabitha stood by Anakin and smiled at him, patting his shoulder proudly. "She's beautiful!"

Anakin tilted his head to one side, nodding, then glanced anxiously at Gann.

"We've had difficulties," Gann said, his expression dark and tired. "A client has caused substantial damage at Middle Distance. He injured some of our people, and he escaped. But that's not the worst—there's an invasion squadron within our system. Four small craft are approaching Zonama. We fear they are fighters. Someone has followed you here. Or—you led them here deliberately."

Sheekla and Shappa had stayed a few paces back until now. Sheekla stepped forward. "We have sent a message to the Magister," she said. "The ship cannot be delivered until we hear his response."

"We had nothing to do with bringing ships here," Obi-Wan said. "But if there is a hostile force nearby . . . How will you defend yourself? Perhaps we can help."

"We trust no one, not even Jedi," Sheekla Farrs said, her expression stony. "We've learned this the hard way."

"We have to stay with the ship!" Anakin cried out.

"You will be near the ship," Gann said. "You will remain here, in fact. But the ship will stay on Zonama. We have no clear picture of the threat. It may be small—petty traders, a troupe of pirates."

"I suspect they are not pirates," Obi-Wan said. Anakin agreed.

"Then why so few?" Gann asked, turning to Obi-Wan. "It doesn't make sense. A Trade Federation invasion force would encircle us with a fleet. They may have made a mistake, or there may be a malfunction."

Obi-Wan shook his head. "We can only help you if you tell us certain things."

Jabitha stood back, eyes wide, frightened by the talk. Shappa pushed between Gann and Sheekla Farrs. "I believe we can trust these Jedi," he said. "Perhaps it is time to tell the story of Vergere—"

Obi-Wan thought of the brief message carried by the seeds. That Vergere had had to leave Zonama Sekot, to follow an even greater mystery.

"No!" Gann cried. "We must defer to the Magister!"

"No one has seen the Magister for months!" Shappa replied. "He issues his orders from the mountain and defers to us more often than not. Not even his daughter has seen him."

"The Magister is in command! He always has been, and he always will be!"

The two Ferroans seemed about to come to blows. Fitch was embarrassed by their loss of dignity.

"What happened to Vergere?" Obi-Wan asked, thrusting an arm between the two men.

"No one knows," Sheekla Farrs said, her voice high and clear over the grumbling breaking out among the technicians on the platform. "We were afraid you would think we had murdered her."

"We have lived in fear since the Far Outsiders!" Shappa said. "They were the first to challenge our way of life."

"Who are the Far Outsiders?" Obi-Wan asked.

"You do not know?" Sheekla seemed at a loss that Jedi would be so ill-informed. "The female Jedi—" She caught herself and flung her hand over her mouth.

Gann was beside himself. "The Magister must decide!" he insisted.

"Then take us to him," Obi-Wan said, irritated by the confusion. He could sense they had little time to waste. "Let him tell us personally."

A moment of silence among the Ferroans.

"Do we trust the Jedi?" Shappa asked them. "If the Trade Federation is here—"

"Then they are operating illegally, and they might as well be pirates," Obi-Wan said. "The Trade Federation is handing over all its weapons and ships to the senate. The rule of central law is being restored in the Republic."

"That is what we have heard from our factors," Sheekla Farrs said. "But we considered it of no consequence, since Zonama is so far from all that."

"The Magister must be consulted," Gann persisted, but his voice was weakening. He wrung his hands, close to despair. "It has *always* been our law."

Anakin stood by the Sekotan ship, his hand brushing the surface. His eyes were half-closed, and he seemed lost in a dream, perhaps of flying. Obi-Wan called his name, but he did not immediately respond.

"Anakin!" Obi-Wan called again, more forcefully.

The boy jerked and came to attention. "We're in danger," he said, his voice almost a whisper. "We should leave here."

Obi-Wan needed no more warning, but he stopped as more Ferroans rushed along the bridge, calling for Gann. "There is another!" they cried in unison.

"Another what?" Gann asked.

"A second fleet within the system, even larger than the first!"

"Now, Obi-Wan!" Anakin cried.

Obi-Wan looked up and saw descending flashes of light in the sky—two of them. They were swooping down out of orbit, still trailing hot plasma tails. With his keen vision he could see their glowing outlines. He recognized them instantly.

He had faced them before, on Naboo, with Qui-Gon. The most capable and deadly of all the Trade Federation droids.

"Starfighters!" he shouted, and tugged Anakin down beside him, just in time to avoid four slashes of laser fire. He pulled his lightsaber—Qui-Gon's lightsaber—from his belt, and the glowing green blade hummed to full length. Smoke from the melted rock rose on either side, cutting off their view. Obi-Wan shifted into a state of full-sensory alertness. His ears tracked the engine whine and sonic booms of the maneuvering starfighters. They were turning for another attack. He faced in that direction to deflect their fire with his blade.

"Stay down," Obi-Wan told Anakin, seeing the boy climb to his knees.

"The ship—"

"Forget the ship," Obi-Wan said. "We need to find shelter."

"We can escape in the ship!" Anakin insisted. "She's ready to go!"

Obi-Wan took hold of his shoulder and pushed him low to the smooth rock surface. Thus distracted, he could not raise the lightsaber in time to provide even a partial deflection for the next laser salvo. The blast knocked him several meters and tumbled him over and over. Flecks of broken and molten rock flew through the air, burning his clothes, drilling into his skin. Instinctively, he held up one arm to shield his face and the other to protect Anakin.

But the boy was out of reach. Obi-Wan could not get up. Something had slammed into his solar plexus—a sharp piece of rock. He found blood there and a hole in his tunic.

Then he heard footsteps. People shouting, crying out in pain.

Anakin made a sound through the smoke, a cough and then a sharp grunt, as if he had been struck. Obi-Wan tried to roll over, tried to reach out for his Padawan, but he could not regain control of his body, even with the most extraordinary concentration of effort.

A figure loomed out of the murk and stood over Obi-Wan: tall, dressed in dark blue, many-jointed, with iridescent golden skin. A booted foot came down on his arm and pinned it.

"I could kill you now, Jedi. Your death will restore my honor."

Small black eyes focused on Obi-Wan. He grasped the hilt of his lightsaber and extended the blade. The foot stomped his arm again, nearly breaking it, and kicked the lightsaber out of his hand, out of reach. The blade skittered and sizzled across the rock.

More laser salvos slashed through the air behind the Blood Carver, blowing apart the suspension bridge and setting the buildings on an adjacent pillar ablaze. The glow of destruction made his shining skin dance like a flame, part of the destruction.

"Yes, Jedi, I live," the Blood Carver snarled. "I *still live*."

Anakin had done his best to elude the nightmare that rushed forward out of the smoke, but the laser blasts had stunned him as well as Obi-Wan. He could only crawl backward on his elbows and grimace up at the shadow, trying to make his body hurry or time slow. Time slowed, all right, but he did not speed up.

The shadow disappeared in a fresh billow of smoke, reemerged, became clear.

"Slave boy!"

It was the same Blood Carver Anakin had encountered in the garbage pit. He carried a long shaping lance with a wicked blade on the end and moved quick as lightning. He swung the lance down so quickly Anakin hardly had time to begin his roll to one side. The flat of the blade struck the boy across the back of his skull and neck. His head exploded with sparking pain.

The blow stunned him, but he did not lose consciousness. He felt himself lifted by one ankle, like an amphibian delicacy on Tatooine, and swung through the smoke, dripping blood from his nose. As his assailant whirled him about, he saw the Sekotan ship still in her tendril sling, undamaged.

The Blood Carver casually plucked out and threw aside an engineer who poked up from the dilated opening in the hull, then hoisted Anakin over the ship's side lobe and dropped him in. Then he crawled after.

Anakin found he could move a little, but pretended to be inert. *Where's Obi-Wan? Is he still alive? How could this all happen so fast?*

But he knew. This was the trial, the test no Jedi Temple could provide, no Jedi Master could oversee.

The Force is never a nursemaid.

Anakin was on his own. The first thing he did, while the Blood Carver poked around the interior, looking for any other engineers, was to still all his resentment, all his feelings of failure and inferiority, and most important, his self-anger at having distracted Obi-Wan with his own foolish regard for the ship.

That regard was not so foolish. The ship is part of your power—it is essential in the here and now. It is the beginning of your trial—and it will end with the trial of Zonama Sekot. Your master cannot help you now.

He thought for a moment this might be the suspended voice of Obi-Wan, or even Qui-Gon Jinn, but it was not. If the voice had any quality whatsoever, it was his own—older, more mature. *The Jedi I will become. All I have trained to be.*

The Blood Carver growled and Anakin heard a small shriek. Jabitha was pushed forward from the back of the cabin, where she had hidden behind a thick cross brace.

She glanced at Anakin, eyes wild with fear like a small, trapped animal. The Blood Carver yanked her arm and tossed her lightly into an alcove beside the rear acceleration couches.

"Be still! He's dangerous," Anakin warned her.

Jabitha dropped her jaw as if to speak, but the Blood Carver slapped her hard across the face, then swiveled gracefully, grabbed Anakin by the shoulders, and yanked him into the pilot's seat. The seat automatically adjusted to Anakin's body, and he felt a greeting from the ship—a tremulous recognition of his presence.

The seed-partners had united. They spoke now as one, reporting the ship's condition, her readiness—and their concern. The ship knew something was wrong, but Anakin was still too groggy, his movements too uncoordinated, for him to hazard any action.

Jabitha crawled into a rear passenger seat, whimpering. Her face was bloody.

Anakin's blood seemed to chill. He felt her pain.

The Blood Carver took the seat that had been made for Obi-Wan. He squirmed uncomfortably, then reached into his jacket pocket and produced a small, glassy green bulb.

Anakin watched through mostly closed eyes, slumped in the couch, as the long, triple-jointed arm swung out and slender, strong, golden fingers crushed the bulb under his nose.

Again, Anakin's head seemed to explode—but this time with outraged life. He flung himself away from the bulb's acrid stench and slammed his shoulder into an instrument panel. He shook all over and stared hard at his kidnapper.

"Young Jedi, there is no time to explain." The Blood Carver's tone of voice changed suddenly, became more subdued.

"Is Obi-Wan dead?"

"Not your worry," the Blood Carver said. "This ship needs *you*, not him. And I need this ship. You will fly it to orbit above Zonama Sekot."

"What if I don't?"

"Then I will kill your female." He swung the lance around in the close quarters and poked the blade against Jabitha's chest. She gasped but kept very still.

Anakin tried to feel for his master's living presence, but there were too many voices outside the ship, too much confusion—he could not detect Obi-Wan. Uninjured, his master would doubtless survive any attack the Blood Carver could mount. But if he had been hit by the laser fire . . .

The Blood Carver climbed up out of the second seat and swung one long arm back to the hatch. "I assume silence means courage and you will not fly. So my mission has failed. I will kill the female now and dispose of her body."

"No!" Anakin shouted. "I'll fly. Leave her be."

He probed once more, and sucked in his breath with relief. He could feel Obi-Wan—he was injured but still alive. Anakin could not imagine a universe without his master.

Good. It would be the end of your trial to lose your master. Now . . . begin.

Anakin ran his hands over the controls. They were not marked, but their design and placement were reasonably standard.

The ship once again explained her condition. She was ready to fly, but her fuel reserves were low—the tanks had not yet been filled by the technicians.

"We don't have enough fuel to get far," Anakin informed the Blood Carver. The Blood Carver grabbed the placket of his ritual robe and pulled Anakin close, breathing hot, peppery breath into his face.

"It's true," Anakin insisted. "I'm not lying."

"Then fly to a place with fuel. We must preserve this ship."

"You're the one who couldn't get a ship made! The seed-partners hated you."

"Yes, I am a disgrace," the Blood Carver said coldly. "Now fly."

Anakin brought his hands down over the controls, pulled back on the aft thrusters, and the ship's engines sang to life instantly, smoothly, unlike the engines in any other ship he had ever flown.

The hatch closed.

Some maiden voyage.

Anakin pushed the control levers forward. The console reached up around his fingers and hands. The ship spoke to him, taught him what to do. Anakin, in turn, suggested that the ship should break free of her cradle and fly straight up for a few hundred meters, then level off and head southwest.

The ship did all these things.

He was taking the Blood Carver away from Obi-Wan, giving his master time to recover. It was unfortunate that Jabitha had crawled into the ship. Anakin was more than just concerned for her safety.

He could feel his strength returning, and then building. To his dismay, the primary component of that strength was a red heat of anger.

It is the way, boy. Anger and hatred are the fuel. Stoke them, gather strength.

Again, the voice, terrifying in its power. Anakin could not identify its intent—it was raw, the voice of loyalty and survival, and it seemed to sneer at any second-guessing.

Anakin did not want Jabitha to see what that voice would make him be, what he would become, in order to save Obi-Wan, defeat his enemies, and survive.

Raith Sienar looked out from the command bridge and saw the newly arrived fleet of twelve ships maneuvering to join up with his squadron. He recognized two converted midsized Hoersch-Kessel Drive cargo haulers—smaller than the ungainly craft that had blockaded Naboo, but of the same type. The remaining ten ships were Corellian Engineering light cruisers designed to escort the large Republic Dreadnoughts, the most powerful weapons in the Republic armory.

Yet Tarkin had not managed to procure any Dreadnoughts. His connections were not that strong.

Captain Kett surveyed the new ships with some satisfaction, no doubt anticipating the time when he would no longer have to take orders from Sienar.

The extent of Tarkin's betrayal was all too clear to Sienar. The starfighter droids had accepted Sienar's programming, but had enacted hidden code anyway—code designed to sabotage Sienar's plans. For all he knew, the starfighters had killed Ke Daiv, aroused the inhabitants of Zonama Sekot, and completely ruined any chance of getting a Sekotan ship.

Perhaps all Tarkin cared about was making himself look good before the Supreme Chancellor.

Kett walked up the steps to the command deck. Sienar turned to meet him.

"Captain Kett," he said, "prepare to receive Commander Tarkin. I empower you to coordinate with his command and tender my resignation as commander."

"Sir, that is not regulation."

"Nothing done so far has been according to regulations. You are at the mercy of rogues once again, Captain Kett. I will not be one of those rogues anymore."

"Sir, you don't understand—"

"I understand only too well."

"I have orders from Commander Tarkin."

"He's here already?" Sienar asked with a lift of his lips, neither surprise nor amusement.

"He will board *Admiral Korvin* and assume command at any moment. He does not need your permission."

"I see."

"You cannot resign, because you have been placed under arrest. Your rank is frozen pending a formal hearing."

"Have they communicated charges?"

"No, sir."

Sienar shook his head and laughed. "By all means, then, do what must be done. Lock me away."

"Commander Tarkin requests the security codes to all of the new programs installed in the ship's droids, sir."

"You told him?"

"I told him nothing, sir. He seems to have anticipated you would do some such thing."

Sienar laughed again, even more falsely. His face flushed with anger. "Tell him the droid programs are burned in and cannot be modified. Also, tell him attempts to remove the computer cores or engage in a memory wipe will initiate droid self-destruct."

"Sir, that would put our entire complement of droids out of action!"

"It did not stop the starfighters, Captain Kett. I'm sure Tarkin can figure out some work-around. I just don't want to help him do it."

Kett examined Sienar with a puzzled expression. "Sir, what is all this about? Some dispute between you and Commander Tarkin?"

"Not at all," Sienar said. "From the beginning, I've been assigned the role of patsy. Our mission was meant to go wrong. It *has* gone wrong. We've alerted Zonama Sekot to our presence. Subtlety and finesse are out of the question. From now on, it will be brute force and coercion. More Tarkin's style. Nothing I do or don't do now can change that. I'll be in my quarters, should Tarkin wish to see me."

He climbed down the steps and made his way forward, to the commander's quarters. Along the way, in the wide main corridor that ran above the cargo holds of the *Admiral Korvin,* Republic troops blocked his path.

Tarkin walked through as the troops parted, and greeted Sienar with a curt nod.

"We need to talk," Tarkin said, and took him by the elbow. "Things have gone badly wrong here, and I need to know why.

The senate is concerned by your actions. Even Chancellor Palpatine has taken an interest."

"Perhaps you briefed him yourself?" Sienar's expression was stony. "We should go to my quarters. We can talk there."

"What, and have some lackey droid kill us both? Honorable, arguably, but foolish, Raith. We'll go to my ship, where I know what to expect."

Sheekla is injured," Shappa told him. "The medics are seeing to her. Gann is in shock."

Obi-Wan quickly stripped off the ceremonial robe. Underneath he had worn his more familiar tunic. The large chip of rock had punched him hard, bruising a nerve center and scrambling his bodily control, but had not penetrated deeply. The pain was intense but no problem for a Jedi Knight. He removed the tunic, took a long bandage from Shappa, and wrapped it around his midriff. Then he slipped back into the tunic. The architect held up the lightsaber, and Obi-Wan lifted it from his hand.

Gann stumbled across the platform, face racked with confusion. "What are we to do? The Magister must rule on this. Who will order activation of the defenses? Perhaps it is time. We must flee!"

Shappa pushed him gently aside. "The leadership seems to devolve upon me, now," Shappa told Obi-Wan. "How may I help you, Jedi?"

"I need a transport. A spacecraft, if possible," Obi-Wan said. "To follow them."

"You shall have my ship," Shappa said. "I flew her here from Middle Distance. I will fly you myself."

"What about the defense of the planet?" Gann insisted, fingers wrenching at the sky.

"That is the Magister's concern," Shappa shot back. "You've worked with his group for so long . . . Everything is in place, is it not?"

"*They* brought the invaders here!" Gann shrieked, pointing a trembling finger at Obi-Wan.

"They're Jedi," Shappa said. "They would do no such thing. Would you?" He glanced at Obi-Wan.

"Never knowingly," Obi-Wan said.

Shappa's face was dark with angry blood. "Not the first time we've fended off invaders. And probably not the last. We'll get your boy back . . . and then, who knows what will be done?"

Shappa whistled sharply. His Sekotan ship rose beyond the edge of the platform, wheeled about gracefully, and dropped her landing gear. Shappa went aboard first, and Obi-Wan followed.

Shappa laid his hand on the instrument panel. The panel's living surface closed around his remaining fingers. "They've flown south," he said. The ship began to rise, and the hatch closed silently. "They're already a hundred kilometers away. We'll have a difficult time catching up with them, especially if they go into space. But first, they'll have to find fuel, or they'll never make it to orbit."

"Where else can they get fuel?" Obi-Wan asked impatiently.

"Middle Distance. But I doubt they will go there . . . it's very well defended and on alert. They will have to return to Far Distance, or fly even farther north, to the polar plateau. Or to the Magister's mountain in the south." Shappa glanced at Obi-Wan. "Perhaps it's time we were completely open with each other.

There is something special about the boy. Can you tell me what it is?"

Obi-Wan trusted Shappa. The architect seemed more sensible than any of the other Ferroans, and perhaps more in tune with the ways of the Force.

We need another ally.

Obi-Wan understood the inner voice now. As he had suspected, though not as he had hoped, it was not Qui-Gon. It was his Master's teachings that lingered, the memory of countless days and weeks of patient training, the voice of so many years together.

There was no spirit. Qui-Gon had not vanished upon dying. He was truly dead.

"First, I'll ask our ship in the north to join us. Charza Kwinn can help."

"And I'll instruct our people to let it go. Now . . . tell me, please. Why are you here?"

"A year ago, our Temple sent a Jedi Knight named Vergere to Zonama Sekot."

"Yes. I was going to design her ship."

"What happened to her?"

"You tell first."

"We came here to buy a ship from you, and to find out what happened to Vergere."

Shappa chuckled grimly. "It's all tangled, isn't it? She's gone."

"Where did she go?"

"She left with the Far Outsiders."

"Who are they?"

"We still do not know for sure. They arrived two years before Vergere. They lurked outside our system, sending in exploratory ships. We thought they might be customers who stumbled upon us without a guide or factor. But they were very strange . . . They knew nothing of our politics, our economics, not to mention simple manners.

"And very curious they were about what we had done on Zonama Sekot. They, too, seemed to build all their ships and goods from living matter. We managed to communicate, a little. The Magister spoke with their ambassadors, and quickly learned that they wanted all of our secrets. They wanted complete control of Zonama Sekot. We were naive at first, but in time, we realized they were a threat, and began our defensive preparations. When we refused to submit, they were, shall we say, offended.

"Vergere arrived with money for a ship—old Republic aurodiums in ingot form, just like you. When the situation became tense, she volunteered her expertise. She acted on behalf of the Magister and tried to reason with the Far Outsiders. At first, they refused to listen to reason. Did you see the scars around the equator?"

Obi-Wan nodded.

"Their weapons were powerful." Shappa listened to his ship for a moment, then said, "The boy is alive. He is talking with the being who hijacked your ship."

Obi-Wan felt a sudden shudder of relief. He would have known if Anakin had died or been injured, but even so . . . "You can hear them?"

"Of course. We install trackers on all of our ships. I shouldn't tell anyone this . . . But I have a feeling it isn't going to matter much now. I have no idea how the Magister will react to this second attack."

"What can he do?" Obi-Wan asked. "Your planet is almost defenseless."

Shappa smiled. "And you a Jedi! How little you know. Did the boy suspect more?"

"He said the planet's living things form a symbiotic unity. I could feel that myself."

Shappa smiled. "That is just the beginning. Believe me, Jedi, we are not weak. We defended ourselves very ably. We drove off the Far Outsiders. Perhaps Vergere did some convincing of her own, I do not know. But we sent them packing."

Obi-Wan could hardly believe this. "With what?"

"That *would* be telling, wouldn't it?" Shappa said. He cocked his head to one side, listening. "There are large ships dropping from deep space. I think Zonama Sekot is about to be invaded . . . again. And I cannot predict how the Magister will react. We are so much stronger now than we were a year ago."

Obi-Wan opened a comm channel to Charza Kwinn.

You messed with the droids," Tarkin said, shaking his head in pity. "Didn't you trust me?"

He and Raith Sienar faced each other in Tarkin's cabin aboard his headquarters vessel, the converted hauler *Rim Merchant Einem.* The cabin was less luxurious than Sienar's had been, but it was in a larger vessel filled with many more weapons.

"No more than you trusted me." Sienar held up his hands and pointed a long finger at Tarkin. "You meant for all my efforts to come tumbling down, and then you'd show up and save the day. Well, I damned near had a Sekotan ship, Tarkin, and you've messed it all up. Now, who knows what's going to happen?"

"I see," Tarkin said, and paced back and forth across his cabin floor. "Droid starfighters going off on their own . . . highly unusual." He could not hide his expression, as much grimace as grin. "Interfering with droid intelligences is a tricky operation. Are you sure you didn't do something wrong?"

Sienar did not reply.

Tarkin called up an image of Zonama Sekot in the middle of

the cabin and walked around it, chin in hand. "Our sensors tell us something is going on down there, perhaps set off by the starfighters . . . a kind of chase between three ships. Where is Ke Daiv now?"

Sienar pointed at the planet's image. "Unless your trickery has killed him."

"Captain Kett informs us you had a long talk with Ke Daiv, and then reassigned him. Was he impressed by what you had to say?"

"I told him he could procure a Sekotan ship and save us all a lot of bother. He seemed to look upon it as an adventure."

"You haven't heard from him, I assume?"

Sienar shook his head.

"Very tough to kill, these Blood Carvers. Useful in so many ways, resourceful, yet mercurial." Tarkin waxed philosophical. "This competition . . . how ridiculous! What has either of us accomplished, Raith?"

"I take it you're going to conquer and take command of Zonama Sekot . . . you're going to invade?"

"I've already given the orders. The ships are assuming their positions around the planet," Tarkin said. "The Republic has a strong chancellor, a true leader. And the senate is remarkably docile these days. But they can be persuaded, if you have the right contacts. And I do. I always have, Raith."

"What weapons?"

"We were given more Republic sky-mine delivery ships, and we took control of many more Trade Federation droid starfighters than were assigned to you—with intelligences intact. We also have sufficient firepower aboard the cruisers to lay waste to any inhabited areas should they defy our diplomatic requests. I have long suspected this planet could create ships and arms for a rebellion."

"How subtle," Sienar said.

"How *effective*," Tarkin corrected. "But let's watch this little race drama, while my fleet demonstrates its power." The view magnified until they could see the outlines of the three ships, flying just above the tops of dense jungle growth along the equator. "I recognize a YT-1150. Are the other ships Sekotan? Spacecraft, or atmospheric?"

Sienar kept his silence. In truth, he did not know.

"I do believe the YT-1150 is an aggressor, chasing native ships," Tarkin mused. "I believe we will inform whoever is in charge on Zonama Sekot that we have begun our police action by capturing or incapacitating that ship, and then we will sit down to discuss protection agreements."

Captain Mignay of the *Rim Merchant Einem* presented a small image of herself. "Commander Tarkin, there appear to be other ships emerging from hidden hangars on Zonama Sekot. There are also large constructions buried on the planet that we cannot identify."

Tarkin frowned and concentrated his attention on new pictures. Dozens of craft were rising from the Sekotan jungles around the long, inhabited canyon known as Middle Distance.

"You've caused some commotion, I see," Sienar observed.

"They may have a few light defenses," Tarkin said. "Nothing starfighters can't handle. Captain Mignay, release our first rank of starfighters, and coordinate their actions with the sky-mine layers."

"Any warning to the planet, sir, before we begin?" the captain asked.

"No," Tarkin said huffily. "If they don't recognize the rule of law, enacted by Republic ships, I doubt we can reason with them."

Tarkin would not be swayed by anything less than complete submission. Sienar ground his teeth. Even among rogues in a degenerate age, this seemed to overstep the bounds of decency. But then what did he know? He obviously was out of touch with the senate's mood.

Sienar doubted Zonama Sekot would be able to match the combined firepower of two squadrons, or the horror of an atmosphere filled with drifting sky mines seeking anything that moved.

He almost felt sorry for them.

Anakin, fully recovered now, could feel the ship's immediate response, the wonderful surges of instant power, the way she cut through the air almost as effortlessly as if they were in a vacuum. The hull created subtle lift and was remarkably stable. On any world with an atmosphere, she would land sweetly. It took very little of his attention to fly the ship. Information arrived in comfortable flows through his contact with the ship's mind. She truly was a dream, alive to his touch.

But any joy he might have taken in this first flight was tainted by his concern for Obi-Wan. His face was deeply carved by a grim frown.

The Blood Carver stared at the young human, nose flaps closed, sharp as a blade. "I did not kill your master," Ke Daiv said. "It would have served no purpose."

"But you would have killed me, once," Anakin said through clenched teeth.

"I follow orders," the Blood Carver said.

"So you're an assassin. Do you even know my name?"

"You are the only one named Skywalker."

"If you're going to kill me, I'd like to know your name."

"Ke Daiv."

"I've never met a Blood Carver before," Anakin said. "I can't say it's a pleasure."

"Just fly. We need to find fuel."

"I don't know where to get any!" Anakin lied. The seeds knew—they were talking with other parts of Sekot.

And something or someone else flowed through his fingers where they were enmeshed by the controls. Anakin kept seeing misting ghosts around the cabin, like afterimages from bright sun—he had to work to concentrate on the scene around him.

"I have been busy in Middle Distance," Ke Daiv said. "I have learned where secret reserves of fuel are kept. Fly due south."

"Why would they need secret reserves?" Anakin asked. He turned the ship.

"There are mysteries on this planet," Ke Daiv said with a slight hiss. "Not long ago, there was a great war."

"We saw the damage."

"Did you learn what caused the war?"

"I really don't think I should be talking with you." *But I should see how well he reacts to Jedi compulsion. I've never been trained in mind tricks, but I know I can do it. Maybe even better than Obi-Wan.*

The boy shook his head, distracted by seeing a vague image wrap over the Blood Carver's features. The wraithlike form drifted with his attention to different parts of the cabin.

"Who are you, really?" Anakin asked to hide his confusion.

"I am from an old clan, an even older nation, swallowed by the Republic, taken in after our defeat at the hands of the Lontars."

Concentration was becoming increasingly difficult. Anakin

fumbled to keep up the conversation, to keep it away from his main concerns. "That was hundreds of years ago. The senate forced the Lontars to stop their aggression."

"Not before my people had been nearly wiped out," Ke Daiv said. "The few survivors were taken to Coruscant and kept in seclusion. We were warriors. We were called allies, but we could not be trusted. Few understood us. In time, when the rulers of the galaxy lost interest, we made our livelihoods selling crafts."

"So you've lived on Coruscant all your life."

"You said you should not be talking to me," Ke Daiv reminded him.

"What else is there to do? Why didn't you get a ship for yourself?"

The wraith took on form—an oblong head, torso shifting, still too vague to be identifiable. Then he made out the feathers, the elliptical eyes. Anakin held back an exclamation, and sweat broke out on his forehead. *I don't need this now!*

"I am not appealing to the seed-partners," Ke Daiv said.

"Too bad. These ships are really great."

"I have always hoped for independence," Ke Daiv said.

"Yeah, me too," Anakin said sharply. "Fly all over the galaxy . . . Freedom to see everything, no obligations, no . . ."

"No history, no future," Ke Daiv said.

"Right," Anakin said. *He's losing focus. He's weak. Now's the time to move on him. I have to keep control. No distractions.*

But he could not push aside the feathered being's image. She was trying to say something, repeating something over and over, like a muted recording.

Anakin raised his hands, and the panel let go with a soft sucking sound. The image vanished. He made as if to wriggle the tension out of his fingers. "Got to get used to these controls." He looked at the Blood Carver. His fingers instantly formed the graceful shape of compulsion.

Ke Daiv seemed unconcerned.

"You should let me take you back to Coruscant," Anakin said. "I could show you the Temple where I live."

Ke Daiv regarded him, eyes small and somehow sad, his oddly handsome face almost unreadable. "We are not destined to share clan."

"No, just a visit."

Anakin moved his hand to another position, a milder form of persuasion, and felt for connections in the Force. *Jedi must be in sympathy and understanding with what they seek to control. You and he are not that different.*

"We're not that different."

"We *are* different, Jedi. You have honor. I have merely the duty to work my way out of disgrace."

"Tell me about it," Anakin said. "I was a slave."

"You are valued among the Jedi. And those who command tell me the Jedi pose a danger."

"We defend, we don't cause trouble."

"That is young talk," Ke Daiv said.

"You're young, too."

Ke Daiv looked at his set of controls. One of several displays spun into view in front of him. He tensed in the seat, which would not let him sit comfortably. "There is a ship chasing us. It is the ship that brought you here. And . . . there is another. Go faster."

Anakin squinted at him.

Ke Daiv swung his flexible arm back, and the lance nearly caught Jabitha in the face. She screamed.

"Faster, to the Magister's mountain," the Blood Carver insisted, his voice chillingly calm.

"We're going as fast as we can!" Anakin cried. He did not have the training or the concentration now to compel the Blood Carver to do anything. He placed his hands on the controls.

The little creature instantly returned, filling his eyes and his mind. There was no sense fighting her. The image was crystalline. Her expression, what he could read in the piebald arrangement of feathers and whiskers, was stern, and her large, slanted eyes darted left and right, anticipating danger.

Anakin recognized her now. This was Vergere.

"Jedi," she said. *"Whoever you may be. I have left this message in my seed-partners, in the hopes they will find you, or you will find them. There is little time left. I am leaving with the visitors who have provoked a war here and wiped out half of Zonama Sekot. It is the only way to study them, and the only way to avoid a greater war and save this world."*

Anakin tried to stay calm. The integrated seeds contained all of the message that Obi-Wan had caught only a fragment of. That the ship was delivering the message now, in the middle of his trial, when he was at his most vulnerable, seemed grossly unfair.

But fairness had never played much of a part in Anakin Skywalker's life.

"The Zonamans call these visitors Far Outsiders. They are different from all the living things we have studied. The Far Outsiders know nothing of the Force. And the Force knows nothing of them. Yet they are not machines, they are definitely alive, and they may pose a great threat to us all. They are fascinated by me, by my abilities, and they have accepted me in exchange for breaking off their attack and leaving this system.

"I go with them to learn their secrets, and I vow, as a Jedi Knight, that I will survive and report my discoveries. But also, I

lead them away from a planet I have come to love. Know this, Jedi—"

Vergere's face seemed to glow with enthusiasm. "There is a great secret here, which you may discover in time. The heart of a great living creature has started to beat, and a great mind has become aware of itself. I have witnessed the birth of an amazing being—"

Vergere turned aside, and the message ended abruptly.

There was no more.

"What are you staring at?" Ke Daiv asked, thumping the lance on the bulkhead over Anakin's seat. The lance tip left a mark that quickly closed up and healed.

Anakin jumped. "Just let me fly," he said, frowning.

Suddenly, the Sekotan ship, his childish enthusiasm for machines, his resentment at the turns his life had taken, everything that had before now defined Anakin Skywalker, seemed vague and unimportant.

Vergere might have sacrificed her life to pass this information to another Jedi.

Anakin now saw more clearly the shape of his trial. He knew why he was important, and why he must defeat Ke Daiv and all the others who might try to destroy him.

The survival of the Jedi themselves could be at stake.

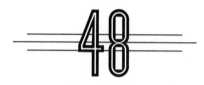

Shappa rose high into the mesosphere, on the edge of space, and pushed his ship until her skin glowed from the heat of friction. They were catching up with Anakin's ship, now about forty kilometers ahead and thirty kilometers below them. The air was a deep purple here, and the curve of Zonama Sekot was clearly evident. The forward ports had narrowed against the transmission of heat from the ship's skin, but Obi-Wan could still make out the endless blanket of clouds below, and the peak of the Magister's mountain on the horizon.

Charza Kwinn was now a thousand kilometers behind them, and trouble was following the *Star Sea Flower*.

"My people won't hold fire for much longer," Shappa said. "I wonder if they know what they're getting into, attacking us?"

"Clearly, they don't," Obi-Wan said. He could not figure out a reason for any attack on Zonama Sekot. Something had gone awry during the transition, the assimilation of Trade Federation ships into the Republic forces. Perhaps outlaw elements in the Trade Federation had broken ranks and gone off on their own.

That would explain the presence of droid starfighters, but not their actions.

"Those are Republic vessels," Shappa said, glancing at Obi-Wan. "Minelayers, I think."

Obi-Wan studied the images from Shappa's sensors. They were indeed sky-mine delivery ships, and above them, ten thousand kilometers out, Corellian light cruisers found only in the Republic forces.

"Forgive me," Shappa said. "But if you represent the Republic . . ."

"I know nothing of this," Obi-Wan said grimly.

"Little matter," Shappa said. "We have regarded ourselves as outside the jurisdiction of the Republic, the Trade Federation, or any other governing body. Our Magister foresaw our need early on—and the Magister before him. We knew that in time we would have to find an even more obscure hiding place. It is the will of the Potentium."

That word again, a discredited concept from the past.

"Was the original Magister given Jedi training?" Obi-Wan asked.

"Yes," Shappa said with an odd reluctance.

"What was his actual name?"

"That name is sacred to Zonamans, and must not be spoken," Shappa said.

Obi-Wan tried to recall the more obscure bits of the Jedi history he had been taught in the Temple. The Potentium had meant a great deal of trouble for the Jedi a hundred years before. Advocates of the concept had believed that the Force could not push one into evil, that the universe was infiltrated by a benevolent field of life energy whose instructions were inevitably good. The Potentium, as they called it, was the beginning and ending of all things, and one's connection with it should not be mediated or obscured by any sort of training or discipline. Followers of the Potentium insisted that the Jedi Masters and the Temple hierarchy could not accept the universal good of the Potentium because it meant they were no longer needed.

But in the end, those Jedi apprentices who had been caught up in the movement had left the Temple, or were pushed out, and dispersed around the galaxy. As far as Obi-Wan could remember, none of the believers had actually succumbed to the dark side of the Force—something regarded as a prodigy by Jedi historians. From time to time, young Jedi caught up in their first experience of the Force broached the Potentium philosophy and had to be patiently retutored in the history of the Force, in the many and various reasons why the Jedi understood there were definite divisions and pitfalls in life's tenure in space and time.

For days now, a name had remained on the tip of his tongue—a particularly prominent young Jedi apprentice who had left the Temple voluntarily and renounced his training.

"Was your original Magister named Leor Hal?" he asked Shappa.

Shappa stared straight ahead through the port on the pilot's side of the cabin, jaw tight. "I knew you would figure things out soon enough," he said.

"He was a powerful student," Obi-Wan said. "Even after he left, he was regarded with respect."

"He was regarded as a dupe and a fool," Shappa said.

"An idealist, perhaps, but not a fool."

"Well, his own prejudices against any political system or philosophical organization . . . they established much of the character of Zonama's settlement."

"He recruited among the Ferroans?" Obi-Wan ventured.

"He did. My people have always been a sunny people, believers in independence and basic goodness. We came here to escape and raise our children in a new state of bliss."

"And when the Far Outsiders arrived . . ."

"It was a rude awakening," Shappa said. "But the Magister's heir insisted they were outside the Potentium. They knew nothing of its ways, and we must teach them."

"How did he react to the presence of Vergere?"

"He shunned her, for his father's sake," Shappa said. "He gave her no assistance."

"But he built weapons."

"He did. He knew that many could misinterpret the Potentium, and that they might try to destroy us for our differences."

"What did the original Magister build?"

"He was the one who began selling ships. He told us we needed to raise enough money to buy huge hyperdrive cores. And to import huge engines, study them, and use the Jentari to remake them as even more powerful engines, for our own purposes."

"To what end?"

"Escape," Shappa said. He drew himself up. "Now, I believe the time has come."

"But he is dead," Obi-Wan said.

"Nonsense. You met with him."

"No. It is clear now."

"The Magister is not dead!" Shappa cried out, and shook his fist at Obi-Wan. "He sends instructions to us from his palace!"

"Perhaps even the palace no longer exists," Obi-Wan said.

"I will not hear of this!" Shappa shouted. "I will help you rescue your boy, and then . . . you must leave!" He turned away, intensely agitated, and studied his displays. "Perhaps the Jedi *did* send you here to disrupt us. And the Republic ships—"

The sky ahead filled with tiny points of light. Sky mines were descending through the upper reaches of the atmosphere, spreading out for thousands of kilometers around like diffuse orange blossoms.

"They're trying to destroy us all!" Shappa groaned, his face a mask of fear and disappointment.

Anakin brought his ship low around the peak of the mountain, flying in a smooth, beautiful arc, with perfect control.

All was quiet within the cabin. Jabitha had curled up on her couch and seemed to be trying to sleep. Anakin felt very protective toward her, but there was nothing he could do now. Rash behavior would get him killed, and now was not the time to indulge his brash and youthful tendencies.

"The palace should be right around here," Anakin said. Ke Daiv remained silent, the tip of his lance blade poised near Anakin's neck. "I don't see anything . . . no landing field, nothing!"

"You have been here before?" Ke Daiv asked.

"Just a few days ago," Anakin said. "It was huge . . . it covered the peak of the mountain."

"And this is the only mountain," Ke Daiv mused. "You wouldn't trick me, Jedi?"

"No," Anakin said, frustrated. "I tried that . . . it didn't work."

Ke Daiv made a small clucking sound. "Circle again."

Jabitha spoke up. "Are we at the palace?" she asked. Anakin did not know how to answer.

"Come here and show us where to go," Ke Daiv ordered. She rose from the couch and stepped forward gingerly.

"I don't see it," she said tremulously. Then her eyes widened. "Wait—that's the Dragon Cave, full of steam right next to an underground glacier . . . We used to hike there, years ago. But what's that? I've never seen that." She pointed to a long slope of talus, huge pieces of rock tumbled into temporary stasis on one side of the mountain, jumbled terrain dropping below the clouds. "That's new."

"You said you haven't been here in a year," Anakin said. "Not since the attack?"

Jabitha's face colored. "Father said never to discuss the attack with strangers."

Ke Daiv watched and listened with cautious interest.

"It looks like the mountain's been hit by laser cannon fire, or something even more powerful," Anakin observed, mindful that this was probably not what the girl would want to hear.

"Ridiculous! Father told us the mountain was—"

She clamped her mouth shut and shook her head stubbornly. "I won't tell secrets."

"Too late now for secrets," Ke Daiv said. "Tell all."

"I don't know what to say!"

"She doesn't know anything," Anakin said. "I was here just recently, and I saw a palace."

"It is still on the maps at Middle Distance," Ke Daiv said, by way of agreement. "We must find fuel, whatever has happened."

"We have to find the palace!" Jabitha insisted. "It's here. My father's here. They have to be!"

Anakin swung the ship up for a higher-altitude sweep. It was now that he spotted the blossoms of sky mines spreading out overhead. Ke Daiv saw them at the same time.

"Looks like they won't mind losing you," Anakin said tersely.

The Blood Carver stared through the port, his face unreadable, but the lance tip fell slightly. Anakin knew that now was the time to bring the ship down, release Jabitha, and take on Ke Daiv once again, all by himself.

The sky mines would provide the perfect excuse. They were designed to prevent ships from leaving a planet; they rarely if ever exploded on the surface.

"We have to land somewhere," Anakin said.

"Do it," Ke Daiv said.

Jabitha had crowded up beside Anakin to stare through the port. Suddenly she gave a sob. "There!" she cried.

They had come halfway around the peak of the mountain. Buried in a massive landslide from the higher elevations lay the ruins of a huge complex of buildings. The area had been altered so drastically, and the complex covered so completely, that they had missed it on their first circuit.

Anakin saw the spare edge of the old landing field, with its reddish black lava surface. "I'll put down there," he said.

"Where's Father?" Jabitha asked, her cheeks wet with tears.

The sky mines zigged and zagged in search of prey, their contrails catching the sunset light over the clouds like flaming letters in the sky. They numbered in the hundreds of thousands, tiny highly explosive oblate spheroids equipped with fierce tracking ability and split-second maneuverability. They were forcing Shappa to drop lower and lower.

"We won't be able to stay in the air for long," he said. "A few minutes at most, and then they'll find us."

Obi-Wan said nothing for a long moment. Following the sky mines would come hunter-killer starfighters, and the air over the clouds would be filled with swift destruction. The Sekotan ship was unarmed. They wouldn't stand a chance.

"Then take her down," he said.

"They've landed on the Magister's mountain. At least they will have some protection in the palace." Shappa glared at him, challenging Obi-Wan to contradict his beliefs, his hopes.

The Sekotan ship dropped through the cloud deck, and they were surrounded by a silvery gloom. Winds whipped them this way and that before Shappa brought his craft down on a scourged prairie of bare, blackened rock. All around, jagged outcrops of twisted stone showed that a fury of destructive energies had melted and rearranged the landscape, killing all life.

Shappa removed his hands from the controls and bustled around the rear of the cabin, making checks on the equipment installed there. He came forward and found Obi-Wan still in his seat, lost in intense thought.

"Look what they did," Shappa said softly, peering through Obi-Wan's port. "What did we ever do to deserve such destruction? How could the Potentium have allowed such evil?"

Obi-Wan rose from his seat. No sense contradicting Shappa now. Didacticism—always a tendency in him—was of no use here. Shappa was an ally and had to muddle through as best he could with the beliefs that gave him strength.

"How far are we from the mountain?" Obi-Wan asked.

"About a hundred kilometers."

"And where is Charza Kwinn?"

Shappa looked at his displays. "The other ship has also descended below the clouds."

There was nothing Obi-Wan could do for now. His sense of the future was as clouded as the sky. Anakin's fate was pushed up against a knot, a fistula in the pathways to different futures. What struck Obi-Wan most was the terrifying connections between so many futures that bunched up in these next few hours. So many events whirled around his Padawan, so many interconnected lives.

He wished he could speak with Mace Windu, Yoda. Qui-Gon. This was completely beyond his comprehension.

If he felt this way, after more than a decade and a half of Jedi training, Obi-Wan could hardly imagine how Anakin felt.

Obi-Wan closed his eyes to consult the wisdom that Qui-Gon had left behind.

The boy's trial . . . he will face it alone. You must trust in your Padawan. And you must trust in the Force. After Qui-Gon's death, in a way, you lost that trust. You relied on a sense of duty and a daily regimen of work and study and training to replace what had once been a marvelous sense of awe and wonder at the ways of the Force.

The Force disappointed you, did it not, Obi-Wan?

It allowed your Master to die.

It could allow Anakin to die.

And if it does, that will kill any chance of your remaining a Jedi.

The future could not be read. The Force was silent and compressed around them all, as if holding in a giant breath.

Jabitha walked across the barren field, climbing up and over ribbons of once-molten rock. She breathed in thin, ragged jerks. The air was too thin for her. She was used to the luxurious and rich atmosphere of the northern valleys, not the desolate and dead atmosphere on her father's mountain.

"The palace should be over there," she said, her voice little more than a whisper.

Anakin's vision swam for a moment, and he worked a small Jedi technique on his blood pressure and chemistry to give himself more strength and clarity with less oxygen.

Ke Daiv stood a few steps behind them, lance blade ready. Anakin measured all the distances, estimated the times. The Blood Carver was closer to Jabitha. He could easily kill her before Anakin could reach him, and what would Anakin do to him anyway?

Bank the anger. Bank the frustration. Convert them and store the energy.

Anakin gave a small nod. Jabitha turned. "There's almost

nothing left," she said. And then again, "Where's my father? Where are all the others who worked here?"

"They are all dead," Ke Daiv suggested. "Our only concern is fuel."

"There were fuel reserves near the palace," Jabitha said with a strange tone of defiance. "If we can't find the palace, we won't find the fuel!"

Anakin saw a corner of stone masonry jutting from a pile of rocky rubble about a hundred meters away. He turned to Ke Daiv. "Maybe over there," he said.

Jabitha was on the edge of collapse. The Blood Carver seemed to find the thin air no trouble at all. Anakin wondered why they hadn't noticed it when they were first taken here. Surely the palace had been in this condition already. Something had worked an even more startling deception on them.

The girl stumbled, then turned in a daze and walked for the ruin as fast as she could. Anakin and Ke Daiv followed. Anakin made sure he was closest to the Blood Carver. He tracked the motions of the lance, the yellow and red glitter of the blade in the last of the sunset light. The mountain's peak, black and deep brick red at other times, was now a ghastly orange, backed by the cryptic glyphs of the sky mines, endlessly and hungrily searching. Beyond the violently calligraphed sky rose the pinwheel of the distant companion stars, purple against the orange and red and gold.

Anakin looked over his shoulder at their ship. *We haven't even given her a name yet,* he thought. *What would Obi-Wan call her?*

Jabitha's shoulders trembled. She was expending her little remaining energy on racking sobs. "The messages were all lies. Nobody came here, he said everything was fine . . . But you!" She turned on Anakin. "You came here!"

"We saw the palace," Anakin said. "At least, we thought we did—"

"Fuel, and quickly," Ke Daiv insisted sharply. "The sky mines will drop low enough to find where we've landed. And others may come soon, as well."

"They'll sacrifice you, won't they?" Anakin said. The wall of the building loomed above them. A small door, possibly a service entrance, showed to the right, half-obscured by rubble. "They don't care what happens to you."

Ke Daiv did not dignify this with a response.

"Just what did you do to earn such disgrace?" Anakin asked. Without thinking, he tilted his head to one side, and three fingers on his right hand curled.

"I killed my benefactor's son," Ke Daiv said. "It was prophesied he would die from a severe head wound in battle. So his father beseeched the clan that his son would never fight. The clan agreed, but ordered him to go on a ritual hunt to fulfill his training. I was an orphan brought into their family, and the head of the clan appointed me to protect my benefactor's son. I accompanied him on the hunt. We fought with a wild feragriff in the ritual preserves on a moon over Coruscant." The Blood Carver's nose flaps had spread wide now, a motion Anakin had learned to interpret as uncertainty, questing for sensation, information, confirmation. *He's weaker now. His past makes him weak, just like me.*

Anakin saw Jabitha enter the doorway. She would not see.

"The prophecy came true. You killed him with a stray shot," Anakin finished the story.

"It was an accident," the Blood Carver murmured. Ke Daiv straightened. His face became sharp again, and he pushed the lance forward, poking at Anakin to get him to go through the door after the girl.

"No," Anakin said.

Sky mines jagged wildly just a few hundred meters overhead, their engines screeching in the thin air. Anakin saw another silhouette at an even greater distance: a droid starfighter. Just one. The invaders were concentrating their forces in the north, but sky mines were cheap. They could be spread everywhere. In time, they might even blanket the planet. Someone might be planning to kill all living things on Zonama Sekot: Jabitha, Gann, Sheekla Farrs, Shappa, Fitch, Vagno, Obi-Wan. And all the others.

"You still have honor," Anakin said. "You can still make up for what you did." But something else built inside, a shadow far thicker than the descending night. It could easily fill his being.

The Blood Carver had hurt Obi-Wan, threatened Jabitha, called Anakin a slave. For these things there was no possible redemption. The banked anger threatened to spill over, unconverted, pure and very raw, hot as a sun's core. Anakin's fingers curled tighter.

"My benefactor cursed me," Ke Daiv said.

Let it be done now. Anakin had made his decision, or it had been made for him. No matter.

Anakin let the fingers go straight.

Ke Daiv closed on the boy, swinging his lance.

"Stop that," Anakin said coldly.

"What will you do, *slave boy?*"

It was the connection Anakin had sought, the link between his anger and his power. Like a switch being thrown, a circuit being connected, he returned full circle to the pit race, to the sting he had felt with the Blood Carver's first insult, with the first unfair and sneaky move that had sent Anakin tumbling off the apron. Then, back farther, to the dingy slave quarters on Tatooine, to the Boonta Eve Podrace and the treachery of the Dug, and to the last sight of Shmi, still in bondage to the disgusting Watto, to all the insults and injuries and shames and night sweats and disgrace piled upon disgrace that he had never asked for, never deserved, and had borne with almost infinite patience.

Call it instinct, animal nature, call it the upwelling of hatred and the dark side—in Anakin Skywalker, all this lay just beneath the surface, at the end of its journey out of a long, deep cave leading down to unimaginable strength.

"No! Stop it, please!" Anakin yelled. *"Help me stop it!"* The rumbling of his ascending power drowned out this plea for his master to come and prevent a hideous mistake. *I am so afraid, so full of hate and anger. I still don't know how to fight.*

Jabitha appeared in the doorway, eyes wide, watching the boy crouched low before the Blood Carver. Ke Daiv lifted his lance. What would have once seemed quick as lightning was now, in the eyes of the young Padawan, a slow, curiously protracted swing.

Anakin raised his hands in the twin and supremely graceful gestures of Jedi compulsion. Pure willful self flooded his tissues. The urge to protect and to destroy became one. He straightened and seemed to grow taller. His eyes became black as pitch.

"Stop it, *please!*" Anakin shouted. "I can't hold it back any longer!"

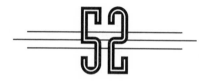

They have many more ships than we suspected," Tarkin observed. He looked down in wonder at the battle unfolding
on the planet below. Sweat appeared on his brow. Sienar, re-
signed to whatever might happen, took some comfort in Tarkin's concern.

Magnified scenes of conflict spaced themselves around the
command bridge of the *Rim Merchant Einem*. The sky mines
themselves were sending signals back to their delivery ships, and
the ships forwarded them to the command center.

Droid starfighters engaged countless ships rising from opening hangars in the jungle, swarms of ships like green and red insects.
These defenders seemed lightly armed but highly maneuverable.
Their principal tactic was to catch up with the starfighters, grasp
them in tractor fields, and drag them down to impact in the jungle
below. Tarkin was losing a great many starfighters this way.

"They will not escape the sky mines," he said. Indeed, many
mines were finding their targets, destroying the red and green
defenders before they could fly far from their concealed bases.

But Sienar saw something else was happening. It was subtle at first. The rectangular bulges in the jungle they had noticed earlier now cast long shadows as the terminator between night and day approached. Natural enough, but the shadows were lengthening faster than the lowering angle of sunlight would explain. The rectangles were rising.

Sienar estimated the tallest of them stood more than two kilometers above the jungle.

They reminded him of trapdoors slowly opening.

But he said nothing to Tarkin. This was no longer Raith Sienar's fight.

Tarkin murmured under his breath and moved his viewpoint farther south. Thousands of projected images flashed before him like revealed cards. "There," Tarkin said, a note of triumph in his voice. "There's our prize, Raith."

Parked on the extreme edge of a talus-covered field on the only mountain to rise above the southern cloud deck was a Sekotan ship. No figures were visible in its proximity. It seemed to have been abandoned.

Raith leaned forward to see the ship in more detail. It was larger than any he had heard of and different in design, as well. The very sight of it made his mouth water. "Are you going to destroy it?" he asked Tarkin bitterly. "To complete my disgrace?"

Tarkin shook his head, saddened by Sienar's mistrust. To the captain he said, "Direct sky mines away from the mountain. And let's take care of that pesty YT-1150. Put all the mines in that sector on its track." He faced Sienar with the expression of a beast of prey about to pounce. "We're going to capture that ship and take it back to Coruscant. To be fair, I'll give you credit, Raith. *Some* credit."

The mines are dropping below the clouds," Shappa observed. "We won't be safe here much longer. But they seem to be abandoning the Magister's mountain."

Obi-Wan flexed his fingers and leaned forward in the seat. "Is Anakin still on the mountain?"

Shappa swallowed hard and nodded. "Your ship reports her passengers are outside, not visible. Her mind is young, Obi-Wan. She does not understand what is happening, and she misses contact with her pilot. But something else is causing alarm. I'm not sure what."

"The mines?"

Shappa shook his head. "I doubt it."

"If we are not safe here . . ." Obi-Wan ventured.

"Then we should attempt a rescue," Shappa concluded. "The Magister's daughter was on that ship."

Shappa raised his vessel from the dark and desolate rocky prairie and quickly ascended through the clouds. "Our sensors will warn us of immediate mines, but these ships are not designed to be weapons of war, or to understand defensive maneuvers. I will do my best."

Obi-Wan nodded, still flexing his fingers. He knew that Anakin was alive, but he also knew that something significant had happened, a minor unknotting in the boy's pathway. He could not tell if the outcome was positive or negative.

To bring back a spiritually damaged boy of Anakin's abilities might be worse than finding him dead. It seemed cruel, but Obi-Wan knew it was a simple truth. Qui-Gon would have agreed.

"The sky mines are concentrating on your YT-1150," Shappa said, studying the displays closely as they flew toward the mountain. "It is eluding them, so far."

"Charza Kwinn is one of the best pilots in the galaxy," Obi-Wan said.

Jabitha walked across the landing field toward the two figures crouched next to each other. Their struggle, if struggle it
had been, had lasted only a few seconds, and yet somehow they
had moved into the shadow of a huge boulder, where she could
barely make out their outlines. She walked slowly, fearful of what
she might find. She did not want to feel the Blood Carver's lance
once again, nor did she wish to find the boy dead. But she
dreaded something else almost as much.

Her skin crawled at the thought that this young boy could
have survived against so formidable an opponent.

"Anakin?" she called, a few steps away from the rock.

The Blood Carver emerged from the shadow, triple-jointed
arms loose by his sides. He seemed exhausted. In the last of the
daylight, his skin glimmered a deep orange color, and Jabitha's
heart filled her throat. He was still alive. The boy had not moved
from beneath the overhang.

"Anakin!" she called out again, her voice trembling.

Ke Daiv stepped toward her and lifted a hand. She was almost too afraid to look at his face, but when she did, she screamed. His eyes had turned white, and the flesh around his head and neck had cracked. He was bleeding profusely, and his dark orange blood dripped down over his shoulders. He was trying to say something.

Jabitha backed away, speechless with terror.

"I tried to control it," Anakin said, and emerged into the twilight. The pinwheel's purple glory illuminated them with the fading of the dusk. The Blood Carver lurched forward step by step toward the edge of the field, away from the Sekotan ship.

"Stop him," Anakin said. "Please help me stop him."

Jabitha walked beside the boy toward the pitiful figure of their enemy.

"Is he dying?" she asked.

"I hope not," Anakin said as if ashamed. "By the Force, I hope not."

"He was going to kill you," she said.

"That doesn't matter," Anakin said. "I should never have let it loose like that. I did it all wrong."

"Let what loose?"

He shook his head, trying to erase a nightmare, and grabbed the Blood Carver's arm. Ke Daiv swung about as if on a turntable and fell to his knees. Blood dripped from his mouth.

Jabitha stood before the two, the young boy with the short, light brown hair and the tall, gold-colored Blood Carver who might be dying. She shook her head in desperate confusion. "You saved us, Anakin," she said.

"Not like this," he said. "He was being brave in the only way he knew, the only way they taught him. He's like me, but he never had the Jedi to help." To Ke Daiv, he said, "Please be strong. Don't die."

Jabitha could stand this no longer. "I have to find my father," she said. She turned and ran toward the ruins.

Anakin gripped Ke Daiv's arm and glanced up at the sky. The awful glyphs written by the mines were fading, contrails pointing east now, drifting and diffusing in the winds over the clouds.

Ke Daiv spoke in his native language. Each sound cost him an agony. By the cadence, he was repeating something familiar, a poem or a chant. He fell to one hand, then lowered himself to the ground.

Anakin stayed beside him, holding his arm, until he died. Then the boy rose, turned around once, and screamed, heard only by the mountain, the skies, the broken and charred stones, the crumbling ruins of the Magister's palace.

Anakin Skywalker understood the nature of the Force—the many *natures* of the Force—better than a century of teaching in the Temple could have taught him. And he understood now that his trial was far from over. He had to remove Jabitha from the mountain and get back to Obi-Wan, and he had to wrestle with what he had discovered about himself.

But the wrestling would have to wait. A Jedi with responsibilities had to put away the personal and get on with his duty, no matter what it might cost him.

The entrance to the ruin was dark. Dust sifted from a shattered stone lintel. He wiped the dust from his eyes and crawled into the darkness, until the rubble cleared and he faced a long, black corridor.

His senses had become marvelously acute, sharper and more intuitive than ever before. Despite the darkness, the corridor offered no mysteries. It was simply a hallway in what was left of the palace. He saw himself at the end of the hallway, turning right.

And when he reached the end of the hallway and turned right, he saw ahead to another corridor, larger, its thick roof supporting much of the mass of talus and rubble that covered the ruins. That corridor led to the chamber where Obi-Wan and Anakin had first met the Magister.

Jabitha was in the chamber already, so it was not far away. He walked there, his footsteps sure but his thoughts a painful riot.

The ceiling shuddered with a sound like a dying bantha. Other groans and shrieks of rock grinding against rock echoed down branching hallways, and somewhere, very close, rock tumbled into a corridor and sealed it off, then crushed it completely. A blast of air and dust blew out over him like the penultimate breath from the dying palace.

He stepped over tendrils that crept along the cracked floor, new tendrils. Sekot still lived here, still felt its way through the broken shafts and voids. There was still life here, and something like the voice of their ship, soft in his thoughts, almost drowned out by the tumult of Ke Daiv's death.

Anakin thought for a moment that he saw Vergere gleaming softly ahead, and wondered if she had died on Zonama and left behind a spirit to guide him. But the image was not there when he reached that point, and Anakin shook his head. He was dreaming, hallucinating. Perhaps he was going insane.

His mother had many waking dreams, disturbing and strange, she had once told him. That had scared him a little.

He came to the circular chamber with its high, thickly vaulted roof, the skylight now collapsed, and a thick pillar of rubble fanning out. Jabitha stood by one side of the rubble, on her knees, her head bowed.

Anakin approached her. She looked up and held a powered

torch beam on his face. She had found the light somewhere in the rubble, perhaps in her rooms in the palace.

Sticking out between two large carved stones was an arm, most of the flesh gone now. On one finger gleamed a thick steel ring set with a pentangle of small red stones. Anakin recognized one of the old signet rings once handed out to Jedi apprentices.

"He's dead," Jabitha said. "Only the Magister could wear this ring. It meant he was linked with the Potentium."

"We have to go," Anakin told her softly. The corridors echoed with more groans, more shrieks and rumbles. The floor beneath them trembled.

"He must have died during the battle with the Far Outsiders," Jabitha said. She shone the torch beam around the chamber, looking for any others. The chamber was deserted. "But who was sending his messages?"

"I don't know," Anakin said. Then once again, from the corner of his eye, he caught a gleam of light in the darkness, away from Jabitha's torch. He turned and saw the feathered Jedi Knight standing on her reverse-articulated legs, feet splayed as if prepared to leap, staring at him with no apparent emotion.

Jabitha could not see her. Nor did the girl see the figure become the Magister, her father. The transformed figure stepped forward.

Anakin felt no fear. He felt instead in the presence of another young person very like himself, a friend. This made him consider once again the real possibility that he was going insane.

"I sent the messages," the figure told Anakin.

The girl remained crouched over her dead father. Anakin bent and touched the top of her head, and she fell asleep, slumping gently to one side. He caught her and made sure she was comfortable, then stood and faced the image.

"Who are you?" he asked, his voice cracking.

"A friend of Vergere," it said. "I think my name, to some, is Sekot."

To prepare the way for a retrieval ship to land on the mountain, Tarkin ordered a swarm of droid starfighters to take on any other ships in the area. He watched with satisfaction from his lofty orbit, Sienar at his side, as the starfighters harried the outmoded YT-1150 and another Sekotan ship.

"We'll sacrifice one to gain another," Tarkin said.

"Take care with the larger Sekotan vessel," Sienar said, though he was not at all sure that Tarkin was willing to hear reason. "It may be exceptional."

"Sir," the captain said, "we are losing most of our starfighters over the inhabited valleys in the north. Their defenses are relentless and apparently without limit. And there are—"

"Quiet!" Tarkin shouted. "I think you overestimate these primitives. Once we are done with our primary mission, we will sweep up the rest by main force. No more delicacy. If they do not submit, we will destroy them utterly."

Anakin stayed close by Jabitha, as much for his sake as for hers. The atmosphere within the chamber was thick with dust. Dust sifted from the ceiling, puffed from the outer halls as ceilings collapsed elsewhere in the ruin.

Tendrils on the floor moved with deliberation toward Jabitha, encircled her. Sekot itself would protect the Magister's daughter. In some fashion Anakin could not yet fathom, the figure before him regarded the Magister's children as brothers and sisters.

"You are the Jedi apprentice," the image said.

Anakin nodded.

"And your master is elsewhere, fighting the new invasion."

"I feel him out there," Anakin said.

"How I would love to learn the secrets of the Jedi! What can you teach me?"

"Who are you?" Anakin said. Like Obi-Wan, he was now finding mystery and delay to be a real irritation.

"I don't know for sure. I'm not very old, but my memories

go back billions of turnings. Parts of me saw the pinwheel grow in the sky."

Anakin thought of Vergere's message contained within the seeds. "You're the mind I sensed, aren't you?" he asked. "The voice behind the seed voices."

"They are my children," the image said. "They are cells in my body."

"You really *are* Sekot, then, aren't you?" Even under the present circumstances, he could not help but feel awe and wonder.

"I tried to be the Magister, but I can't continue. I grieve for him. He was the first to know me. The Magister was going to reveal me to his people, but the Far Outsiders arrived. I had never known anything like them. The Magister's peoples were gentle."

"Can you see around the entire planet? What else is happening outside?"

"I see wherever my parts reach. I am almost blind down here. They burned me down here. I've never known such pain. The Magister told me to burn them back, so I helped him make weapons. But I did not know what to believe."

"Why?" Anakin knelt beside Jabitha. The tendrils encircled them, rustling faintly across the floor.

"He told me I was the Potentium, the force behind all life. He thought I reached everywhere. I don't. I'm just here. He saw what he wanted to see, and told me what he wanted to hear me speak into his own ears. He said there was no evil in the universe, only good. I did not see how wrong he was until he died. Then I reached out with the weapons we had made, and I killed. The Magister had said that would be good, but I knew it was not."

Anakin sucked in his breath. "Just like me," he said.

"I killed more, but it was still not enough. It was Vergere who drew away the Far Outsiders. She did not kill them; she persuaded them. I wish she was still here, but there is only a little part of her. The message to you and your master."

"Did she know the Magister was dead?"

"No one knew, until now."

Anakin held out his hand to fend off a questing tendril.

The image seemed to be hurt by this. "Why do you distrust me? I want to protect her."

"I don't distrust you. But I don't think either of us knows what we're doing. We should get her outside and wait for my master to arrive."

"It is you I feel closest to," the image said. "The Magister's peoples made me their servant, and you were a slave. I did what they told me to do. You did what your owner told you to do. So like me! I tried to be like the others, but I am not like them. My mind is made up of so many parts, spread out over so much of my world. And your mind is so different from the others. I have no real parents, and your parents—"

Anakin interrupted with a stammered question. "What m-made you wake up? Why did *you* suddenly appear, after billions of years?"

"I had to come into being to communicate with the new arrivals, the Magister's peoples. All of me came together, reached up to talk with them, and I was—"

A large chunk of the roof collapsed on the far end of the chamber, showering them with splinters and shards of broken stone. "We have to go now!" Anakin said. "Can you help me?"

The image emerged from the swirling dust, glowing faintly in the darkness. "I will shore up the hallways. You will carry her outside."

Tendrils grew from trunks that pushed up through cracks in the floor. They spread ahead of Anakin, forming red and green vaults overhead, as he picked up Jabitha and slung her over his shoulder. As a deadweight, Jabitha was not easy to carry. He was beginning to regret putting the girl to sleep, but it had been the best thing to do at the time.

She came out of her trance as they passed through the last open doorway, and struggled to get down from his shoulder. "Where are we?" she cried out, and then stared up at the pinwheel in the night sky and the rolling blanket of stars beyond.

A shadow passed over the landing field and their Sekotan ship. It blocked out the pinwheel and then dropped down to cover the ship like a predator pouncing on its prey. This was not another Sekotan ship, and it was not the *Star Sea Flower.* Anakin heard the whine and roar of repulsor engines pounding against the rock.

It was a sky-mine delivery ship, doing double duty now as a landing craft.

A shaft of light appeared in one side of the hulk. Troops marched down the ramp in quick tight cordons and surrounded Anakin and Jabitha. A squad circled the body of the Blood Carver.

Two officers walked down the ramp with more dignity, as if they had all the time in the universe. Anakin thought they might be brothers, they so resembled each other, though they wore quite different uniforms. Both were thin and carried themselves with assurance and perhaps too much pride. Both looked arrogant. He knew instantly, with instincts he had developed long before becoming a Jedi, that they were very dangerous. They turned toward the boy and the girl.

In the ordinary scheme of things, neither would have cared

much for the fate of two children. The taller of the two, by a spare centimeter or two, lifted his hand and whispered something into the other's ear.

"Him," the shorter man said, pointing imperiously at Anakin. "Leave the girl here."

Anakin tried to stay with Jabitha. She reached out for him, and their fingertips gripped for an instant before a bulky soldier dressed in a Republic Special Tactics trooper uniform pulled him away. For a second, the boy's anger threatened to flare again, but he saw they were not going to harm Jabitha, and he could not kill them all.

And would not if he could.

"My name is Tarkin," the shorter of the officers said to him in deeply mannered tones. "You're the Jedi boy who collects old droids, no? And marvel of marvels, you're now the pilot of this ship?"

Anakin did not answer. Tarkin rewarded his silence with a smile and a pat on the head. "Learn some manners, boy." Two soldiers hurried him, struggling, into the innards of the dark ship.

"What about Ke Daiv?" Raith Sienar asked.

"A failure from the beginning," Tarkin said. "Leave him here to rot."

Jabitha yelled for Anakin, but the ramp closed with a hiss and a metallic bang. He felt the ship rise abruptly and climb. Tarkin and Sienar immediately escorted him to the bay where the Sekotan ship had been hoisted and stowed in a catchall harness.

"Stay with your ship, boy," Tarkin said. "Keep it alive. You are very important to us. The Jedi Temple awaits your speedy return."

They'll keep the sky mines away from that ship," Obi-Wan told Shappa as they ducked in and out of the mountain ravines at the cloud line. "No one trusts them in close quarters not to go after friendlies."

Three droid starfighters still doggedly followed, but Shappa's craft was too swift and maneuverable to be caught.

"They'll take the Magister's daughter!" Shappa said grimly. He pushed his hand even deeper into the console, which wrapped its tissues up to his elbow, shoving back his sleeve.

"I don't think so," Obi-Wan said, brow furrowed in intense concentration. He closed his eyes, feeling ahead for all futures, for the knot rapidly coming unwound, for the strands of fate whirling off in all directions, not unlike the pinwheel that filled the sky.

"You're right," Shappa said as they leapt up over the rim of the field and circled. "They've left her behind, and she's alive!"

"Move in and retrieve her," Obi-Wan said. "Leave me on the field."

"But the starfighters will kill you!"

"Perhaps," Obi-Wan said. "But there's nothing more you can do for me, and nothing I can do for you."

Shappa opened and closed his mouth, trying to think of something appropriate to say, then nodded and concentrated on bringing his ship down.

There was no time for farewells. One moment the Jedi Knight sat beside him, and the next, just as the hatch opened, he was gone like a twist of smoke in the wind.

The next thing Shappa knew, the Magister's daughter dropped through the hatch, kicking and screaming.

"Now go!" Obi-Wan shouted after her, and slammed the ship's hull with the flat of his hand.

Shappa did not need encouragement. Starfighters buzzed up over the rim of the landing field. Jabitha held on for dear life as Shappa lifted the ship away.

Obi-Wan Kenobi flung aside the bandages that impeded his free motion and simultaneously drew forth his lightsaber. The blade hummed into angry green life. Once, the weapon had belonged to Qui-Gon. Holding it in his hands, Obi-Wan felt he now had the strength of two. He needed every gram of hope, and if sentiment gave him strength, helped him focus and emulate his former Master, then so be it.

The Force did not disagree. Qui-Gon had had a special relationship with the Force, and he had taught his apprentice well.

"Come on," Obi-Wan whispered as he stalked across the field. Two starfighters had remained to see what prey they could find on the mountain. The other had gone off after Shappa's craft. "Come on," he repeated a little louder this time.

He walked up to the Blood Carver's body. It lay in a crumpled heap surrounded by boot prints. Something about it troubled him, but there was little time.

As Obi-Wan rose from his stoop, a starfighter dropped from the sky, laser cannons lighting up the shattered landscape. Obi-Wan deflected two of its blasts with his blade, but their force nearly ripped the lightsaber from his hands. A third blast pulsed brilliant red to one side and hit the Blood Carver's corpse square.

Ke Daiv received his ritual cremation then and there.

The second starfighter joined the first, curving high up into the sky.

From out of nowhere, as if sneaking suddenly between veils of stars, Charza Kwinn's old YT-1150 screamed over the field, guns yelping out quick bolts that shattered the two starfighters before they could even think about a return run. Their smoking remains slammed into the side of the mountain and started a rumbling avalanche that spilled down over the palace ruins. Boulders tumbled across the field, huge and implacable, worse than any phalanx of warriors.

Obi-Wan raised his blade and swung it over his head as a beacon.

The *Star Sea Flower* whipped up on end and glided backward like a falling leaf just meters above the smoking, grinding flow of rock and dirt. Its loading ramp dropped like a jaw. Obi-Wan vaulted over the edge of the ramp, and the ship lifted him away just as the last of the landing field was reclaimed by the mountain.

Obi-Wan sloshed through the dank corridors to the pilot's cabin. Food-kin scampered out of his way, snapping with excitement.

"They have your Padawan," Charza Kwinn bristled, bending over backward to peer at the Jedi. "Sit down and buckle up."

Anakin felt as if he had been swallowed alive. He huddled next to his ship, hand on the fuselage, feeling her quiver in the capture harness. Shoulders hunched, he controlled his rapid breathing and tried to come up with a plan, any plan, to regain control over his life.

He could not shake the vision of the dying Blood Carver. Firing lasers at droids was no preparation for his first personal kill, and the way he had done it . . .

Anakin moaned. The four guards in the bay turned at the sound, shrugged, and looked away. Just a frightened youngster.

Jabitha appeared beside him. Anakin looked up and blinked. Again the image shifted, and Jabitha became Vergere, then the Magister. Anakin stood and sidled up against the nose of his ship. He did not know if he could stand any more of Sekot's illusions.

"They are trying to destroy the settlements," Sekot said, seeming to kneel beside him. "I can't let this go on much longer."

"What can you do?" Anakin asked in a low whisper.

"The Magister prepared for this, but we have never . . ." Sekot seemed at a loss for words. "Practiced? We have never had a drill and tried everything all at once."

"Tried what?"

Sekot stared straight ahead. "The engines, the hyperdrive cores."

"What, you're all going to escape in big ships?"

"We will do what we need to survive. Do you know where you are?"

"In a sky-mine delivery ship. I'm a prisoner," Anakin said.

"You are in orbit around me. You are part of the fleet I may have to destroy soon. I would regret harming you."

"You can do that? Blow up all these ships?"

"It's possible. I'm trying not to be too destructive all at once, but the Magister never had time to teach me everything. I do not know what we are all capable of, the settlers and me, working together."

"Did you kill any Far Outsiders?"

"I must have," Sekot said.

"Would this be any different for you?" Somehow, that seemed important.

"I don't know. Every experience is new. I do not know myself very well. I am only now aware of how much death there is in my own parts, how they compete with each other and keep a balance of coming and going, being and ending. All across my surface there is death and birth, all the time. Do I feel bad about this? Do you know when the parts of your body kill invading organisms?"

"No," Anakin said. Some Masters were fully aware of all the minute living things within their bodies. Padawans were rarely taught such skills. They could be distracting.

A guard came over to check him out. "Who are you talking to?" the guard asked, glancing at the ship in her harness.

"The planet," Anakin said. "It's getting ready to blast you out of the sky."

The guard grinned. "It's a backwater, a jungle," he said. "Putting up a pretty good fight, I hear, but nothing we can't beat."

Anakin pressed his lips together. The guard could not face the boy's direct gaze. He backed away, then returned to his post, shaking his head.

Sekot returned. "I wish there was another way. I mean you no harm," it said.

"You have to defend yourself."

"I wish there was more time."

Anakin shivered. "So do I," he said. Time to calm his inner turmoil and prepare for the proper passage, for the death of a Jedi apprentice.

Tarkin was beside himself with pride. "They thought they could keep their secrets from us," he said to Sienar as they emerged from the turbolift onto the bridge. The captain of the mine ship, a disheveled, scum-yellow-haired fellow well into old age, received a look of disdain from Tarkin and scuttled back into the recesses to get out of the way of the commander of the fleet.

"The Republic's forces need a manicure and a heavy trim," Tarkin confided to Sienar, a display both of good humor and determination. "And after this success, I'll be the barber, Raith."

"I shall sweep up after you," Raith said tonelessly.

Tarkin chuckled again. "My success will reflect well on all around me," he said. "Even that *cuticle* hiding from his superiors. I can't wait to get back to the *Einem* and finish our work."

"We could just leave them with this warning—as a resource for future investigation," Sienar suggested halfheartedly. "I doubt they'll be going anywhere."

Tarkin did not reply. He stared down through the captain's broad viewport at the cloud-shrouded southern hemisphere, and above the equator at the battle still being fought between the planet's defenses and droid starfighters. Flashes and sparkles of laser fire and blazing jungle illumined the night-bound planet beyond the orange and gray band of the terminator.

He was not pleased with what he saw. "Still not subdued."

"You're trouncing their defenses badly," Sienar said. Other lights glimmered in the darkness, as well, and Sienar, less arrogant and less pleased with himself, traced their outlines with interest. Longitudinally oriented rectangles hundreds of kilometers long were outlined by what looked like lightning. Some large change was disturbing the atmosphere.

He doubted starfighters could be blamed for that.

"How soon until we dock with the *Einem?*" Tarkin called back to the captain, still hidden in shadow.

"Fifteen minutes, Commander," the captain replied in a croak.

"Antiquated," Tarkin murmured in disgust. "Time for the new and for the young." He turned for the turbolift. "Let's interview the boy before we dock."

I don't know what shape he's in," Obi-Wan told Charza Kwinn as the *Star Sea Flower* pulled up through the atmosphere. The sky darkened and the faint sound of rushing atmosphere diminished beyond the port. "I think he's shrunk inward, pulling all his signs with him."

"But he is still alive, you are certain?" Charza Kwinn asked.

"He was captured with the ship. They'll keep him alive to keep the ship alive."

"I can't believe the Republic would do such a thing, attack this planet," Charza said. The food-kin arrayed themselves on the instruments, eyes fully extended, alert and ready for action.

"I suspect there's confusion during the assimilation," Obi-Wan said. "Some ambitious and unscrupulous elements are taking advantage of it."

"You are sworn to protect the Republic," Charza said. "Can you fight against them?"

"I am sworn to protect my Padawan," Obi-Wan said. It was a deeper law, a more ancient tradition, but Charza's question still hit home. How did Obi-Wan know what had been decided back on Coruscant?

Charza anticipated his thoughts. "They would never allow the destruction of a helpless world," he said. "That is more like the Trade Federation of late. And if they know the boy is Jedi—"

"It doesn't matter," Obi-Wan said. "We are under illegal attack. We will rescue the boy." *And the senate will have to sort it all out when we get back to Coruscant.*

"I have already plotted a course," Charza said, and showed Obi-Wan the projected orbit and rendezvous. "The mine ship will be more vulnerable just before it docks. These big old control ships have poor eyesight from above and below. I will slip in through the lower blind spot, push up against the underside of the mine ship, where its hull is thinnest, and try out a new toy." Charza made a high, brushy, sloshy sound to show his amusement.

"What sort of toy?" Obi-Wan asked.

"Perfect toy for an age of pirates," Charza said. "I have to make plans, in case the Jedi no longer need my services, no?"

Obi-Wan folded his arms. He was still chilled by the memory of the Blood Carver, the manner in which he had died. *Anakin has made his first kill in direct combat. I know it was in self-defense. He did it without a lightsaber, against a much stronger foe. Why then do I feel that something went badly wrong?*

62

I'm very impressed," Tarkin said to Anakin Skywalker as the Sekotan ship was winched out over the closed bay doors, now serving as the bay's floor. Racks of empty sky-mine cradles overhead and on all four sides jangled with the vibration of the old ship. "You made this?"

Anakin stood still, head bowed, and said nothing. He could feel the ship's mind, quiet, waiting. Like him.

Raith Sienar climbed up on the harness and walked around the top of the ship, kneeling at one point to examine its hull with a special instrument. "Very healthy," he pronounced.

The taller one, Sienar, is smarter, Anakin thought. *The shorter one is very powerful and resourceful. Ruthless as any man I've met.* This was the older voice speaking once more. Anakin realized that in his present situation, with no real chance of rescue, he would have to listen to this voice very carefully in order to survive. And survive he would, at all costs. There was too much unfinished business in his life, even if his career as a Jedi was now at an end.

He did not believe they would return him to the Temple.

Believe nothing they say. You are just a part of the ship to them.

"Are these ships as special as the rumors say?" Tarkin asked him in a conversational tone.

"I haven't had much chance to try her out," Anakin said. "You attacked the planet and nearly killed us all."

"I'm sorry you had to experience that," Tarkin said, focusing on the boy intently. "Strategy is a tough master at times, as any Jedi should understand. We protect the greater interests, sometimes at the expense of the smaller."

"Zonama Sekot did you no harm," Anakin said.

"It did not respond to our authority, and these are troubled times," Tarkin said. The boy was interesting. A very strong character, well beyond his years. "Did you kill the Blood Carver?"

"His name was Ke Daiv," Anakin said. "I killed him after he threatened Jabitha."

"I see. A clumsy misunderstanding of our orders. Well, you can never trust his kind, can you? I prefer dealing with humans, don't you?"

Anakin did not answer.

"Tell me about your ship. We shall let you command it, of course, and fly it, once we return to Coruscant."

"They could make many more for you if you just paid them and—"

"Enough," Tarkin said, his voice gathering a rough edge.

Sienar stood atop the Sekotan ship with his hands on his hips, listening. Anakin looked up at him. Sienar smiled and nodded, as if in agreement.

"Will you allow me aboard your ship?" Tarkin asked, recovering his calm tone. He stroked the long upper edge of the starboard lobe as he walked around the ship.

Anakin stood still, head lowered again.

Tarkin glanced over his shoulder and frowned at the boy's quiet concentration, thought of the condition of the Blood Carver's body, and shot a brief, commanding look at his personal guards, spaced around the bay. They touched their weapons.

"I say once more, will you—" Tarkin began again.

Anakin looked up suddenly and stared directly into Tarkin's eyes. "Do whatever you can," he said. "I will not help you." There it was again, the contrariness, the defiance that seemed completely illogical. The older, wiser self chafed within.

He could feel another part of the trial approaching. It was far from over. His hopelessness was a weakness and had to be banished, and if he cooperated with these men, or showed any signs of giving up, giving in, then all would be lost, wiser self or no.

Sienar shrugged and climbed over the hull to the upper hatch.

"We'll have to wait until we transfer it to the *Einem*," Tarkin said with a sigh. "The boy will see reason eventually."

Loader droids rolled across the deck, preparing for the docking. They beeped around Anakin's legs, warning him that he should move. The bay doors would be opening shortly.

"Come," Tarkin said, taking the boy by the shoulder. His hand burned, and he jerked it aside, waving it through the air in pain. *A very impressive lad!* He stopped himself from swatting the boy's face.

Anakin looked up at Tarkin, and his eyes seemed to lose all focus. Tarkin felt something twitch in his chest, in his abdomen.

Alarms rang out all around the ship. Sienar jerked his gaze away from Tarkin and the boy and squinted at the flashing red lights, the wailing of horns.

Anakin stepped back and pulled in his anger. *I was going to do it again!*

Something heavy clanged against the bay doors and the ship quivered. Hot spatters of metal spun outward from the seam where the doors met, and a vortex of hot gases and smoke spiraled up into the empty mine racks like a questing finger.

The personal guards escorted Tarkin out of the bay. Sienar jumped down from the Sekotan ship, glanced around wildly, felt the air pressure drop, and ran after the guards with barely a glance at Anakin.

Other guards remained, slapping pressure masks over their faces. They dropped to their knees and drew laser weapons.

Out of the twist of smoke and metal vapor, through a meter-wide hole in the doors, rose a hooded figure clutching a brilliant green lightsaber. Before he was completely inside the ship, laser fire surrounded him, and in a blur of motion, the lightsaber deflected each and every beam.

Anakin cried out for joy, and then felt a hot flash of shame. He had not believed in his master or in the near miracles a dedicated Jedi could work, and that shamed him.

But there was no time to waste. Obi-Wan stood at the hub of a dozen spokes of laser fire, and beams sizzled against the walls all around.

The boy stood by the ship, bent his legs, and leapt the three meters to land on top. The hatch opened at the touch of his boots. The ship instantly switched on her engines, and heated air blasted through the bay.

Obi-Wan, wielding his blade with supreme skill and blinding speed, stepped up on the bay doors and marched toward the Sekotan ship. Pieces of rack dropped around him, cut down by errant and deflected laser fire. Nine guards broke ranks and retreated.

"Anakin!" Obi-Wan shouted. "We're leaving now! Prepare our ship!"

The alarms within the bay grew more strident. Seeing they could do nothing more, the last three guards exited through the last open hatchway, firing as they fled. Obi-Wan jumped to the top of the ship and sliced the harness cables expertly with the lightsaber, working three on one side, three on the other, and then back again to finish the job. With the severing of the last three cables, the ship hovered on her own engines.

"We're almost out of fuel!" Anakin called from inside the ship.

Obi-Wan looked up through the smoking ruins of the racks, saw fuel hoses snugged up tight below the bulkhead. They had fittings to service droid starfighters as well as powered sky mines.

All used high-grade fuel, just like the Sekotan ship.

"Three minutes!" Obi-Wan shouted, and climbed up a precariously swaying rack to bring down a fuel hose. Anakin lifted the ship above the floor another meter to ease his master's task.

What Obi-Wan did not tell his Padawan was that the *Star Sea Flower* was even now setting a delayed charge on the bay doors of the mine ship.

They had just seconds more than three minutes before it blew.

63

Tarkin was beside himself with cold rage, his face almost purple. He hunkered beside Sienar in the escape pod as the elderly mine ship captain sealed them in with a sad, fatalistic nod.

"Two minutes from docking!" Tarkin shrilled, pounding the thin bulkhead with his fists. "We were *that close!*"

"Careful," Sienar said. "These interiors are none too sturdy."

Tarkin froze, quivering with anger, and stared very hard at Sienar.

"Lowest bidder, you know. I designed them for lightness, not strength," Sienar said.

Tarkin grabbed for a comlink and yanked it from the wall. He was connected directly with the *Einem*. "Captain, whatever you do," he shouted, "destroy that damned cargo ship, and destroy all that remains on the planet!"

Charza Kwinn pulled the *Star Sea Flower* away from the mine ship and retracted the boarding tunnel. He had left a plug in the hole, and attached to the plug, a charge sufficient to blow the bay doors wide open.

He surveyed with many sharp eyes the ever-changing network of defensive fire spreading out from the *Rim Merchant Einem*. The mine ship was drifting dangerously close to the hull of the control ship.

An escape pod shot out from the port side of the mine ship and was instantly snared by tractor fields from the *Einem*.

Obi-Wan and his Padawan had only a few seconds remaining before the charge went off, and it was time for Charza to make his own escape.

Obi-Wan kicked aside the high-pressure hose and ducked a spray of corrosive fuel. Smoke billowed within the bay. Gravitation within the bay was failing; Charza's bore must have severed grid cables in the doors. Debris drifted up from the floor.

He jumped through the hatch and closed it tight behind. Anakin waggled their ship back and forth to free her from two fallen mine racks. He clasped his master's hand firmly as Obi-Wan settled into his couch.

"Ready?" Obi-Wan asked.

Anakin had never been more ready to leave a place in his life.

"Brace," Obi-Wan warned.

The charge blew and the doors drew up and ripped aside in less than the blink of an eye. Racks and smoke and debris shot out into space, and the extra nudge pushed the mine ship against the hull of the *Einem*. The control ship shields braced its hull against the intrusion, but the smaller mine ship did not have a chance. Older, built to be expendable, it cracked along its main structural elements like an egg, and all its fuel—and three defective mines kept in storage—exploded.

The shock wave propelled the Sekotan ship through the breach in the doors. A rack punctured one lobe, and in Anakin's mind the ship gave a small cry of pain, then sealed the wound. He could not control her motion yet; the turbulence was too extreme. He felt more punctures and then a rip across her stern, and again the ship made healing repairs, but her pain was intense.

As the brilliant light of the explosion faded, Obi-Wan saw they were tumbling end over end away from the control ship and the expanding wreckage and plasma ball of the old mine ship.

Anakin brought them up and around, through bursts of aimless laser fire, and directly into a swarm of starfighters. The fast, deadly droid ships seemed to flock out of nowhere, two nearly solid walls flanking the *Einem*. Anakin had no choice but to reverse course, swoop into the control ship's shadow, and make a desperate run down toward Zonama's atmosphere.

Every other route was blocked.

"She's intact," Anakin told Obi-Wan. He gave his master a quick smile. "She's brave and she's beautiful. She'll go anywhere we tell her to."

Obi-Wan gripped his Padawan's shoulder. "Shall we live to fight another day?"

"You bet!"

Anakin buried his arms in the control panel, and the ship told him everything that she knew about the planet, where they could fly, and how they might escape.

"The sky is still full of mines," Obi-Wan said. He touched his set of controls lightly. His fingers sank into the panel, and rows of small green lights flashed around his hands. Impulses passed up his arms, and he was directly connected with the ship and with Anakin, as well. The ship fed him her specifications and characteristics. In a few seconds, he learned almost all a pilot needed to know—but Anakin had spent hours attached to the ship, and his expertise was much greater. *There is only one pilot.*

"I think it's best if I just supervise," Obi-Wan said.

"You can keep track of what's going on down below. Sekot talks to the ship while we're in range."

"Sekot?"

"The mind Vergere was talking about."

"Vergere?" Obi-Wan was at a loss.

Anakin quickly explained.

The ship skipped lightly along the upper atmosphere near the equator, reentered with six quick shudders, and shed her friction-generated heat.

"She likes being warmed that way," Anakin said.

"I can tell. She's frisky."

"She's *great*." Anakin could feel relaxation and reassurance smoothing up along his shoulders, into his neck and back. He sighed and wriggled in the seat. Being connected with the ship was like conversing with an old friend, and they had so much gossip to catch up on.

She almost made him forget the last few hours.

But Tarkin's forces were not about to let them go. All the sky mines and most of the starfighters that had fled the ruined mountain were now massing directly west of them, and another tide of mines was dropping from the east. They were about to be enveloped once again in devious, automated death.

Above, a tight-packed ceiling of starfighters flowed in like a storm. Whatever damage the *Rim Merchant Einem* had sustained had not reduced its ability to command and control.

Anakin could easily imagine the grimly determined face of Tarkin, tracking them with gray hunter's eyes.

"We have to go lower."

"The factory valley," Anakin said. "Our ship says the canopy has withdrawn and they've stopped manufacture."

Obi-Wan could piece together the ship's message, but not as quickly as Anakin.

"But they've been stockpiling a lot of ships, Obi-Wan. And something else . . ."

"What?"

"She says the settlers are going to escape."

Obi-Wan narrowed one eye. "*Everybody,* in one big ship?"

"That's what she seems to think. Could they make something that big?"

"With the Jentari, I don't see why not. But it would take days to assemble all the settlers, even if they were willing to go."

Starfighters climbed from behind a low chain of hills and fanned out in a V behind them. Anakin accelerated and dropped down to the level of the tampasi, as he had done earlier when Ke Daiv rode beside him.

The starfighters tracked close behind, weaving around the taller boras.

"There it is," Anakin said. The factory valley's concealing canopy had shrunk away, exposing the basalt floor and leaving the stone pillars thrust up like snaggled peg teeth.

The sky over the valley was alive with the still-raging battle between the Sekotan defenses and yet more starfighters.

"It looks very narrow from up here," Obi-Wan said.

"It is," Anakin said.

Obi-Wan kept track of the Sekotan ships defending the planet. They came in a bewildering variety, none larger than sixty or seventy meters in any dimension, and none as sleek or fast as their ship. But all pursued starfighters with impressive determination, clamping them in implacable jaws and bringing them down to the tampasi, or to the valley floor, where they exploded in brilliant red flashes and arcing showers of metal debris. Smaller craft took on the sky mines by simply ramming into them.

"They don't have pilots," Obi-Wan said.

"I think Sekot is the pilot. It's controlling all of them."

Obi-Wan was still absorbing the idea of a planetwide mind, but he did not doubt his Padawan.

"It's going to be real close," Anakin said. "Any other ship and we'd get creamed for sure."

"They're forming up all along the valley," Obi-Wan observed. "We have about three minutes until we reach the end." He suddenly accessed different eyes, and seemed to rush along the valley walls well ahead of them, seeing patterns of enemy ships in much greater detail. The tampasi was supplying their ship with its own sensory data, and the ship was translating for her human occupants.

"Don't you just love her?" Anakin said softly.

"She's showing us we don't have a chance," Obi-Wan observed. "More starfighters from orbit, and more mine delivery ships—"

"Never give up!" Anakin reminded his master.

Pillars of brilliant light rose into the sky, three to the north, one to the south. The air all down the valley pulsed with an immense pressure wave. Starfighters overhead were blown high into the stratosphere and churned as if with a giant paddle. Only by staying within a few meters of the valley floor did their ship maintain her course.

The terminator between day and night was sweeping toward

them, brightening one wall of the valley with what, in other circumstances, would have been a lovely yellow dawn glow. Clouds rushed to fill in the wake of the pressure wave, and they, also, caught the dawn glow, which painted them with an uncanny purple and gold aura.

Yet to the north, the dawn was interrupted by what looked at first like steep mountain peaks shooting up from the planet's crust. They were too regular and smooth to be mountains, however.

They were vanes of some sort, and they looked oddly familiar to both Anakin and Obi-Wan.

"The ship says if we don't want to go with them, we'd better get out of here," Anakin said. "We'd better find some way to go into a solar orbit. And fast."

Obi-Wan, using all the new sources of vision, examined the vanes from many angles. *They're hyperdrive field guides—and they're over three hundred kilometers high! And the shafts of light—those are the plasma cones of engines. Huge engines.*

He looked across the console at his Padawan.

Another pressure wave shot down the valley and shook the ship. Boras all along the rim were being uprooted and tossed to the bottom of the valley.

"This is insane," Obi-Wan said. "We don't know where they'll go."

"Or if they can survive," Anakin said.

"Let's take our chances up there."

The starfighters were in disarray, their sensors blinded by the sudden shafts of light rising beyond the valley. Cracks formed in the valley floor, and magma rose sluggishly. The entire crust was strained by the force of the huge new engines.

"We'll have to maneuver through a lot of mines," Anakin said.

"Do it." Obi-Wan frowned in concentration, trying to see

where all the pathways were going, where *their* tiny path might converge with much greater events in the immediate future. But nothing was clear.

Anakin brought the Sekotan ship up above the valley walls just as another funnel of searing brilliance scorched a hole through the atmosphere a hundred kilometers north, incinerating all in its path, friend and foe alike. The light seemed to blossom at its base, then darkened to smoky orange and went out, and a wall of debris pushed outward. If that was an engine, it had just failed, but it had cleared a path for them into space.

Anakin bared his teeth, expecting to die at any moment—

"Never give up!" Obi-Wan reminded him.

—And drove them straight up through boiling atmosphere, through fragments of ruined engine and flaming wreaths of fuel.

The stars gleamed clear in a black spot at the end of the tunnel of ionized air. The black spot closed rapidly.

The little ship cleared the atmosphere and climbed with un-believable speed into space, reaching orbital velocity in seconds. Starfighters gathered on all sides to pursue.

The YT-1150 of Charza Kwinn pushed up from behind. Charza had followed them down the valley floor but could not keep up with them now, so he fell back and drew away the droid ships, spiraling higher and higher, finally achieving orbit. The last they saw of him, he was engaging a defense escort ship.

Then, from the *Rim Merchant Einem,* just visible over the limb of Zonama Sekot, came a concentrated bolt of turbolaser fire, expertly aimed. It caught their little ship broadside and blinded them for a moment, crisping one lobe.

Anakin felt the ship's high-pitched, bone-grating signal of pain.

Obi-Wan looked behind, using the senses still supplied by Sekot, and saw engines flare to life across the planet's northern hemisphere, their intense plasma cones pushing Zonama Sekot slowly, majestically, out of its own orbit. All the renegade ships surrounding the planet had to scramble to keep clear of both the flares and the planet's new vector through space.

Zonama Sekot had never been more beautiful. She shimmered against the backdrop of the pinwheel and the far, rippling sheets of stars. Her clouds and vast tampasi faded beneath a sunrise that could not compete with Sekot's own, self-generated energies.

"She's leaving!" Obi-Wan cried out. He reached out to grab hold of something, an instinctive reaction, completely futile.

All the stars around the planet's circumference seemed to suck inward and then bounce back. In the pit of his stomach, Obi-Wan could feel a huge emptiness in space and time, unlike anything he had ever experienced.

He lost his extra senses, his connection with Sekot. Only a brief farewell lingered, the last touch of a far-reaching tendril, ancient and young at once.

Anakin was still lost in their ship's pain. Behind them, Tarkin's confused fleet scattered as if caught in a great wind. All the ships' orbits had changed unexpectedly, and the navigational systems could not compensate. Mines collided with mines and starfighters, delivery ships smashed into defense escorts, and at least two escorts rammed the *Rim Merchant Einem*.

Not his concern. Anakin knew they had only a short time to go where they needed to go. *Take us,* he told their ship.

He entered a state where he understood the ways of the higher spaces. The vastness of the universe no longer frightened him. The ship rooted him to their reality. Even in her pain, she was teaching him how to navigate the more difficult dimensions.

Anakin in turn gave the ship what considerable skills he possessed.

Together, they took themselves into hyperspace and fled the triple star system that had once held the secret promise of Zonama Sekot.

The ship was indeed faster than anything that had ever flown before.

Obi-Wan slept. Exhaustion caught up with him, and sleep came without his even being aware of it. He awoke a few hours later and saw Anakin also asleep, arms still embedded in the console. The boy's eyes twitched. He was dreaming.

Obi-Wan stroked the ship lightly. "Any friend of Anakin Skywalker's is a friend of mine," he murmured.

The console rippled beneath his touch. A display of the ship's vital systems appeared before him. She was giving everything she had to get them to where they wanted to go, but that wasn't going to be enough. The ship's injuries were too great.

Obi-Wan leaned forward. "There's another station," he said. An emergency outpost, a barren, rocky world thousands of parsecs closer than Coruscant, sometimes used by Jedi, unknown to anyone else, and otherwise almost deserted. He had been there only once, after a particularly harrowing adventure with Qui-Gon.

The ship accepted his coordinates. A new display affirmed that the ship could reach this destination.

"And when you can, send a message to the Temple." He provided the transponder frequencies. "Someone should meet us at the outpost. Mace Windu, or Thracia Cho Leem. Or both. It is very important that my Padawan be counseled by another Master after his ordeal."

Anakin came awake and blinked owlishly in the warm cabin lights.

"You were dreaming," Obi-Wan said.

"Not me. The ship," Anakin said. "Or maybe we were dreaming together. We were traveling around the galaxy, seeing wonderful things. It was so great to just be *free*. You were there with us. I think you were having fun, too."

Anakin held out his hand, fingers spread, and Obi-Wan met it with his own hand. A few more years and the boy would reach his full growth.

In more than just size.

"I'm going to give her a name," Anakin said, looking away.

"What?"

"I'm going to call her *Jabitha*."

Obi-Wan smiled.

"It's a pretty name, isn't it?"

"It is a pretty name."

"Do you think they're still alive?"

"I don't know," Obi-Wan said.

"Maybe they all just vanished and no one will ever see them again."

"Perhaps."

Anakin had a hard time asking the next question. "Our ship is dying, isn't she?"

"Yes."

Anakin stared straight ahead, face blank.

The boy loses everything he loves, and yet still he is strong.

"Vergere . . ." Anakin began.

"Tell me more about what Vergere said."

"I'll get the ship—I'll get the *Jabitha* to show you the entire message."

Vergere appeared once more in the cabin, head feathers awry, slanted eyes wary, communicating the news of her discoveries to any Jedi who might follow in her path.

The *Jabitha* lay in a cold and flimsy hangar on the outpost world Seline. The Sekotan ship's skin was rapidly losing its color and iridescence.

Anakin sat on a bench before the ship, chin in his hands. Outside, winds howled and spicules of ice shattered with a harsh, tinny rattle against the hangar's thin metal skin.

Anakin tried to imagine the *Jabitha* back in her birthplace of warmth and lush, tropic beauty, back with her family . . . wherever they might be.

Seline was a poor place for a Sekotan ship to die.

Obi-Wan and Thracia Cho Leem entered the hangar. Thracia removed her weather gear. Anakin looked up, then returned his gaze to the ship.

Thracia approached the boy.

"Not so young now, Anakin Skywalker?" she asked, sitting on the bench beside him. Anakin slid over a few centimeters to make room for the diminutive Jedi Knight.

Anakin did not answer.

"Young Jedi, you have learned some hard truths. Power and even discipline are not sufficient. Self-knowledge is the most difficult of our many journeys."

"I know," Anakin said softly.

"And sometimes wisdom seems impossibly far away."

Anakin nodded.

"You must let me feel what is within you now," Thracia said gently. Then, with the faintest tone of warning, "You are still being judged."

Anakin screwed up his face, then relaxed and let her probe.

Obi-Wan slowly turned his eyes to the dead ship, now good only for cold and heartless research, and left the hangar. This was not for him to witness. There had to be an objective evaluation; that was half the essence of Jedi counseling.

As for the other half . . .

That was Thracia's greatest skill—healing.

There would be many more battles for his apprentice, many more disappointments. And many more joys. More joys than sadnesses, Obi-Wan fervently hoped.

This was how it was, how it felt, to have the heart of a Master.

Coda:

No more Sekotan ships are made. In a few years, all of them are dead or destroyed.

Tarkin and Raith Sienar manage to bring the crippled fleet home. Inspired by what he calls a "great example," Tarkin redeems himself before the Supreme Chancellor with secret plans for a moon-sized battle station. Tarkin claims sole credit for the design. Sienar does not dispute him; it is a brainchild he is eager to disown. Sienar has a bad feeling about such an expensive concentration of might.

The new order will find both Tarkin and Sienar useful.

Charza Kwinn and his shipmates survive and reach Coruscant, where they are assigned new missions. In later years, with the rise of the Empire and a decline in cordial relations with nonhumans, Charza becomes a smuggler and pirate to feed his food-kin. He limits his prey to Imperial vessels.

A legend grows in the galaxy: of a rogue planet that wanders between the stars, forever lost, ruled by either a madman, a madwoman, or a saint, the legends are never clear which.

Months after Thracia Cho Leem counsels Anakin Skywalker, without explanation, she leaves the Jedi order.

Obi-Wan Kenobi has his work cut out for him. The young man, his Padawan, is growing stronger, overcoming disappointment, acquiring discipline. But the knot in Anakin's future has not completely loosened. The trial is not over; it may not be over for decades.

No balance.

No balance yet.

ABOUT THE AUTHOR

GREG BEAR is the author of twenty-four books, which have been translated into seventeen languages. His most recent novel is *Darwin's Radio*. He has been awarded two Hugos and four Nebulas for his fiction. He was called the "best working writer of hard science fiction" by *The Ultimate Encyclopedia of Science Fiction*. He is married to Astrid Anderson Bear. They are the parents of two children, Erik and Alexandra.

Visit the author online at www.gregbear.com